Under a Different Sky

Deborah Savage

Penguin Putnam Books for Young Readers

For Bob M., who has made all the difference

I greatly appreciate the help of Elaine and Janice Kachavos for the information about dressage, and of Mike Mollo and Kristen Livengood for their conscientious reading.

The poems quoted in the text are from:
"The Man with the Blue Guitar," from *Wallace Stevens: The Collected Poems*.
  New York: Vintage, 1982.
"The Waking" and "Memory," from *The Collected Poems of Theodore Roethke*.
  New York: Doubleday, 1966.
"Do Not Go Gentle into That Good Night," from *The Poems of Dylan Thomas*.
  New York: New Directions, 1971.

Library of Congress Cataloging-in-Publication Data
Savage, Deborah. Under a different sky / by Deborah Savage. p. cm.
Summary: A boy with Olympic dreams and an extraordinary horse struggles to transcend his impoverished family background as he falls in love with the emotionally troubled daughter of a wealthy family. [1. Horsemanship—Fiction. 2. Horses—Fiction. 3. Love—Fiction. 4. Boarding schools—Fiction. 5. Schools—Fiction. 6. Family problems—Fiction.] I. Title. PZ7.S2588Un 1997 [Fic]—dc20 96-27238 CIP AC ISBN 0-698-11697-6

10 9 8 7 6 5 4 3 2

Prologue

Was it a dream? Was it?

The boy knelt in the grass in the June night. Everything was familiar. The thick grass smelled wet and sweet, and hidden close to the earth the crickets sang. Lightning bugs floated above the grass tops, and beyond the barn the mockingbird babbled, just as it did every night. The boy turned. Behind him, his father smiled. That was familiar too.

But the old mare lying on her side near them filled the boy with an excitement so close to fear he leaned back until his shoulder touched his father. The mare's body was a dark mound rising and falling in time to her labored breathing, and the boy involuntarily breathed in the same rhythm. He could see only the mare's belly above her twitching legs. When he shut his eyes, the mare's panting filled the whole night. He opened them quickly. Yes, it was old Nell. It was still Nell.

And then the sky burst open over them. The boy threw back his head and opened his mouth as if to drink in the cascades of light. "Dad!" he cried softly. "Dad!"

"Northern lights," said the man. The sky seemed to tremble in ribbons of ice-green light, sweeping the stars and fireflies into a wild dance. On the boy's bare skin the lights flickered until his whole body seemed to be moving, though he held himself completely still.

"Dad," he whispered. The man crawled to the mare's haunches. Her dark tail spilled over his hands and he pushed it aside. Under it, a small black muzzle appeared. The boy watched, transfixed.

"Go up to her head," said the man, but the boy did not hear. "Go on — get up there," he urged.

But the boy was caught in the dream now. In the white-green light spilling over the field, the boy saw the mare's muscles bulging as her belly moved with a violent, mysterious life of its own, until . . . he did not know how . . . he was lying on the ground next to the slippery black foal. He stretched out his arm along the foal's thin black leg, and when the leg twitched, his arm twitched too. He moved his head closer to the foal's in the sweet grass.

Even when his father laughed softly in exasperation and said, "All right then, lie there. I'm going for some water," the boy still dreamed. The foal seemed to be looking straight into his eyes, and when he heard the first fluttering in the foal's nostrils the boy knew it was his own expelled breath the animal was breathing in. He tasted the returning breath from the newborn lungs, warm and thick with the mysterious fluids of life. They lay there, the boy and the foal, breathing deeply into each other.

His father returned with a bucket of water and handed the boy a rough burlap sack. He knelt by the mare's head and spoke softly to her. In a moment the boy heard the bucket rattle and his father's laugh. "There! She drank the whole thing. Now let's get you up, old Nell." His father peered around at him. "You gotta rub him hard with that sack, kid. He's all wet. You want him to catch cold? You gotta help old Nell out."

The burlap was stiff and he couldn't bear for it to touch the delicate body. Instead, he pressed even closer to the foal, so close he felt the heart beating through the tiny rib cage. He could feel his own heart too, and soon he could not tell where one heartbeat began and the other left off.

"That ain't gonna do it," said the man. "C'mon, now. Nell would do it herself, but she's too worn out. C'mon – don't you remember her last one, how she practically knocked it over with her licking? You ain't gonna hurt him."

His father gathered the foal up in his arms and scrubbed the sack vigorously over the wet fur. On his knees, the boy watched in silence, feeling cold. He put his hand against his chest a moment, to see if his heart was still beating there. He could almost feel the rough sack, as if it were his own skin being rubbed. "Let me do it, Dad," he said. "I can do it now."

He scrubbed until he was panting and messy from mucus and blood. His father smiled down at him. With a grunt the mare suddenly lurched to her feet, lowered her head, and tore a mouthful of grass as if nothing had happened. The boy watched her anxiously. "She knows it's her baby, don't she, Dad?"

"Sure she does," said the man. "She's just getting her strength back." He shook his head and studied the mare. "That sure was some trick old Nell pulled on us, wasn't it? Grass bloat! I thought she had grass bloat! What a trick . . . Keep rubbin' him, kiddo. He ain't near dry yet."

"Was it that big stallion, Dad? The one from the school?"

The man grinned ruefully. "You know of any other stallions around here a year ago? Course it was him! Musta got her right through the fence, too . . . " He caught the boy's eye and winked.

The foal was dry and silky to touch now, but the boy still held him across his cramped legs, stroking the sleeping body. The man picked up the bucket. "Okay, kid. Best leave them be now. The little guy'll sleep for a while till he gets on his feet."

When the boy did not move, the man squatted down beside him. "He sure was born under a different sky, wasn't he, son?" He smiled softly. The foal's coat was blacker than night, but spilling over the tiny haunches was a white galaxy of stars. Following his father's caressing hand with his own, the boy found the center of the galaxy just above the foal's tail. All he had to do was close his eyes and he was in the dream again, he and the foal together, breathing the light-struck sky.

But when he opened his eyes there was his father, and old Nell placidly grazing, and the foal sleeping. Above them, the night was filled with stars, just as it had always been. The boy craned his neck to look up. "Where are the lights?" he whispered.

The man shrugged. "Don't know," he said. "Guess they just come and go. Only saw them once before in my whole life, and they weren't nothing like that. What're you doing? You gotta come in now."

"Let me stay, Dad," the boy pleaded. "I'm warm . . . I'm okay. Honest! I just want to see him stand up."

"Could be an hour yet. Your mom won't like it."

"I have to, Dad," he begged. The foal shuddered in his sleep and the boy gazed into his father's eyes. "What'll happen if he wakes up and I'm not here?"

The man grinned. "What d'you think he's got a mother for, kiddo?" He hesitated, glanced toward the house, and shrugged again. "I don't blame you," he said gently. "Ain't nothing so beautiful as a newborn thing gettin' to his feet for the first time. You come in when you want. I'll handle your mom."

The boy lay down again beside the sleeping foal. He stroked the swirl of stars on the bony rump. "Galaxy," the boy whispered. "Galaxy." He was tired, and fell asleep.

Chapter One

It was the hottest August Ben could remember. Even in the shade under the truck, sweat stung his eyes. He sighed. He'd promised Marty Webber two weeks ago he'd have the truck running before school began, but now school was three days off and he'd just discovered a new leak in the oil line.

He was too hot to care. He'd been working on the truck for three hours. Across the cluttered yard a hot breeze rattled the greenhouses his father had built years ago to raise rare orchids. Around them the weeds grew waist high and the torn plastic clung to the rotting frames like shreds of skin on the deer skeleton Ben had found in the woods earlier in the spring. He scrubbed at the sweat running down his neck.

A cock pheasant strutted near the truck and scratched in the dirt near Ben's head. He swatted at it in sudden irritation. The pheasant had been magnificent once, with golden speckled feathers and a banded tail trailing like a royal train. Two years ago, when Ben

1

was fifteen, he'd helped his father build the expensive pens for the exotic game birds Thomas Stahler was determined to breed and sell. He remembered how proud he'd been of those pheasants, resplendent in multicolored plumage. But now the few remaining Chinese ring-necked and Golden pheasants were as thin and moth-eaten as the chickens that ranged free around the dusty yard.

Like the orchid houses, the pheasants reminded Ben that not one of his father's projects had ever been a financial success. For years, most of the money for the farm mortgage and taxes had come from his mother's wages at the supermarket in Jonesburg while his father peddled himself out to odd jobs and drew up endless plans for new projects.

The kitchen door slammed and a pair of boots appeared, poking at Ben's outstretched legs. "Quit it," he muttered, squirming farther under the truck out of his brother's reach. Tom squatted and feinted at him with a cold beer can. "Mom wants you in for supper, Bennie boy," he grinned, peering under the truck. "Shoot. This thing's in worse shape than before. You got half of it layin' all over the ground. Sure you know what you're doin'?" When Ben did not answer, Tom stood up, and Ben heard him gulping the beer. "Well, better get inside. Mom's waiting."

"Okay, okay — tell her I'm coming." Ben hesitated, trying to gauge his brother's mood. "You going out?"

"Yeah, I'm outta here. Dad's on my case again. So

2

what else is new, huh?" Tom growled, then leaned down, grinning again. "Why'n't you come with me? You don't ever have no fun, Bennie — that's your problem. You're too damn serious." Tom was so close now Ben could smell the beer on his breath.

"Naw," Ben said. He waited until he heard the pickup roar off down the drive, wondering if Tom had spun the tires on purpose to stir up the dust. He squeezed his eyes shut, ran his tongue around his gritty mouth, and spit. Then, his eyes still closed, he pressed his palms flat against the earth. Cicadas buzzed in the butternut tree, the pheasants squabbled nearby, and from the house came the jabber of the television. He concentrated on the warm texture of the earth under his hands, on his breathing, on the pulse of his heart until a stillness grew around him.

So faint at first it was a sensation in his body rather than a sound, the steady beat of hooves came. He breathed aloud: "Galaxy." The stallion was waiting for him at the fence by the time Ben stood up, black coat gleaming and the spill of stars over his rump even brighter than the afternoon sun. "Hey!" called Ben softly. "Hey!" The horse tossed his head and nibbled the fence, but his eyes never left Ben as he walked toward him. Ben ran his hand down the muscular neck. He'd always been able to call the stallion without words, to feel the drumming hooves before he heard them, as if they were his own heartbeat. But he did not know how to explain it.

The sound of a car interrupted his thoughts. The stallion threw up his head. Ben squinted through the dust and grimaced. "Dad!" he yelled. "Those guys from the school are here!"

He stayed by the fence while the two men in the car sat talking. From time to time one of them gestured toward the barn or pointed to the fields, and the other nodded. There was a possessiveness to their gestures that made Ben uneasy. When both men got out, they were still talking. " . . . Become a real eyesore — the guy's dirt-poor," he overheard, recognizing Bob Crighton, headmaster at Huntingdon, the private school that bordered the farm on the east. As Crighton spoke, the other man kept nodding. "He'll have to sell eventually — no way he can hold out much longer at this rate —"

"Dad!" called Ben again. Both men looked around, noticing him for the first time, and he met their eyes squarely.

"Hello there, Ben," said Crighton, strolling toward the fence. "How's that big mule of yours today?" Galaxy shifted nervously and Ben stroked his neck. Behind Crighton the other man was studying the horse with sudden interest. "He's a real beauty," he commented. "Hanoverian, is he? What's his breeding?"

"He's nothing," Ben muttered. "He's just a horse . . . he's an Appaloosa."

The man made no further comment but Ben saw a

4

quick frown pass over his face. The kitchen door banged and Thomas Stahler came across the yard, wiping his mouth with the back of his hand. "Hey, Bob," he smiled. "Thought you weren't coming over till later. Just havin' my supper —"

"We won't take much of your time," Crighton said smoothly. "But we've only got our consultant — Ed Richards here — until tomorrow. Mind if he looks the place over to get an idea on upgrading the barn and the riding ring? What we discussed last week?"

"Take your time." Thomas nodded and glanced at Ben. "Hey, kiddo — your mom's got supper waiting. Thought she called you in half an hour ago."

As he walked toward the house, Ben wished his father was not always so polite to Crighton. Huntingdon School might be the richest place in Jonesburg, but they were renting property from Thomas Stahler, after all — not the other way around. The school had been using the barns and ring in their riding program for years and made no secret of wanting to buy the whole farm to expand their campus. Ben paused and looked back at the men talking with his father.

"Ben!" his mother shouted from the kitchen window. The tension he'd been feeling gave way to an anxious exhaustion. He ran up the steps before she could yell at him again. At least Tom wouldn't be around tonight.

Before he could sit, Betty Stahler snapped, "You're a mess, Ben. You could at least wash your hands." When he leaned against the sink without answering, she said more gently, "You get that truck fixed yet? You sure look beat."

"It needs another part," Ben said, avoiding her eyes. She was counting on his pay to cover the cost of his school clothes and supplies. "I mean, I thought I had the problem worked out, but now I got to —"

Thomas came in, slamming the door and laughing, and the kitchen seemed to expand to contain him. They might look alike, his father and he, with the same wiry, compact frame, the same unruly brown hair, but Thomas Stahler at fifty-five had such an unconstrained, generous vitality that Ben sometimes felt dwarfed in his presence. Ben scrubbed his hands, as blunt and worn as Thomas's, but while his father's seemed to exude a gentle strength, Ben's own hands appeared merely rough and broken-nailed, creased with indelible grime. He clenched them into fists under the water.

"Benjamin Stahler, are you trying to run us out of water? Just sit down and eat. I didn't make this food to have it get cold," said his mother. Ben sighed. His mother's peevish voice made him wish he could shut his ears, but when he glanced at her, he flushed with remorse. For more than a year she'd been working weekends and extra shifts at the supermarket, getting home in time to shove frozen dinners in the microwave. She'd often sit staring into space until the timer rang, and it seemed to Ben that everything he did would make her yell.

6

He poked without appetite at the cold fish sticks, and Thomas thumped him on the shoulder. "You hear what them guys want now?" he chuckled, leaning his chair back until it creaked. "They want to rent that big field for a cross-country riding course. Said they're ready to expand, they want more diversity or something."

Betty looked up sharply, but before she could speak, Thomas continued. "Diversity!" He snorted. "They want more rich kids, is what they want. Rich kids have fancy horses, and fancy horses gotta have fancy places to live —"

"You could sell that field for good money," Betty interrupted. "You don't need all this land, Thomas Stahler, and you know it. You ain't done nothing with it in fifteen years."

Thomas let his chair fall forward with a deliberate thump. Ben stared down at his plate. All their arguments began the same way.

"You oughta sell the whole place," his mother went on bitterly. "I mean it! What good has this farm ever been? You can't make it work. Nothing you do comes to anything on this dirt farm. The place just sucks up money like water." Her voice had become thinner, as if the subject itself was sucking the life out of her.

"I told you a million times there's no way I'm selling this farm," growled Thomas. "You think I only want it to make money off of? I thought you knew me better'n that —"

Ben stared out the window while their voices battled

around him. Beyond the barn, the late summer fields sloped up to meet the dark forests of the Buckhorn Mountains. Bordered on three sides by Pennsylvania state forest and on the fourth by the Huntingdon School, the one-hundred-and-eighty-acre farm was Thomas Stahler's life. But Ben knew that to his mother, the farm had become a prison.

They went on like this evening after evening, never getting anywhere, just scratching at each other the way children dig at scabs so they never heal. In three days school would begin and then Ben would shuttle back and forth between the monotony of classes and the automotive shop at Clayton County Vocational-Technical School, and evenings in a house sour with bickering and his brother's sullen silence. Although he sat without moving, staring away with his hands clenched under the table, Ben felt like the rabbit he'd once cornered in the barn that had thrown itself against the walls over and over in a panic until blood came from its mouth.

His mother wanted to move to the subsidized housing development on the other side of Jonesburg, close to her job. Selling the farm would clear them of the debts that kept growing with each of his father's failed ventures. He wished desperately that her life could be better. But without the farm, Ben was sure his father would wither and die. And where would he keep Galaxy if the farm was gone?

"I don't know why you gotta keep buggin' me about this place," Thomas was saying, tired. "Crighton wants

8

to fix up the barns, put in more stalls, build a covered ring out there. . . . There's plenty of money in that. We'll be fine. He'll pay good rent for it." His bad mood shifted as quickly as it had come and he punched Ben again lightly on the arm. "Say – there's your big chance, kiddo," he grinned. "You an' Galaxy show them what you can do, I bet they'd hire you on as a riding teacher. Wouldn't that be something! Teaching at Huntingdon –"

"He's got a perfectly good job all lined up waiting for him at Hawley's Garage soon's he graduates, so don't you go putting any dreams into his head, Thomas Stahler," protested his mother. "Dave Hawley's not going to keep that offer open forever, and there ain't enough jobs around here for Ben to get choosy." She stacked the dirty dishes in the sink, each word she spoke poking Ben like a sharp pin so that he squirmed in his chair. "I gotta go," he blurted at last. Thomas followed him out the door.

They walked together without speaking toward Galaxy grazing quietly along the fence near the barn. In the early evening light the stallion appeared larger than he really was, the white nebula over his hindquarters glowing.

"He sure is the most beautiful animal that ever was," smiled Thomas. "You remember the night he was born? What was you then – twelve? Thirteen? You wasn't any bigger'n him when he come out. And you remember that sky?"

9

"I remember, Dad," said Ben. He glanced toward the house and Thomas caught his look. The gray eyes that Ben knew looked so much like his own darkened. "Look, Ben — don't you worry none," Thomas murmured. "I ain't gonna let you lose that horse. I promise. Can't figure out why your mom don't understand about anything anymore. She used to . . ."

"She just gets so tired, Dad!" cried Ben in a low voice. "She don't mean what she says — not the way it sounds. It's just . . . I don't know anymore what I should do. I mean, once I graduate I got that job at Hawley's, and there won't be any time for Galaxy anyway then, so maybe —"

"You'll make the time," said Thomas firmly. "You won't be no different from other people, trying to fit something they love around a job."

The stallion whickered, raising his head to look toward the slopes of the Buckhorns, and Ben was overwhelmed by an inexplicable sorrow. Suddenly he longed to race away on Galaxy, up into the clean, shadowed solitude of the forest.

"Go on for your ride, kid," said Thomas gently, following his gaze. "Don't you worry none about Webber's truck. It ain't goin' nowhere. I might just take a look at it myself, see what I can do. Go on — get outta here."

In the woods it was difficult to define the boundaries between Stahler's farm, the state forests, and the school property. This was old forest, massive hardwoods giving way on the higher slopes to hemlocks and white pine so dense the sun barely filtered through. But the division between his father's neglected, scrub-choked fields and Huntingdon's manicured campus was easy to see, and Ben rode up a narrow trail along a hedgerow through which he could catch glimpses of ivy-covered stone buildings. The school was quiet at the end of August, but by next week it would be home to more than six hundred students. He shifted his weight and the horse stopped, head turned and ears pricked in the direction Ben was looking.

For the past three years, Ben had been the same age as the students who went to Huntingdon. Now he was almost eighteen; in the spring, he would graduate from Clayton County Vo-Tech. The same spring, a hundred or so seniors at Huntingdon would also graduate, leaving the school to go to Harvard, Princeton, and Yale.

Ben had never found it difficult to like Huntingdon students. Over the years he'd come across them on the trails during their cross-country practice or when they came to the farm to ride, and sometimes he got to know one or two for a while. His mother complained that they acted as if the farm was their personal property, but Ben knew they never gave it a thought. They assumed they could go anywhere they wanted, assumed the barn and the riding ring was like everything else in their world and belonged to them. It wasn't that they were snobs, either, he thought now as he gazed across at the elegant buildings. He liked them better than most of the kids he went to school with.

With a stab of shame for his disloyalty, Ben studied the campus with a puzzled frown. What was it that made Huntingdon students so different from the students at Clayton County Vo-Tech? Was it only money that made Huntingdon seem like it was on a different planet than Jonesburg? Today, sitting on Galaxy and staring through the hedgerow, Ben sensed with more conviction than ever before that what was different about Huntingdon had to do with something much more important than money.

Huntingdon students were always discussing their plans in lively voices, always talking about what they were going to do after school, or over summer break, or when they graduated, or after college. The world was a place of infinite promise to them, a place where everything was possible. It was as if they all knew some secret about what being alive was supposed to mean.

The stallion shook his head impatiently and Ben leaned forward to hug his neck. "No point wondering about things like that, is there, boy?" he whispered. "Even if I did know what I wanted, I'd need a lot more'n we got to start with." The horse half reared then, almost unseating him, and Ben forgot his thoughts in the exhilaration of a wild gallop. He rode without a saddle, as he always had; Thomas had long ago sold the tack when the Appaloosa project failed. Leaning low over Galaxy's whipping mane, he thrilled to the stallion's strength as they flew effortlessly up the steep trail. He and Galaxy seemed to be one creature, so he had only to imagine what he wanted for the horse to do it.

But it was more than simply *thinking;* it had taken years of practice for them both. He had never taken riding lessons. But on videos taped from television coverage of Olympic and Grand Prix equestrian events, Ben had studied every nuance in the extraordinary communication between dressage riders and their horses. Once, on his birthday years ago, his father had taken Ben to Scranton to see the Royal Lippizaners from the Spanish Riding School in Vienna. There, awed by the graceful performance of those white stallions and by the single heart each seemed to share with his rider, Ben had recognized that mysterious alliance as the one he had with Galaxy. In the hours he spent with the stallion, Ben felt as if he and Galaxy together formed something much larger than either of them could ever be alone. With Galaxy, the world was all promise — but of what, he did not know.

The late August evening was cool, the trail along the north slope of the mountain in deep shadow. The stallion surged up the trail like a rocket breaking free of a launch pad, leapt a windfall pine without breaking stride, and Ben leaned into the black mane and laughed. Now Galaxy had broken the sound barrier, now he seemed faster than the speed of light, leaving far behind the orbiting questions Ben had no answers for.

Two miles up the power-line trail, a smaller track led off to a clearing. This was Ben's secret world. In the clearing two years earlier, he had first climbed onto Galaxy's back. Although the colt had followed him everywhere since birth, riding deepened their relationship into an utter certainty that he and Galaxy shared a single purpose in being alive.

But Ben could not define that purpose. He knew only that when he rode the stallion, he lost the debilitating sense of himself as Benjamin Stahler who went to Clayton County Vo-Tech, whose mother was a cashier at the Jonesburg Superette, and whose father dreamed visions of beauty far beyond his ability to carry them out. In the clearing with Galaxy, the boundaries of himself seemed to dissolve – he could be the fox slipping into shadowed thickets, or the red-tailed hawk swooping over the crest of the mountain, or the wind itself. Then, mysteriously, he was more truly *himself* than any other time.

The sun was down over the Buckhorns when Ben and Galaxy arrived at the clearing. Mountain laurels and hemlocks massed around this natural break in the forest. The wild meadow sloped gently toward low cliffs over which, on the far side, a stream added its delicate sound to the rich stillness. From the ledge Ben could look out over the Buckhorn range and see, far in the distance, the steeple on the Lutheran church and the white gleam of the Jonesburg Town Hall pierce the

14

indigo depths of the mountains. Ben felt deliciously alone up here on top of the world, such a welcome solitude compared to the suffocating aloneness he often felt at school.

School. School in three days. And winter coming, with snow drifting more than six feet deep, making the riding trails impassable. And after that, graduation — and full-time work. Galaxy pawed the ground and Ben reached out to pull his ears affectionately, then turned the stallion toward the center of the clearing.

Over the last two years they had worn a pattern of paths across the grassy space. Scraps of birch bark with letters drawn in pencil marked out a makeshift dressage ring. Here Ben and Galaxy worked, slowly and painstakingly, on the intricate dancelike movements of dressage. He had never told anyone about the clearing or about what he and Galaxy did there. His mother would complain that it was a waste of time, and his father . . . his father would understand and would want to share it with him. And Ben did not want to share it. There was no good reason to work with the stallion in this way — it would not bring him a job or serve any practical purpose. There was only this yearning that had to be answered, this demand to create something from the most secret heart of his being. When he and Galaxy worked together in the clearing, nothing divided them from the sky, the earth, the wind . . . and Ben could dance with what he did not understand.

Chapter Two

Lara McGrath leaned against her father's limousine, glanced around the campus of the Huntingdon School, and shoved a tape into her Walkman. Private schools stifled her with their pretentious air of good taste and discreet wealth. After being expelled from five of the most exclusive boarding schools in the United States and Europe – six, if she counted that one in Mexico City – Lara scorned them all.

She pointedly ignored her father, who was supervising the driver in the unloading of her bags, and refused to help. "This is so absurd," she muttered, staring off at the mountains. When the driver glanced at her she returned his look with bland defiance but felt suddenly diminished by the vastness of the Buckhorns. This school she was being forced to come to was so remote she felt trapped.

She took a deep breath and shook the feeling away. She could handle this place, just like she'd handled all the others. It wouldn't be difficult – she'd manage to find someone, a teacher or a counselor or the nurse, who would buy into whatever tragic story she could come up with. They'd look the other way then, and convince everyone else to leave her alone. They didn't have a life, teachers at these schools, she thought in disgust. But at least it made them easier to handle. She could do whatever she wanted, once she could get one of them wrapped around her little finger –

"Lara, you're going to have to let Juan know where you want him to put your things," called William Mc-Grath, checking his watch. "I've got a conference call in five minutes — I'll take it in the limo. So look, honey, just go on up with Juan. I'll be there as quick as I can." He was already getting into the limo as he spoke, so his voice disappeared with him behind the tinted glass. She did not respond and looked away, trying to ignore Juan Marquez struggling to carry a box of her books.

Juan was a small man, one leg shorter than the other from a childhood bout with polio, and he grunted softly under the weight of the box. Lara shifted against the limo. "You're the one who wants me here! You should do the work!" she muttered, addressing her father under her breath. A boy walking by with his parents gave her a startled, inquisitive look and her cheeks burned.

Everyone would think Juan was her father . . . and he might as well be, she raged. They were both Mexican, after all. She'd probably seen more of Juan than her father anyway. Running a big international corporation left little time for family . . . though her father always seemed to have time for Timothy. She yanked the Walkman headphones off and let them dangle around her neck, still playing. "Do you need help?" she asked Juan, sullen.

"I do not need help," he shrugged. She could not read his eyes, but she wondered uncomfortably if he'd placed a slight emphasis on the word *need*. She grabbed a suitcase and followed him into the dormitory.

As much as she'd tried to prepare for it, she was shocked by how familiar the place seemed — the musty smells, the noise of girls clattering down steps, the dim corridors with tiny rooms. She refused to acknowledge the house parent who was welcoming everyone at the door and trudged after Juan to the second floor. She wasn't fooled by the first-day atmosphere of excited camaraderie; it would change quickly. No one in these schools cared about anyone but themselves.

Juan placed the box of books on an empty desk in the room. The other desk was piled high with bags, so her roommate had already moved in. Lara kicked her suitcase out of the way and sat stiffly on the bare mattress, swallowing down the bile of panic. From now on, for months, she would never be alone, never have a moment of quiet to herself. Every day would be structured and supervised, a communal labyrinth of noise, instructions, rules, and expectations from which it would be impossible to escape. Roommates, classmates, coaches, teachers, deans, dorm parents — all watching, correcting, commenting . . . She jerked up her knees and wrapped her arms around her legs, rocking slightly on the mattress. Juan lugged another bag into the room.

"These are your clothes," he said. "Where would you like me to put them?"

She hated that he treated her like a stranger. He always had, keeping his distance as the hired help, although he'd been with her family since they'd first lived in Mexico City. Over the years, he'd moved her in and out of every school she'd ever gone to. She wanted to shake him, to cry, Don't act like that with *me,* Juan! Not with me. But he had never allowed her close, so she could never find out what she most wanted to know: What is it like to know who you are, Juan? What is it like to be Mexican? To have a family who looks like you, to have a past, to have grandmothers and grandfathers in old family photographs with features that look like your own?

But she could only stare at him wordlessly now, indicating the closet with a nod of her head. He put the bag down and left her alone in the room. She got up miserably and poked through the box of books. She opened one and read aloud softly: "'They said, "You have a blue guitar, You do not play things as they are." The man replied, "Things as they are Are changed upon the blue guitar."'" Wallace Stevens – she held the book tightly against her. Something deeper in the box, half exposed, caught her eye, and she stared, stunned, at a photograph in a silver frame of her and Timothy. She recognized it – it had been taken early last summer at Greenwood, her father's Connecticut estate, where they'd spent almost every weekend since they'd been in New York. There was her brother Timothy, with Conquistador looking over his shoulder in that lop-eared way he always had. Timothy, immaculate in his riding gear, was beaming his usual friendly grin. She remembered how they'd made her hold Daisy, the barn terrier, although she never trusted the runty creature not to bite. Next to Timothy, Lara looked as much his sister as Daisy did.

Her mother must have packed the photo in at the last minute. Why? To make sure Lara would never forget? She ran her finger over the glass. She hated posed photos, but this one did show Timothy as he really was, light shining in his hair and a smile just as bright, his white-gloved hand holding Conquistador's bridle. She jammed the photo to the bottom of the box and turned quickly as a girl came in the door.

She was short and round, with pale freckles, and she spoke first. "Are you Lara? They said my roommate's name was Lara." The girl gave her an eager smile and Lara thought in disgust, Oh great, she's going to try to be friends. Those were the worst kind, the ones who wanted to be friends. It was better to have a sullen roommate, even a nasty one — at least she always knew where she was with that kind, and they'd leave her alone. She gave the girl an abrupt nod and fiddled with the things on her desk so she wouldn't have to speak.

When Juan came in with the bedding, Lara cringed to hear the girl say brightly, "Hi, I'm Lara's roommate, Emily . . . " Lara swung around and grabbed the blankets from Juan. "This is not my father. This is our driver," she snapped, and busied herself making the bed.

First Juan and then Emily left the room, and all at

once the chatter in the halls seemed briefly to recede. Lara sat on the bed and closed her eyes until the stillness surrounded her. She could breathe again. Her whole body felt cloaked in an unexpected warmth. She didn't know what made her open her eyes, because she had heard no sound.

A woman stood in the doorway. She seemed to have been conjured up from the spell of silence, so Lara did not recognize her at first as the dorm parent who had been greeting people downstairs. It threw Lara so off guard that she blurted "Hello" before she could catch herself. Startled as much by her own voice as by the woman's appearance, she tried to compose herself into haughty indifference. But she came in and held out her hand with such directness Lara had to shake it. In confusion, she met the woman's eyes which were looking at her with a straightforward smile. "Hello," the woman answered. "Your father wanted me to tell you he's still on the phone."

"He had some conference call," Lara muttered, pushing herself as far back as possible on the bed. "They always take hours. I don't care."

"There's a meeting downstairs for new students and parents." Again the woman smiled so openly it took all of Lara's reserve not to smile back. "We'll be starting in ten minutes," the woman added.

"My father won't go," Lara interrupted. "He never goes to those things. I don't need to go either. They're all the same, anyway."

21

"What's the same?"

She tossed her head. "Oh, what they always talk about at those meetings. Rules. Curfews. Everything you have to do — I've been to a million of them."

To her surprise, the woman only nodded and said, "Well, I live in the apartment downstairs at the end of the hall if you need anything. My name is Clara Mikolaczuk. You don't have to remember how to pronounce it — just call me Miss Mik."

Lara waited for her to leave then, but Miss Mik chose a book from the box and leafed through it. After a minute, without comment, she put the book down and said, "You're welcome to come if you want to."

Lara held her breath after the woman left, then slipped out the door to the stairwell. She heard the indistinct murmur of voices and an occasional laugh from the lounge on the first floor. The air in the hall smelled stale. The walls, paneled with age-darkened wood, were gouged with the names of generations of girls. Hesitantly, Lara leaned over the banister. She heard the girls asking questions and giggling, but she had to take a few steps down to hear the quiet voice of Miss Mik.

Maybe she would go. . . . It wouldn't hurt, after all, to find out what she was up against. She'd moved halfway down the stairs when she heard the slam of the limo door outside, and she scurried back to her room. When her father came in, she was sitting on the bed as if she hadn't moved since Juan left.

William McGrath wiped his forehead with a handkerchief. "Hot, isn't it, sweetie?" he laughed. "Still, it's a lot nicer here than the city. I don't mind being out of New York on a day like this."

"You don't have to stay, Daddy," Lara said. "I've got everything, if you want to go."

McGrath glanced awkwardly around the room, then pulled the desk chair out and sat facing her. "I don't have to go just yet," he assured her with a smile. "Your mother said you might need to get some things in town."

"Town's ten miles away," said Lara, meeting his eyes blandly. And you know that, Daddy, she added to herself. You picked this school on purpose. There's nothing here. There's nowhere for me to go.

"I could send Juan," McGrath said. "Why don't you make a list, honey? You must need something."

"Don't you think Juan's tired of driving?" she snapped. "It took four hours to get here and he's got to drive all the way back, and he's sitting out there in the hot —"

"All right, Lara," said McGrath, getting up. "I don't need one of your lectures on exploitation. It's what he's paid for. He's glad enough for the work, I can tell you. If you want to be in a bad temper, perhaps it would be best for me to leave. If you need anything later, you can call — you know if we aren't home, we'll be at the hospital."

At her intake of breath he stopped, and for a moment neither spoke, each staring at the other. Over and over inside her head, she heard herself chanting: No, Daddy, don't talk about it. Don't say anything. Don't say it. I don't want to hear. Please don't talk about it.

She stared at her father, helpless against the force of the unspoken words between them. But William McGrath turned away first, his shoulders drawn tensely back in his linen suit. She could not see his face as he looked out the open window, and after a moment a curl of smoke lifted above his head. She took a deep breath.

"You're not supposed to smoke in the dorm," she said. Her father stubbed out his cigarette on the outer windowsill. "I forgot," he grunted sheepishly. "And see that you don't, either. I take it you're still smoking those filthy things?"

"You do," Lara reminded him.

"That's not what I asked."

When she didn't answer, he sat again and addressed her seriously. "Lara, I'm sure I don't need to spell out one more time what the situation here is — no, honey, you better listen. Huntingdon took you on probation. You've got good grades, but . . ." He shook his head at her when she tried to speak. "That attitude of yours — well, honey, you just won't get another chance. You know that."

She glared at him but he met her eyes without flinching. "You've got one year of school left, Lara," he continued in the impenetrable businessman's voice she hated. "I lose money every time you're expelled, damn it. And there aren't any schools left that would take you. If you had any idea what it took for me to convince Huntingdon . . ." He paused, then told her bluntly, "If you get into any more legal trouble — any at *all*, Lara — you could be treated as a legal adult. Do you know what that means? You're seventeen — they can do it. You've used up your chances."

Lara looked down at her hands. How brown her skin was — like honey and chocolate, her father used to say when she was little. Hair black as molasses. Eyes dark as Hershey's Kisses. Good enough to eat. She swallowed. "Why don't you just leave me alone, if I'm so much trouble," she hissed vehemently. "You never wanted me in the first place. You only send me to these schools because you feel guilty."

"Don't you dare start that again, Lara," barked McGrath in disgust. "Don't use that psychologist crap with me. I don't care what that stupid shrink said to you. There are millions of adopted kids all over the place."

"You and Mom sent me to those shrinks," she said, sullen. "I didn't want to go. I don't want any of this. I never asked you to spend money on me. I hate your fancy schools — I don't even want to *be* in school. Why can't you understand?"

McGrath stood wearily. "We do it because we love you, honey," he said. "Whatever you think, we do love you. We have the money and we want the best, just like any parent wants. We just want you to be happy."

She wadded up a pillow and clutched it against her.

25

"I'm all right," she muttered. "I just want to be left alone."

She refused to look at him, and after a pause he said in a low voice, "I just wish . . . you weren't always so miserable." Still she kept her face turned away. He sighed and opened his wallet. "Here's the phone card." She looked at the list of numbers: New York apartment, her father's office, her mother's office, Greenwood house and stables, both car phones . . .

"I know them all by heart, Daddy," Lara said. "This isn't the first time I've been away, remember?"

The only way to diffuse the tension was to make him laugh. Her father patted her gratefully on the shoulder. The last time she remembered him putting his arms all the way around her in a hug, she'd been a child small enough to climb into his lap.

At the limo they stood together awkwardly. "Oh – I almost forgot," McGrath said. "The academic dean called last week about your schedule. You weren't around, so I suggested Advanced Photography for your art component. That all right, sweetie?"

"That's okay, Daddy," she said.

"Why don't you let me get that new camera we looked at?" he asked.

You'd feel a lot better then, wouldn't you, Daddy? she thought, but couldn't force the venom into her voice. "I like the camera I have," she said. "It's almost four o'clock, Daddy. You better go."

When the black limo moved slowly around the circular drive and down the long avenue of maples toward

26

the main gates of Huntingdon, she waved until it was out of sight.

Chapter Three

Lara stood holding a field hockey stick at the edge of the playing fields and knew she would not last long at Huntingdon School. Tiny insects swarmed in the humid afternoon and stuck in her eyes. She wiped her hair from her sweaty face and gazed unhappily into the hedgerow separating the campus from Stahler's farm. Only four days. She'd only been here four days.

Huntingdon School was isolated deep in the mountains of north-central Pennsylvania. Nothing but wilderness and poor farms lay between it and the nearest town, ten miles away. During orientation, the dean had read pompously from the school handbook: "'Huntingdon was founded in 1870 as a finishing school for girls from well-to-do families but has since developed into a coeducational preparatory school of the highest and most exacting academic standards.'"

Warily, Lara watched the girls on the far side of the field hacking at the hockey ball, yelling excitedly as they pounded across the grass. The mountains seemed to mute their voices. She took a few steps closer to the shadowy hedgerow, then paused in astonishment as the unmistakable call of a stallion cut through the stillness beyond the trees. She listened for several minutes, but though the cry seemed to hang tangibly in the air, she heard nothing more.

Without further hesitation, she stepped into the hedgerow. Immediately, the sun-dappled solitude relaxed her. Ripe grapes hung on vines tangled in the tree branches and the ground was green with ferns. Through the trees she looked out on the overgrown fields of the farm.

"Lara McGrath, what do you think you're *doing!*"

She dashed back onto the field and was swept up in a noisy mass of jostling girls. She tried frantically to hear what the coach was bellowing but the flailing sticks and the girls' yells flustered her. She couldn't remember which team she was on or the position she was meant to be playing. Something slammed hard against her leg and she gasped. Girls lunged at her from all sides, screaming above the vicious cracking of sticks. "Hit it! Hit it, you idiot! No, not that way! God, are you stupid! Hit it to me . . . no, to *her* —"

Lara stood still, grasped her stick with both hands, and squeezed her eyes shut. Bracing her feet, teeth clenched, she whirled around and around, holding the stick out from her body. When she finally stopped and opened her eyes, the girls were huddled together staring at her in silence. No one moved. Lara kept her fierce grasp on the stick and tried to steady her breathing.

Later, she sat in the dean's office while the coach described what had happened.

"Are you suggesting it was a deliberate attack?" asked the dean calmly, without taking his eyes from Lara's.

"It looked deliberate to me," insisted the coach. "For goodness' sake – she was holding the stick like a . . . like a broadsword or something! She –"

She liked the image of a broadsword and imagined the sun flashing off the keen blade. The dean's cool eyes were unblinking. "Are you smiling?" he asked her, his voice dangerously soft. She sat motionless and refused to respond. He did not release her eyes, but she had learned long ago how to hold the gaze of authority without wavering.

"The girls won't play with her again," said the coach grimly. "And really, Dean Parker, I don't blame them. It's just a game –"

They always say that, thought Lara, twisting her mouth in disgust. *It's just a game* . . . as if anyone believes that! Girls don't play games, they have wars. And the wars, she knew too well, were carried beyond the field into the dormitories and classrooms.

"Did you want to say something, Lara?" asked the dean in his deceptively gentle manner. Under his relentless eyes she was horrified to feel herself weakening. Her leg throbbed. As if by accident, she moved it so the red welt was visible, and the dean, glancing at it, dropped his eyes from hers. She was triumphant.

"They were hurting me," she told him, pressing her advantage.

"Did that happen in the game?" he asked.

"Someone hit me," she whispered.

The coach half rose from her chair in disgust. "If you'd been where you were supposed to be . . . She wasn't even in position, Dean! She was wandering around in the *trees*. What does she expect?"

The dean studied the open folder on his desk. "Your father indicated that you'd played field hockey before, Lara," he said. "That's why he signed you up for it."

She would not answer questions that were not questions. It made her feel as if she was explaining herself. The dean leaned forward. "Lara, what position were you told to play?"

"I don't know."

The coach made an exasperated noise. "Left *wing*," she muttered. "Left wing. I told you three times. You hardly have to do *anything*." The dean ignored her and asked quietly, "Is there some other sport you'd rather play, Lara?"

"No," she answered.

"You are required to play a sport or take part in some equivalent activity each term. You have to choose something."

She allowed her eyes to drop now, so that she would appear confused. The dean waited, pencil poised above the folder. "Could I . . . could I choose tomorrow?" she faltered. "I don't feel very good right now." She knew she was only buying time, but if the dean was taken in by her act, that in itself would be a victory.

But Lara also knew the dean was aware that there was nowhere for her to go from here. She could only conform or leave. Her face grew hot and she turned toward the open window to feel the cool evening breeze.

"I'd like to speak to Lara alone now," said the dean pleasantly to the still-fuming coach. "I'm sure she is aware of what she did, Miss Douglas. I'm sure it was a reflex action and it won't happen again."

After the coach left the dean closed the folder and smiled at Lara. "But everything in your records indicates, Lara, that it *will* happen again — isn't that correct? You are at Huntingdon on probation. Personally, I do not want to see you expelled before the end of your first week — you do want to get expelled, do you not?"

"I don't know," she blurted.

"That's good," he said. "Because if you're ambivalent, that means you aren't sure. And I think, Lara, that you are a person who will do whatever she sets her mind to. So if you haven't quite set your mind to getting expelled . . . well, do you see what I mean?"

"I never wanted to come here!" she flashed, raising her chin scornfully. "I *hate* these schools."

"I can see that," he replied. "But it's not exactly the same as wanting to get expelled, is it? Think about it. Sometimes hating something can give you a valuable insight about yourself. You just have to stay with the hate awhile, try to discover what it means to you."

31

He held the door open for her and directed her to the nurse's office to get her leg looked at. "I think you should give this discussion some thought," he repeated.

That night she lay awake staring at the ceiling, the dean's words swarming in her head like the persistent insects. Hate. Stay with the hate. No amount of swatting at them would dispel the words and she ground her teeth, remembering the girls screaming at her in the hockey game. But she hadn't felt hate then. She'd felt hunted.

She curled on her side. *Stay with the hate*. But all she found in herself was misery. She would not allow herself to cry, so she rocked in the bed for a long time. Then, unexpectedly, the night air blew in through the open window with the cool scent of wild grapes and mossy earth. The solitude of the hedgerow filled her and she lay still, able to breathe again.

At breakfast in the dining hall, the photography teacher announced that all students signed up for Advanced Photography were to bring samples of their work to class. When Lara got back to her room she found Emily looking through a snapshot album. "We're in the same class," she muttered, already intimidated by Lara's glowering presence. Lara ignored her and dragged a large portfolio out from under the bed. Emily continued to flip through the album. "Ugh, these are so bad," she groaned and Lara sniffed in disdain. Hurriedly, instead of choosing any, she tucked the whole portfolio under her arm, grabbed the treasured old Voightlander camera she'd bought at a Mexican market, and left for class before Emily could follow. At the bottom of the stairs, still hurrying, she bumped hard against Miss Mik, who was just coming around the corner. The corner of the portfolio caught in the strap of Miss Mik's shoulder bag, flipped open, and the contents scattered over the floor.

She fell to her knees, trying to shield the photos from Miss Mik's sight. She'd planned on taking out only one or two of the most ordinary photos to show the teacher. But Miss Mik held up several collages and brushed the dirt off them. "Slow down, Lara," she laughed. "Slow down — you're going to bend them. No one's going to step on them."

Lara watched helplessly as Miss Mik studied the collages she held. "These are really extraordinary, Lara," the woman exclaimed, examining each one closely. "They're quite . . . unconventional. What a unique combination of images —"

Lara snatched the collages from her and stuffed them into the portfolio. "I don't like anyone looking at them," she gasped. Shaking with humiliation, she scrambled to her feet, but the woman only gave her a perplexed look and said nothing more.

In English literature class, and later in History of the Western World, Lara kept thinking of the word *unconventional*. She rolled it around in her thoughts as if she was tasting it. Somehow, now, it didn't seem so terrible that Miss Mik had seen her work. But in Advanced

Photography, Mr. Pettigrew frowned at the two photo-collages Lara selected to show him.

"These are interesting experiments," he said slowly. "But it seems you're *trying* to be artistic, Lara. As you know, class, we need to learn the basics before we can deviate from them. Now here —" He picked up Emily's snapshots and showed them to the class with approval. "These, you see, demonstrate a knowledge of contrast, of composition, of light . . . you see? Now, Lara, you need to think about whether you're quite ready for Advanced Photography." He pursed his lips, studying a collage. His finger kept tapping on the work so the class never took their eyes from it. "You've handled the shots of these buildings fairly well," Mr. Pettigrew conceded. "But these cut-out figures over here — they're way over-exposed. And you've colored them in with . . . what? Markers? I see. Well." He handed the collages back to Lara. "You've got a bit more basic work to do, Lara, learning F-stops and so forth. Right? Now, let's examine our cameras."

When he came to Lara's he shook his head and smiled. "Well, here's your problem right here," he told her. "This is such a limited old camera. I think you'll find a real difference working with a more sophisticated tool, Lara. We've got a couple of Minoltas in the lab — you are welcome to use one of them until your parents send you one of your own. I'll be happy to advise you on what to get."

Lara held the Voightlander tighter and found her voice. "But this is what I always . . . this is the only camera I want."

Mr. Pettigrew smiled indulgently. "I understand a sentimental attachment, Lara, but it just won't do for this class. You won't be able to complete some of the assignments."

Lara forced herself to stay calm. "I've been taking photographs for a long time — since I was eight," she explained. "It's really important to me, Mr. Pettigrew — it's what I want to do more than anything. I *do* know about F-stops and light and all that. I have a darkroom at home. I developed these like this on purpose because —"

"Lara, perhaps we could discuss this at another time," interrupted Mr. Pettigrew. "I'll let you stay in the advanced section until I see what you can do with the Minolta. Right?"

Lara trudged to the nurse's office before lunch and asked to be excused from afternoon sports and classes. When the nurse raised a dubious eyebrow, she went into the bathroom and was noisily sick. She'd learned how years ago, and it was effective because after heaving violently for ten minutes she looked and felt convincingly sick.

To her surprise, Miss Mik came into the infirmary during the break between classes and sports. "Things aren't going well, are they," she commented in her straightforward manner.

35

So Miss Mik had learned of the hockey incident and the photography class. Lara twisted her head away, suddenly hating the woman's meddling. "I don't care," she mumbled.

"I've taken you on Trails with me," said Miss Mik, ignoring Lara's words.

After a pause so long she squirmed on the cot, Lara asked sullenly, "What's Trails?"

"Well, to be honest, it's where they put you if they can't figure out what else to do with you." Despite herself, Lara looked up to see Miss Mik smiling. "Don't worry – they don't know what else to do with me, either. That's why I'm supervising Trails. I refused to coach anything."

"You don't coach a sport?"

Miss Mik pulled the curtain back from around the cot so a soft breeze came in the stuffy room. "No. I don't like competitive activities. I've got better things to do with my time."

"So do I."

Miss Mik considered her for a moment. "Such as what?"

"I . . . I just want . . . I need to be alone," Lara stammered, caught off guard. "My parents make me go to these stupid schools, but I'm different from everyone else and I never get any time to myself and it makes me crazy," she finished in a rush.

"Everyone is different from everyone else," Miss Mik said, but she was smiling again. "However, I agree –

someone who makes such intriguing collages and who reads Wallace Stevens and listens to Mozart's Requiem on her Walkman may be a little *more* different than usual. So — what are you going to do about it?"

Again the question caught her unawares. "I don't know," she whispered. "I don't know what to do." Miss Mik waited. Lara sat up on the cot. "Could I be . . . alone, if I did Trails?" she asked finally. "Whatever that is?"

She thought for a moment that Miss Mik had not heard her. The woman was gazing out the window pensively. But at last she answered, "I know that being alone is important in itself, Lara. But some people don't understand that, so you've got to give them a good reason. So — why do you want to be alone?"

"So I can take photographs," said Lara without hesitation. She faced Miss Mik with a mutinous glare. "Mr. Pettigrew thinks I can't do Advanced Photography! He thinks those stupid snapshots of Emily's are better than . . . He's a total jerk! I know exactly what I'm doing! I take pictures so I can make things out of them — that's the way I *see* things!" she cried. "That's how I can make things be anything I want —" She stopped abruptly, dismayed that she had revealed so much, but Miss Mik nodded.

"All right, Lara," she said. "I can arrange for you to have some time alone on Trails."

Chapter Four

Ben skipped school to braid Galaxy's mane. From the doorway of the barn he watched the school bus pause at the end of the drive, then with a belch of exhaust lumber on toward Jonesburg. It was 8:05, twenty minutes after his mother left every morning for work; because of that, she never knew about his stolen days.

Galaxy finished his grain and wandered out of the open stall to butt against Ben's shoulder. Ben grinned, rubbing the stallion's broad forehead. These stolen days had grown more frequent in the last year, but he still felt a momentary letdown at the sight of the bus pulling away without him. No matter how demanding the urge to have a day to himself, he always felt left behind at this moment, and whatever he had planned to do seemed insignificant.

Now he leaned against Galaxy and combed the thick mane with his fingers, trying to avoid looking at Marty Webber's truck. Right now, his mother would be tying on the red supermarket apron, preparing to stand at the cash register for the next ten hours. He shouldered Galaxy back into the barn and began to brush the dust from the black coat. But his enthusiasm had gone strangely flat and he sighed, draping his arms over the horse's back.

He didn't dislike school all that much. There were just times when he wanted to have the farm and Galaxy all to himself. It was an indulgence he felt ashamed of, but he could not help it. When he was alone, he could focus entirely on the stallion without being interrupted; he never realized how much tension built in him until these rare solitary days when he felt he was doing something completely *right*.

The kitchen door banged and in a moment Thomas Stahler poked his head in the barn. "I figured you was still hangin' around, son," he said. "Whole place feels different when you're gone . . . can't explain it. Here — I wrote you this."

Ben took the folded paper sheepishly and put it in his pocket without reading it. "Thanks, Dad," he said. His father's notes always said the same thing: "Benjamin Stahler was ill and could not attend school yesterday. T. Stahler." They smiled at each other, their shared secrets unspoken and warm between them.

"You working at the factory today?" Ben asked. His father smoothed his hand over the stallion's back and gazed past him out the door. "Yeah," he grunted. "It's the damnedest thing, kid — how just knowing I gotta spend the next eight hours fillin' cans with beans makes me want to sit down and die. Can't figure it out — it ain't a bad job, really, an' I'm lucky to have it. . . . Least, that's what your mom keeps telling me. An' the guys I work with are decent —"

"It's a horrible job!" The words burst from Ben passionately. Thomas reached across the stallion to put his hand on Ben's shoulder. "Hey, it ain't for you to worry about, Bennie," he said softly. "I'll be fine. Besides, I got some new ideas."

He knew this expression in his father's eyes. "Another project, Dad?" Ben asked eagerly. "What is it?" They were always exciting and somehow mysterious, his father's ideas, rich with such wonderful promise that Ben could never resist enthusiasm.

"You ever hear of a Saluki?" Thomas asked, and Ben shook his head. "Well, it's a kind of dog — but it ain't like any dog you ever saw. More like a floating cloud than a dog, I'd say — coat like spun silver, huge black eyes, runs like she was on air . . . Guy at work has a bitch he'd sell me cheap. His wife don't want it no more. An' what do you think — the bitch is already bred! Them dogs fetch up to eight hundred or a thousand dollars each in the city. All's I gotta do is —"

As long as Ben could remember, he'd been able to see his father's visions as clearly as if they already existed. It was so compelling to imagine the beautiful silvery dogs racing over the fields with the black stallion, leaping to catch the moonlight. . . . Suddenly he knocked the dust out of the brush and turned brusquely away. "It won't work," he muttered.

"What?"

"It just won't work, Dad!" he cried, anguished. "You know it won't! Mom'll have a fit if you spend any money on a *dog*. Think of all the money for food and shots and . . . and everything . . ." And you'll never be

40

able to sell the puppies, he continued silently, trying not to see the hopelessness in his father's eyes, but you'll keep saying you will, and then we'll have to keep them, and they'll eat a ton, and the lovely silvery coats will get all matted and dirty —

"Yeah, you're right, kid," Thomas said heavily. Ben watched his father walk, shoulders slumped, toward the car, and lost all desire to make Galaxy look like one of the gleaming dressage horses on his videotapes. Instead he wandered aimlessly to the riding ring, the stallion plodding behind. He'd set up a jump course at the beginning of the summer, designing all his obstacles to match the specifications in the American Horse Show Association book of guidelines a Huntingdon student had left in the barn the year before. He'd felt a proud satisfaction when he finally completed it, but this morning the ring looked like a junkyard to him. Jumps and hurdles constructed of old tires, tree limbs, and scraps of tin and chicken wire bore no resemblance to the clean, painted fences in a Grand Prix stadium.

He kicked at a fence post. It would all have to be torn down at the end of the week anyway, when Huntingdon began work on the new indoor ring. Galaxy butted Ben with his head and he smiled sadly. "You want us to do the jumps, don't you, boy?" he said.

Despite himself, he felt a stir of anticipation. Galaxy took the jumps now with such ease, sailing over them with a foot and a half to spare, that he had been planning on raising them. Maybe they could even knock a few seconds off their time, now the farrier had made the stallion a new set of shoes. His spirits revived, Ben went to the barn to get tools, but when he came out there was a Huntingdon truck pulled up by the door. "Now what?" he muttered.

"Hey, Ben!" called Red Schuman from the cab. "Your daddy around?"

"He had to work today," said Ben.

Red and another man got out and let down the tailgate. "Gonna be a real hot one today," grunted Red. "Look, Ben — your dad knew we was comin' today . . . school wants us to finish up them new stalls before the contractors start building that ring. Coupla kids got horses coming in next week."

"Sure," Ben shrugged. Red winked at him. "Kinda early in the year to be skippin' school," he commented dryly. "So, when'd your dad start down at the factory? Last I heard, they was closin' the place down."

"It's just part-time," said Ben. "I guess things picked up or something." Galaxy trotted around the yard snorting, scattering the chickens. Red grinned and jerked his thumb at him. "You ask me, that horse there's worth ten of them fancy showhorses the kids have. Man, the *money* that school has — not that I'm complaining. Decent job, decent benefits. Hey, Ben, why'n't you get a job with them?"

"I got a job with Dave Hawley, soon's school's done," Ben mumbled, knowing what the response would be, knowing he'd have to agree. Red Schuman hauled a sheet of plywood from the truck. "Yeah, well — you're lucky there, kid. He's a good guy, Dave is. Fair an' honest. Jobs like that ain't easy to find. You must be some crack mechanic!"

Ben answered with a wan smile and stood at a loss in the yard while Red and his partner began work. Galaxy snuffled in the dusty grass. It wasn't even nine and already the heat was stifling. He was utterly sapped of energy. The soft morning stillness he had been looking forward to was shattered by the screech of Red's power saw, and then, unexpectedly, his brother roared up the drive in the pickup. Ben didn't need to see Tom to know he'd been drinking. The pickup slewed to a stop by the house and Tom threw a bag of donuts at him from the open window.

"Breakfast, Bennie boy!" he grinned, getting out and sauntering toward him. "Fresh. Got them chocolate ones you like, too."

"Thanks," said Ben. He opened the bag and took one out, giving Tom a guarded smile.

"Skippin' school?" Tom teased. "I sure did that plenty of times! But you got it all wrong, Bennie — you ain't s'posed to hang out at *home*. Trouble is, you gotta skip school *with* somebody. Like a girl. Ain't you got a girl yet, little brother? That's where all the fun is."

"Shut up," mumbled Ben. Tom jabbed a punch at him, but stumbled over his own feet and giggled.

"Shut up yourself," he jeered. "Just trying to give you a little advice. Look, you wanna go up to Scranton? I

43

gotta get something there. C'mon — we could have a blast. Like we used to."

He met his brother's eyes reluctantly. When he'd been younger he'd have given anything to drive around with Tom, had followed after him hungry for his attention. "I got a lot of work to do —" he began uneasily, but dropped his eyes under Tom's sudden glower. "No, really — Webber's truck . . . I got to get that done, 'cause Mom'll —"

"Forget Mom!" said Tom with contempt. "Cripes, Ben, ain't you ever gonna grow up? It'll only be a few hours — have some fun, loosen up!"

Ben took a deep breath. "I don't want to," he said stubbornly. "I don't want to drive with you when you've been drinking."

With a curse, Tom slammed open the truck door and grabbed a beer. "The real trouble is, you think you're too damn good for people like us, don't you, Bennie?" he taunted. He chugged the beer, glaring at Ben, and challenged, "That's it, ain't it? Too damn good for your own brother?"

Ben glanced nervously toward the barn where Red Schuman was working. There was never any predicting what Tom might do. He could work himself up into a drunken fury, yelling for half an hour. He might get bored and stop if Ben didn't react, but at other times that could escalate his rage. Ben hesitated, unwilling to risk the embarrassment of having Red intervene. If he could just get to Galaxy, gallop away into the woods . . .

44

But Tom suddenly swung up into the truck, spat a final incoherent curse at Ben, and spun away down the drive. Ben hoped desperately that the men in the barn had heard nothing over the sound of the saw. It was his own fault, he thought. He should have told Tom he was sick or something. At least it wouldn't have set him off. He wished all at once that he was in Mr. Lapinsky's advanced auto mechanics class where he was supposed to be, in the familiar school shop listening to Jimmy Taylor swearing under the car next to his. He stared around the yard. The day was unredeemable. He could not face Marty Webber's damn truck, he thought fiercely. But maybe he could chop up that wood Dad needed for the stove. Something. Anything.

He put Galaxy in the field and tried not to think, attacking the pile of wood with an ax, throwing himself into the work until he lost all track of time. When Red and the other man left for lunch, he paused to wave. "That sure ain't my idea of skippin' school!" called Red from the window of the truck. "You better get something to drink, Ben — you gonna faint from heat exhaustion."

He drank a glass of water standing at the kitchen sink and looked out at Galaxy. Every few moments the stallion would lift his head and gaze toward the house, until Ben couldn't help laughing. "Okay, boy," he whispered. "Okay." And though he was inside with the door closed, the stallion snorted and pricked up his ears.

It took him half an hour to raise all the jumps to the highest notch. Then, without bothering to get the bridle, Ben vaulted onto Galaxy's back and signaled him with his knees toward the starting point. He grasped the thick mane, cantering around the perimeter of the ring until they'd found their stride. When the second hand of his watch lined up on twelve, Ben urged the stallion at the first jump. So effortless was his takeoff and landing Ben hardly felt a break in the powerful rhythm. There was a moment, at the zenith of each jump, when Ben felt suspended in space. Then the weightless drop back to earth, the surge forward, the black mane whipping in his face. Gathered perfectly, the stallion rose and rose again over the jumps, like a graceful wave cresting against the sky.

Galaxy took the final hurdle with an exuberant snort that matched Ben's triumphant yell. "Four whole seconds!" he crowed, looking at his watch. "I knew it! I knew you could do it faster!" He leaned forward and pounded Galaxy's neck in joy. When he looked up, he saw a girl watching him from the fence. For a long moment they both stared, and then she remarked, "You should braid his mane."

He was dumbfounded. The girl stood beside the gate, her dark-skinned arms folded along the top rail, her black hair tucked neatly behind her ears. Although she was dressed casually in black jeans and T-shirt, there was such an inscrutable element to her composure that she seemed striking, exotic. Galaxy swiveled his ears in curiosity. Under the girl's gaze Ben felt exposed and was uncomfortably aware of his sweat-streaked appearance. Something about her disturbed him. He moved the horse closer to the fence and asked, "Why'd you say that?"

The girl shrugged. "Because you can't see properly with the mane blowing in your face like that when you jump," she said. "And he'd be gorgeous with it braided."

He was at a total loss for what to say. The girl took out a pack of cigarettes, lit one, and nonchalantly flicked the match into the dirt without taking her eyes from his. He felt a sudden annoyance. It was almost as if she was challenging him — but to what, he did not know. "We haven't had rain in weeks," he said. "You could set the whole place on fire doing that."

She picked up the match immediately and asked, with exaggerated courtesy, "Where shall I put it, then?"

"It's your match," he shrugged. The girl's proximity made him restless and irritated, and he moved Galaxy back. But the girl followed.

"He's beautiful," she said softly, stepping close to put her hand on the stallion's shoulder. He could not read the expression in her eyes but was startled when she smiled at him. "I'm Lara McGrath." She held out her hand to him in a peculiarly formal gesture, and he took it. "Who are you?"

When he did not answer, her lips curled and she tossed the hair from her face. "Okay, I'll answer all your questions first and then maybe we can have a conversation," she mocked. "I go to Huntingdon, but I don't plan to be there for long because I've been kicked out of every school I ever went to; I'm adopted, that's why I don't have an accent; my real mother is a street prostitute in Mexico City; my parents are American and they got me from a convent and they have so much money it makes me sick. . . . There. Now I'm supposed to pull weeds around the barn or something, instead of killing girls on the hockey team."

He was so stunned by her outburst he didn't notice she still held his hand, and when he slid off Galaxy he could feel the warmth of her body. "Ben – my name's Ben," he blurted.

"Well, that's a start," she said flippantly. "So show me the weeds. I'll pull some so I can say I did it. I always like to tell the truth if I can." She paused and grinned. "You can begin talking any time, you know. This is supposed to be a conversation."

His face grew hot. "There's plenty of weeds everywhere." He scowled. "Pull as many as you like." He brushed past her, Galaxy at his heels. When he heard the girl following, he grunted without turning around. "Something else you need?"

"I didn't mean to make you mad."

"I'm not mad," he lied. "I'm busy. I gotta go." But he loitered at the steps, pretending to scrape his boots. The girl leaned over and picked up a golden feather off the ground, holding it so the iridescence caught the light. "It's incredible," she said. "What's it from?"

"Golden pheasant," Ben answered shortly. "My dad raised them for a while." He gave up the pretense of indifference and turned toward her. "I didn't think those damn birds had any feathers left that pretty." The girl twirled the feather back and forth between her fingers and Ben watched, half mesmerized. It looked as if she was playing tag with the sunlight. "Look," he said abruptly. "If you're supposed to pull weeds, you better get at it. If you want, I'll help." He frowned. "Don't you guys have a teacher or someone when you come down here to work? There usually is."

"Miss Mik said she'd be back in an hour," the girl said, trailing the feather down her cheek. "She's with some other kids on the cross-country trails clearing brush or something. She just dropped me off here."

They eyed each other. "Do you always tell people your whole life history two seconds after you meet them?" he demanded.

"No," she laughed. "I just thought I'd try it with you. I might try it with others, but I haven't decided." Her expression changed. "Why? Did it bother you?" She narrowed her eyes, defiant. "I wasn't making it up, if that's what you think. I may as well say it first off, since that's what everyone wants to know around here. 'Where are you from? Oh, Mexico? But you don't have an accent. Oh, you're adopted? How *nice*,'" she mimicked, and added, "I was left in a basket on the steps of a convent. If my parents hadn't adopted me I'd either be a nun or a prostitute."

Again he had no idea how to respond. "Well, you don't look much like a nun," he said at last, and immediately regretted it. She gave him a furtive, enigmatic smile and looked quickly away. He kicked the edge of the step. "Look, if we're going to get at those weeds we better start," he muttered.

Out of the corner of his eye Ben watched the girl yank ineffectively at the weeds. All the vitality that had fascinated him seemed to have been subdued and she appeared almost a different person. Restless, he went for a wheelbarrow to load the weeds in, but when he came back she had disappeared.

It crossed his mind that there was something not right about her, and he stood with uncertainty in the yard, provoked at his own anxiety. Huntingdon kids were supposed to be supervised when they worked on the farm, he growled to himself as he stalked around to the front of the house. She disturbed him so much he was not sure he wanted to find her. He could not bring himself to call out her name, else she would become too real.

She was crouching by the fish pond, staring into the water where the lily pads grew thickest. She lifted her head sharply at his approach, and he felt like an intruder. He knelt at the edge of the pond several feet away from her and stirred the water with his hand. In a moment, large red-spotted koi appeared from the murky depths. He wiggled his fingers and the koi drifted up to nibble at them, a speckled one nudging his hand.

Without looking at the girl, he said, "My dad once had this idea he could make money breeding Japanese koi — I don't know who he thought would buy them around here." He laughed softly and kept playing with the fish. With a start, he realized he could sense the girl's mood in much the same way he was able to sense Galaxy's. It was all he could do not to look at her. "My dad loves beautiful things," he went on. "Trouble is, he always thinks he'll make a fortune on it, but it never works out. My dad sees something beautiful and he imagines everyone else in the world will want it too. Drives my mom nuts." He tickled the water. "These here were real little when we got them. My brother Tom and me each got two. Mine got so tame I could feed them out of my hand — like this speckled one. His name is Batman. I was into Batman when I was ten. My other one — Robin — he got eaten. Raccoon, I guess."

The girl was watching him with unabashed interest now. Ben dried his hands on his jeans and the koi sank out of sight. "Gosh, I haven't played with them for ages. They just get along on their own now," he said, walking casually toward her. "If you look around the place, you can see stuff left over from every single one of my dad's projects."

"Like your horse?"

"Yeah," he smiled. "Appaloosas. Dad really loved

spotted horses. He had four or five once, but Galaxy's the only one left." He added with caution, "You want to see some of the other things? He tried to grow orchids for a while. There were a few left last spring, but they might all be dead by now."

She followed him to the greenhouse. Under a mass of ferns where the plastic was still intact, the girl found one pot with a living orchid. She ran her finger over the waxy flower, brown against white. "Like a dancing swan," she said. He looked at her with wonder. "I couldn't stand pulling those stupid weeds!" she cried, suddenly fierce, as if he'd asked her to explain herself. "What a total waste of time! I just wanted to be alone."

"Don't matter to me what you do," he replied, bewildered. "I like being alone, too. But won't you get into trouble with your teacher?"

She smiled, a smug, cunning smile. "Miss Mik won't bother me," she said, and paused. "I just want to take photographs. It's all I want to do."

There was such passion in her last words that Ben was sure she was telling him something important, and equally sure that if he answered her the wrong way, she might disappear again. He said, feeling stupid, "Photos?"

"I take photographs." Her voice was haughty now, as if she thought he could not possibly understand. He could not keep up with her shifts of mood. "I cut them up into bits and make collages of them," she explained.

"Oh. Like an artist, you mean?"

She left the greenhouse without answering. Irritated, he had no choice but to follow, but he wasn't going to be jerked around by this girl's moods like some yo-yo. He slapped the fender of Webber's truck. "Well, look," he said. "I gotta get some work done on this, so if you —"

"You're fixing this?" she asked, ignoring his hint. "I'll just watch you."

"Well —" He hesitated, feeling foolish, unwilling for her to leave and just as unwilling to let her stay and watch him work. He looked at her helplessly. When she smiled he had the uncomfortable impression that she knew exactly what she was doing and the effect it had on him. "I have to get my tools," he said.

The girl was still leaning against the truck when he got back. Nearby, Galaxy pawed the ground, bored. "What do you do?" she asked Ben.

He didn't answer at first, propping up the hood of the truck. How could he explain about Galaxy, about dreams with no names, about being in love with beauty so pure it had no purpose beyond itself? "I fix cars and trucks," he said. "I'm going to be a mechanic."

She peered into the engine as he worked. It made him nervous to have her so near and he dropped the wrench. As if there had been no break in the conversation, she said, "I don't believe that's what you want to do, though."

"What are you talking about?" he retorted, twisting a cap so hard it flipped out of his fingers. "It is so what

I want to do. It's what I'm learning in school, and it's what I'll be doing when I get out."

She leaned even closer to him and in spite of his distress, he could not bring himself to move away. "But do you like it?" she challenged him. "Messing around in dirty old engines?"

He stammered, "Yes," but she seemed to be forcing him into further explanation. "I don't mind it. I'm real good at it. It's decent work," he insisted.

"Well, I think you hate it," she said softly. She was standing so close now their arms touched. He couldn't even remember what he'd just said. It didn't seem to matter. There was some other conversation going on behind their words, so he could no longer think straight.

"I saw you ride the stallion," the girl said. She stooped under the truck and handed the fallen wrench to him. "Here – is this what you're looking for?"

But he answered, "What do you mean?"

She didn't reply for a moment. "I actually hate horses," she said bluntly. "But my brother rides – Olympic level. He's one of the best. Mom and Dad are always dragging me around to Timothy's events." She tossed her head. "I've watched all the best riders. And I've never seen anyone who could ride the way you did. Never. And I never saw a horse like that either."

He felt the way he had the night Galaxy was born – as if a whole new universe was opening inside him. The girl put her hand on his arm. "You were both so perfect," she whispered. She ran her fingers down his arm to his grimy hand, took it and turned it, palm up, frowning. "Maybe you do fix trucks. Maybe you're great at it. But it's not what you *do*. I mean, it's not what you were *born* to do."

A car was coming down the drive. The girl dropped his hand. "That's Miss Mik," she said. "I have to go. If she asks, tell her I pulled a million weeds."

Halfway across the yard she turned and looked back at Ben. "You never said hello to me," she called. "You haven't even said my name."

"Lara," he answered. "Lara. Hello."

Chapter Five

Ben stared blankly at Mr. Mercer scribbling algebra problems on the blackboard. He had not copied one into his notebook. He slumped, stretched his legs into the aisle, and waited for the last class of the day to drone to an end.

It had been a week since he'd seen the girl from Huntingdon. Red Schuman and his men were busy building new stalls, and no students would be sent to the farm to work until they were finished. Ben forced his attention to the textbook but could not focus on the print.

"It's all I want to do." He remembered the intensity

of the girl's voice speaking those words more than he remembered her. He could recall certain momentary aspects of her: the impact of her eyes when she smiled for the first time, the feel of her hand on his arm, her brown finger tracing the orchid petal, the curve of her shoulder as she crouched by the koi pond. But if he tried to contain an image of her whole in his mind, she eluded him like a mirage. Only her voice retained a coherent form in his memory, every nuance vivid. "It's all I want to do." In her words he'd caught a mixture of defiance and sorrow, as if she knew she spoke a truth that kept her a willing captive. But more than anything else, Ben remembered the certainty in her voice.

By Friday afternoon Ben was exhausted with his preoccupation and did not even go into the house before riding Galaxy up the Buckhorns to the clearing. It was mid-September and the trees were already showing patches of color. Ben sat motionless on the stallion, breathing deeply in the clear mountain air. Each breath brought him closer to the horse, until he could feel Galaxy's heart beating with his own. And when they were breathing in the same rhythm, the stallion and he began to move.

He kept the image of what he wanted to achieve focused in his mind and in every muscle of his body. Dressage was more than a neck arched in a certain way, more than legs moving in a particular pattern; it was hidden energy transformed into conscious movement. The stallion responded eagerly, meeting the vision in Ben's mind.

After a time he drew the stallion up and thought about what Lara had told him — that they were perfect, he and Galaxy together. The stallion stood without moving. Little stirred in the now-dark forest around the clearing. But something felt different. Ben listened, acutely aware of a tiny rustle in the leaves, of a brush of air through the hemlocks. Gradually he realized that what he was listening for did not lie outside himself. The words Lara had spoken were now *his* words, his truth. They had been his all along; hearing the girl speak them had been a recognition, not a discovery.

He found in his own heart the image the girl's words had formed: he and Galaxy, in perfect accord, performing the balletlike dressage routine in an Olympic arena. He saw this image as if it were a reality, something waiting only for his acknowledgment to exist.

But later, brushing Galaxy down in the dim barn, Ben's conviction dissolved. "Maybe *she* can do what she wants," he muttered, accenting each word with a brush stroke. "Maybe people like her get to decide what they want to do, but other people are just stuck with what they get." He brushed so vigorously the stallion turned to look at him in mild surprise.

He'd run into Dave Hawley at the feed store two days ago. "Now that dealership over on Route 48's closin' down, I'm getting more work than I can handle," Hawley had told him, clapping him on the back. "So you just get that certificate, Ben — I got maybe fifty hours a week for you."

Fifty hours a week. Fifty *hours*. "I'll *die!*" he whispered. By next winter he'd be at work before the sun was up and out long after it was down. He set his jaw, told himself he was lucky to have the promised job when so many people were out of work. And besides, what more could he expect, graduating from Clayton County Vo-Tech? It wasn't like it was even the regular high school in Jonesburg . . . not that *it* was any better, he thought sourly. Tom had gone to Vo-Tech, but his cousins Brenda and Mike had gone to Jonesburg High, and look where that got any of them. Tom's a drunk, Brenda got pregnant in her junior year and dropped out, and Mike's — but lots of people were like that in Jonesburg. If you were lucky you got a decent job, married and had a family, worked hard, maybe went out bowling Friday nights, watched Sunday afternoon football — plenty of chance to make a good life, if you kept out of trouble. And what was the point, anyway, in dreaming beyond that?

Betty Stahler barely glanced up when Ben came in the house. "We ate," she said. "There's leftovers in the oven."

"Sorry," Ben muttered. He had no appetite, but his mother would comment on the cost of food if he didn't eat. Thomas winked at him over the newspaper. "So, kiddo," he said. "How's that long-legged pig of yours doing?"

"He's okay, I guess," Ben replied. There was an unusual note in his father's voice, but before Thomas could continue, Betty said, "Ben, don't you go fussin' with that horse again till you finish Marty Webber's truck. I mean it, you hear? You said you'd get it done before school started, and now look."

"Mom, I had to order another part, I told you," Ben sighed. How tired her eyes looked tonight. He remembered suddenly how she used to whirl around the kitchen when he and Tom were much younger, dancing to the radio with his father, laughing until they all joined in. Now she erased a square on her crossword puzzle. "You need clothes and I ain't got no way to buy them," she said without looking up. "I hate you goin' around with holes in everything, Bennie. You look so nice when you dress decent."

Yeah, sure . . . as if working at Hawley's Garage was going to leave much room for wearing nice clothes, except maybe Friday nights when he could go out and get drunk like everyone else, he thought bitterly, pushing the food around on his plate. He felt his father's troubled eyes on him. "Betty, leave the kid be a minute," Thomas said. "I got something to tell him." He folded the newspaper with deliberate care. "Crighton was over this afternoon, after you took off, looking at the new stalls. We're gonna have to use that near field for them new horses coming in — but don't worry none, Ben. You can keep Galaxy in the upper field —"

"But then I can't see him from the house!" cried Ben.

"Sure you can — all's we gotta do is move the fence over along the hedgerow . . . see? Just shut up a minute,

59

will you?" Thomas settled back in his chair. "Now the school's building that indoor ring and the jump course, Crighton's hiring some topnotch trainer to work with them kids once a week — Saturday afternoons. Guy from Connecticut, I think he said. Teaches Olympic-level riders. Anyways, that's besides their regular riding lessons. This guy's supposed to be one of the best." Thomas's face creased in a satisfied grin. "So I tell Crighton: You want that big field? You can have that field for no extra rent, if my boy can take lessons on his horse with that trainer, just like the rest of them kids."

Betty slapped her magazine on the table. "That's right, Thomas Stahler. Just keep throwing money away. What on earth does Ben need lessons for? He rides too much as it is."

Ben stared at his father. "What'd he say, Dad?"

"Said it was okay with him. All's he had to do was get the okay from the trainer." Thomas whacked Ben lightly with the folded newspaper. "But don't you worry. That guy'll be lucky to get you, the way I figure it. So what d'you think?"

He looked at Thomas with shining eyes. If he could have real lessons with a real trainer . . . if the trainer worked with Grand Prix–level riders . . . if someone like that could see what he and Galaxy could do together . . . But he was caught short by his mother's look.

He didn't even have a saddle. He didn't have a bridle with the correct bit, didn't have the right clothes or any of the equipment. He didn't have the money to enter shows. Very soon he would not even have time. He rose abruptly and dumped his dishes in the sink. Thomas seemed about to speak, then shrugged and went outside.

Ben scrubbed the dishes long after they were clean, staring out the window at the evening's first stars. In a moment, his mother came to stand behind him. He turned, startled. "It's hard not to believe him, isn't it, Bennie?" she said, her voice so low he wasn't sure he'd heard. "I want to believe him too. I always did. You know how old I was when I met your dad? Seventeen — same as you."

He wanted to bury his face against her the way he had as a child, to hide from the sadness in her voice. "Mom . . ." he began, but she brushed her hand over his hair and continued. "There's nothing like your father's dreams, Ben. Nothing in the world. They're like . . . some beautiful movie. Like a story you don't want to end." She leaned against the sink, both hands clenched on the edge of the counter. "Oh, Bennie," she cried. "It's so awful not to be able to believe him anymore. I want to. But I can't. They just ain't real, them dreams." She stopped suddenly and grabbed the sponge from Ben as if angry with him for hearing her. "You gotta leave things be the way they are, Ben," she said reproachfully, wiping the counter with quick jabs. "There's no use tryin' to make things out to be different than they are. It don't pay the mortgage and it don't feed the kids and it don't put a new roof on the house."

She threw the sponge in the sink. "You want to ride that horse, you go ahead. I can't stop you. But that's all there is to it, Bennie — just a ride. You gonna have a job in a few months and you can't blow it. There ain't nothin' else for you, 'cause we don't have anything to give you."

The next afternoon, as the blue Huntingdon vans sped past Stahler's farm on the way to Saturday games with other schools, Lara McGrath appeared in the doorway of the barn where Ben was stacking hay bales. As at their first meeting, she stood there silently for several minutes before he noticed. Again, he was sweaty, shirtless, and covered in bits of hay, and he flushed when he saw her. Lara was dressed in black as before, a camera over her shoulder. The strap crossed between her breasts so they were defined under the T-shirt, and she was watching him with a slight, secret smile. He stumbled with a bale. "Something wrong?" she asked with studied innocence. He arranged the bale carefully on the pile to give himself time to regain his composure. He couldn't believe how much he'd wanted to see her again.

"They're heavy," he muttered. She came in and sat near him on a bale, but he didn't trust himself to look at her. "So what're you supposed to do here today?"

"I'm supposed to sweep out the new stalls," she said primly. "But of course I'm not going to. I'm going to take pictures. Miss Mik won't be back for a couple of hours."

He caught her mischievous look and grinned despite his discomfort. "So I guess Miss Mik is okay, huh," he said. "She sure leaves you alone like you want."

She shrugged. "Some of them are easier to butter up than others." She jumped up, brushing the hay from her jeans. "You coming?"

"I thought you wanted to be alone," he said but shoved the last bale onto the pile so quickly it toppled to the floor.

"I do," she mused, frowning a little. "But you don't make me feel like I'm with another person. Isn't that funny?"

He wasn't sure it was funny. He wasn't sure if it meant that he was just a nobody to her. "I'm kinda busy," he hesitated.

"You are not," she said impatiently. "You're all done with the hay — I can see that."

Instead of answering, he asked, "What're you going to take pictures of?"

She fingered the camera with a grimace. "I don't know," she said in disgust. "I hate it here. There's nothing interesting to look at."

"What do you *want* to take pictures of, then?" he persisted.

"People," she answered. "All kinds. Like in cities. Especially in the projects, or the street people, or in subways. Things like that."

"Rocks?" he suggested.

She studied him. "Rocks?"

"Yeah. Rocks – kind of a ledge, with caves. I think maybe the Indians used them. There's even a stalactite."

"Where?"

He gestured up the hill toward the lower slopes of the Buckhorns. "Not too far. You could be back in time to sweep the stalls, if I helped." He kept his tone carefully nonchalant. "I could show you, if you want."

As they walked up through the field he felt triumphant, kept looking back at her, anxious that she might suddenly disappear as she had the other day. Galaxy followed lazily, and in the stallion's presence, Ben was more confident. "Why do you hate horses?" he asked.

"I don't hate horses!" she flashed, and he didn't say anything for a moment. Then he muttered, "You said you hated them, the other day."

"Oh, don't believe everything I say," Lara said lightly. "I probably meant I hated having to go to all those stupid horse shows. It's really the people I hate. They only care about horses because horses are expensive. It's a great way to show off how much money they have. Money makes me *sick*."

"You oughta try not having any for a while," Ben grunted. Involuntarily, the girl glanced back toward the farm, then met his eyes. "Yeah," he nodded. "That's what no money looks like. Nothing gets fixed. Nothing works properly. Place is falling apart."

"I know what poverty looks like," said Lara defensively. "I've seen plenty of it. Ever been to the projects

64

in the Bronx? I go out there on the subway to take pictures. My dad would kill me if he found out. And Mexico City, where I used to live — there's miles of slums. Shacks made of cardboard and broken crates and rags. After the earthquake, the poor people lived in the rubble, like in little caves. I wasn't supposed to hang out in that part of the city, of course." She laughed bitterly. "But I figured I have a right to, since it's where my real mother lives . . . somewhere in there. Or maybe in Tepito — I used to walk down there and think, Maybe that woman is my mother. Or that one, with the sores on her face. It's real dangerous there. I wasn't supposed to go there, either."

They entered the woods and left Galaxy watching from the fence gate. The girl walked so close behind Ben on the narrow trail he could hear her breathing. Without turning, he asked, "How do you know your real mother is a prostitute? Did you ever meet her?"

"No," said Lara. "But I found the place where Veronica — that's my mom — said they'd adopted me from. Santa Maria-Theresa Convent. And I found out it's a refuge for street prostitutes and their babies. A lot of the prostitutes are children, too. Twelve and thirteen years old."

"I can't believe your mother would tell you about the place, if she knew that!"

"Oh, I can," said Lara darkly. "She wanted me to know." She paused and looked up into the trees. "What's that bird?"

"Wood thrush." He pointed. "There. It's really hard to see. Pretty song, huh?"

He showed her a colony of orange fungus growing on a fallen log and was amazed by how skilled she was with the many buttons and levers on her camera as she squatted to take pictures. He tapped a funnel-shaped web with a twig, and a spider dashed out. "He thinks a fly got caught and he'll get dinner." Ben grinned. "Can you take a picture of something that small?" But she was already lying on her stomach, aiming the camera inches from the web. Her body was small and rounded, and he wondered how she could look so vulnerable and so unapproachable at the same time.

"Don't stand in my light," she demanded and he swallowed, taking a few steps back.

It was always cool under the rock ledges where water dripped even in the driest summers. Ben slapped mosquitoes as he waited for Lara to photograph the pale yellowish gray stalactite he'd discovered years ago in a crevice of the ledge. "Come here," she called, and he scrambled along the rock to the narrow opening. "I need to get down in further," she said. "Hold my legs so I don't fall in."

"Don't you know how to say please?" he grumbled, torn between annoyance and the intense desire to touch her. She glanced up at him. "You sound just like Timothy," she said. Then, as if she'd voiced something that frightened her, she caught her breath sharply and turned her face back to the crevice. But in that instant,

Ben saw her eyes flicker with pain. "What's the matter?" he asked, bewildered.

She only shoved herself deeper into the crevice. "Just hold my legs," she answered savagely, her voice muffled in the earth. He grasped her ankles. It wasn't what he'd imagined touching her would be. She felt unyielding, unreachable, and after a few minutes he called out, "We have to go now or you'll be late. I mean it. You better come out."

By the time they were back in the field, Lara's mood had changed again to an enchanting mixture of playfulness and mystery. She told him merrily about her exploits at the schools she'd been expelled from, but even through his laughter Ben realized that she was trying to shock him. He refused to be baited. "I don't care how many boyfriends you've had, Lara."

"I think you do," she said, laughing.

"Think what you like," he retorted and was startled to see her taken aback for a moment.

"Well, it's the easiest way to get kicked out," she asserted blithely, after a pause. "Sex, drugs, drinking — that's what those schools always have rules about. If you don't want to be there, choose one. . . . Sex is the most fun."

He didn't reply and by the time they reached the lower gate, his head ached. He wished Galaxy was around. Almost at once, the stallion emerged from the thickets and trotted down the hill toward them. When Ben stopped, Lara bumped into him. He didn't look at her, but he didn't move away. Galaxy snuffled them both and the girl reached out to touch him. Against the black coat her brown skin seemed to glow golden in the sun. "See?" she said softly. "I don't hate horses." She ran her hand up the stallion's withers. "You really should braid his mane, Ben. He'd look fantastic." She hesitated, then added, "I know how to do it properly. I always helped Timothy."

It seemed to Ben that she was forcing herself to say her brother's name. They were standing so close he could not turn away this time. But Lara could shift herself from one mood to another with the caprice of a magician transforming air into substance. The elusive shadow in her eyes disappeared and she gave him a smile that was like a secret meant only for him. "I used to braid Conquistador's mane before the shows," she continued. "Timothy only wanted me to do it because I could braid neater than anyone else."

If he said the wrong thing now she might vanish in a puff of smoke. "Next time, you can braid it," he told her. "Next time you come."

They walked slowly through the lower field and Ben told her about Galaxy's birth under the northern lights. "My dad didn't know old Nell was pregnant," he said. "We didn't know anything till the night she foaled. There'd been some champion Hanoverian stallion boarded here the year before, belonged to some kid at the school."

68

She raised her eyebrows. "People pay a lot of money for Hanoverian stud fees," she teased him.

"I figured that," he said uncomfortably. "That's why I don't hardly ever tell anyone. The stallion's owners could've taken Galaxy away, I guess, if they found out. Thing is, it *was* an accident. The fences weren't too good, but no one thought . . ."

Lara giggled. "You're a horse thief, Ben." She paused, then said quietly, "I can see it, though – the stars, and the northern lights. And the little black colt, and a whole galaxy drifting down from outer space to cover him and keep him warm."

Her words filled him with longing. "Dad said he was born under a different sky," he said. "He told me anything's possible under a different sky."

Later, after dark, Ben leaned on the fence and watched Galaxy grazing a short distance away. The spell was still woven around him. "*Lara* was born under a different sky," he whispered into the night.

Chapter Six

The rock ledge emerged in the developing tray under the amber light of the darkroom. Lara lifted out the photo with tweezers, finished processing, and clipped it to a line to dry, then stood back to study her prints. She waved a notebook at them so they would dry faster and glanced anxiously at the clock — her sign-up hour was almost over. The prints had come out exactly as she'd wanted.

An idea for a new collage was emerging in her mind, gaining solid definition like the prints in the developing fluid. She counted five photo papers left in the packet, and she had only two more rolls of film. She had no money to buy anything. She remembered Ben Stahler's words the other day: "Try not having any for a while."

"I *hate* money!" she snarled. And she hated William McGrath for trying to control her by leaving her at Huntingdon with no checking account and no weekly allowance the way she used to have. So she could not leave. So she could not buy anything they didn't want her to have. So she would be forced to ask for everything. "I won't ask!" she said, gritting her teeth. "I'll get what I want some other way." Trying to concentrate, she used the remaining paper to develop the rest of the roll. As she clipped the last print to the line she stopped, startled, and looked at it closely.

The boy stared directly back at her with his candid, steady eyes. He must have been standing so still she hadn't seen him as she clicked the shutter. Even now, if she stepped back, Ben's image melted into the undergrowth. She held the print closer and again the image materialized into focus, as unobtrusive as Ben himself. His presence seemed to fill the small room and Lara felt a perplexing comfort.

70

A sudden pounding on the door made her jump, and she yelled, "Get away, Carmen Ronzoni! I have five more minutes in here, you little worm!" There was silence on the other side of the photo-lab door, and she began to grab her prints from the line. After a moment Carmen's voice whined, "The clock out here says after nine."

Lara pressed her face to the door. "Just shut up, Carmen!" She waited, listening, then pushed the door open so violently Carmen scuttled behind a desk. Lara looked at him scornfully. "That's very smart, Carmen," she said. "You'll be safe there. Maybe you'll get extra credit if you tell Mr. Pettigrew about this."

She was unwilling to break her solitude by returning to the dormitory, so she wandered to the edge of the playing fields. The hedgerow on the far side was nothing but a dark mass under the late evening sky. She squinted, trying to find a light from the house on Stahler's farm. Strangely, the school felt more bearable to her because the farm lay just beyond the trees. Like the slums she'd wandered through in cities, the farm's decrepit exterior concealed a secret life — brilliant fish in a dirty pond, golden birds covered in dust, orchids growing among broken pots. Because it was hidden, the beauty seemed somehow hers.

She remembered taking a picture of a single red geranium on the sill of a shattered window high above a drug-ridden Bronx street, remembered capturing on film the glimmer of a thin golden chain worn by a child who smiled at her from a cardboard doorway in a Mexico City slum. Now, when she closed her eyes, she could see a boy in dirty jeans riding an Appaloosa stallion over hurdles made of junk. In the darkness she whispered the lines from Wallace Stevens's poem: " 'Things as they are Are changed upon the blue guitar.' "

When she got back to the dormitory, Lara paused to look in the window at the girls sprawled across the lounge floor watching a video. A shock of loneliness caught her unexpectedly and she slipped in the door to run up the stairs. She sat at her desk, the newly developed photos spread before her. But she could not concentrate. She fought the urge as long as she could, then went slowly down the hall to the pay phone.

The ringing seemed endless, first in the New York apartment, then at Greenwood, then, absurdly, in her father's office, her mother's office. . . . But she knew all along they wouldn't be at any of those places. Not at 9:30 on a Tuesday night.

She knew where they were, where they always were in the evenings now. Slowly she punched in another set of numbers and listened to a voice answer, "Carrington Central Hospital. May I direct your call, please?" The words were repeated, more impatiently, and the connection clicked off when she didn't answer. She leaned her head against the phone. Not once since she'd been at Huntingdon had she been able to go through with that call.

She sat on her bed and clipped images from her photographs. Gradually her heart stopped pounding and the tension constricting her throat relaxed. She took the picture of Ben and held it cupped in her hand, gazing at it for a long time.

"I thought I'd find you here." Lara jumped when Miss Mik spoke from the doorway. The woman held something out to her. "I thought you might like this. I taped it off the radio." Lara took the cassette and read "Brahms – A German Requiem" in Miss Mik's neat printing on the cover. "You don't already have it, do you?" she asked, and Lara shook her head. She waited for Miss Mik to ask her why she'd been late for check-in after she'd finished in the photo-lab, but the woman only suggested, "Why don't you play it?"

She didn't want to listen with Miss Mik standing there, but she didn't know how to refuse. Trying to shield her photos from the woman's sight, Lara reluctantly slipped the cassette into the tape player. But almost at once she was caught in the haunting orchestral music that built, layer upon layer, until the pure voices triumphed over even the loudest drums. "That's a requiem?" she asked in spite of herself.

"Yes," said Miss Mik.

Lara leaned her chin on her hands and listened, rapt. The music seemed to shed darkness and to rise, swelling with drums and voices, in a crescendo of light.

"'Rage, rage against the dying of the light,'" Miss Mik said softly, and Lara stared at her. "Dylan Thomas,"

73

she explained, smiling and sitting next to her on the bed.

"I know," said Lara. "It's one of my favorite poems." To her horror, her eyes burned with sudden tears, and she jabbed the off button on the tape player. "I'll listen to it later," she muttered, jumping off the bed.

But Miss Mik did not leave. "That's quite a collection of books," she commented, going to the bookshelf and reading the titles.

"They're just my mom's from when she was in college."

"But you read them, obviously."

Lara fussed with some papers on the desk and refused to look up. She wasn't fooled by what Miss Mik was doing, pretending interest in her things, trying to trick her into her confidence.

"You must have inherited your mother's taste in books," Miss Mik remarked.

"I didn't inherit anything from her," Lara growled. "She isn't my real mother. My real mother is a prostitute in Mexico City with sores all over her face. That's who I inherited from."

"You've met her?" asked Miss Mik.

"I have not met her! Why does everyone think I've met her!"

"It sounded as if you had," Miss Mik replied, her voice calm. "It sounded as if you knew her."

"Well I don't."

"But you must have thought about her a lot."

74

"Wouldn't you?" Lara shot back.

"Of course," said Miss Mik. "Yes."

Through the open door Lara could hear laughter coming from the lounge downstairs. "Shouldn't you be down there?" she demanded nastily. "Instead of up here trying to be my friend? I don't need friends."

Miss Mik went to the door immediately. "Well then, there is no point in my staying, is there?" She paused and added pleasantly, "If I see any more evidence of smoking in this room, Lara, I'll bring it to the dean's attention. Understood? And tomorrow –" She interrupted herself to answer one of the girls calling up the stairs to her, then continued. "Tomorrow you can either start clearing the lower brook trail or do some clean-up work over at Stahler's. What'll it be?"

"I don't care."

"Fine," said Miss Mik. "You can help Rick and Jordie at the farm get the stalls ready for some horses. And I expect you to work." She went down the stairs.

Lara jumped up and slammed the door so hard the building echoed. She dashed the photos to the floor and kicked them under the bed. Then, her hand shaking, she took a cigarette from her last pack hidden under the mattress and lit it, gasping down the smoke between crying. She wished Miss Mik would come back and catch her. She listened at the door, but there was no sound.

She could not bear to do nothing. She finished the cigarette hurriedly, not enjoying it, and gathered up the photos from the floor. On a piece of Bristol board, she arranged images of the rock ledge cut from several prints, overlapping each so they formed an uneven tower. She cut out mouths from the crowd pictures she'd taken at a soccer game, then meticulously glued clusters of the screaming mouths in the dark crevices under the ledges. As she searched through the scraps for anything else she could use, she found the photo of Ben. She paused and again held it cupped in her hand.

After a few moments, she filled in with black marker around the tower of ledges so it looked suspended in space. She cut eyes from the soccer photos and positioned them so they peered into the hiding places where the screaming mouths were trapped. She glued everything carefully, then propped the collage up to study it, pleased.

The next morning, Emily said, "Put that where I don't have to look at it, Lara. It's sick. It's really a disgusting picture. What'd you go and ruin all those soccer pictures for? That was our assignment. Mr. Pettigrew will have a fit."

"You think it's sick, Em?"

Emily rolled away in the bed and faced the wall. "It's horrible. Really."

"I wanted it to be sick," said Lara. "*I'm* sick. Didn't you know that?"

When Miss Mik drove them to the farm that afternoon, Lara noticed an unfamiliar truck in the yard. A man in his early twenties lounged against it smoking, an open can of beer in one hand. Lara saw a six-pack on the seat of the cab. The man caught her eye and she felt a startling rush of heat over her face. She turned away, but was acutely aware of him as she followed Miss Mik to the barn. When the woman left her with Rick and Jordie to spread straw in the stalls, she slipped out and casually strolled across the yard. The man shifted against the truck, grinned at her, and swallowed the last of the beer. She gazed back without showing a flicker of interest, but she could almost taste the beer.

"Well, hey there," said the man softly. "You from Huntingdon?"

"What's it to you?"

He chuckled, tossed the empty can in the back of the truck, and snapped the top off another. "Nothing to me. Want a beer?"

She shrugged. She would wait until he wanted something from her. She wouldn't owe anyone a favor. "Maybe," she said, and walked back toward the barn. She could feel him watching and her heart beat faster. He had a truck. He could get her out of this place. All she had to do was play him the right way. Without paying the slightest attention to the man, she lit her last cigarette and shook her hair back as she blew smoke into the air. A thrill ran through her. She could get anything she wanted from him. She smiled.

She was taken aback when she saw Ben watching from the door of the barn. He was scowling. "Don't you know better'n to smoke around a barn? Cripes,

Lara! Put that thing out." Deliberately, Lara dunked the cigarette in a water bucket and followed him inside. Ben ignored her, lugging sacks of grain from a wheelbarrow to a bin.

After several minutes, when he still had not acknowledged her further, she snapped, "What are you in such a bad mood for? I don't want to be here either, you know."

"Then go."

Lara watched a few moments more, her eyes narrowed, then went to stand by the bin where he was dumping the grain. He tried to avoid her, but she shifted so he had to brush against her. "Who's that guy outside?" she asked, a calculated combination of disinterest and suggestiveness in her voice. With satisfaction, she saw Ben's face darken.

"My brother," he muttered. "And you just stay away from him, Lara. He's bad news."

Again she moved closer, let her arm linger briefly against his. She smiled at him when he didn't answer, and he seemed to catch his breath. But he did not move away this time. "He didn't look like bad news to me," she commented. "I thought he looked like fun." She smiled knowingly. "So what's his name?"

"Tom," he replied tersely. He hefted another sack into the bin. "Look, Lara, if you're supposed to be working you better get to it. I don't feel like fooling around today. Aren't Rick and Jordie —"

"Does he live here?"

He swung around and for a second she thought she'd pushed him too far. His eyes darted away, dark with something she could not read. "He lost his job 'cause he's a drunk, so he moved back home. Okay, Lara? If you're so interested, go out and talk to him yourself. I don't care."

"I'm not interested," she countered, uneasy. She was sorry, suddenly, that she had started this. There was an ache in her throat and she swallowed, wishing she could touch Ben, not to torment him but to have him touch her back. But before she could speak again, he turned and stalked away.

Chapter Seven

Lara found herself waiting for Saturday afternoon when she would again be sent to work at the farm. The new stalls were ready and the indoor riding ring was being constructed the following week. She wondered how Ben felt about this invasion of his privacy with Galaxy. Her Western history homework forgotten, she gazed at his photograph propped on her desk. His expression was so clear and direct, she did not know why he confused her. Out of habit, her first response to discomfort was anger. Who did he think he was, anyway — always seeming to sit in judgment of her, always telling her how to behave! But despite the anger, she could not help thinking about him and looking forward to Saturday afternoon.

When Miss Mik dropped the students off at the farm, however, Ben was uncommunicative. "I gotta move that fence up there," he said in answer to Miss Mik's question. "An' them jumps in the ring have to be torn down. If they want to help, they can pile the stuff over there." He gestured with a hammer toward a shed.

"All right — Rick, you and Jordie start in the ring and I'll give you a hand," said Miss Mik. "If you're going to work on the fence, Ben, Lara can help."

Ben thrust the hammer at Lara and grunted without meeting her eyes. "Yank out the staples on the posts. Don't let them fall on the ground for the horses to step on. I'll be up in a minute." With that he turned abruptly and went behind the barn.

Disgruntled, Lara dropped her pack in the waist-high weeds on the hillside and began to struggle with the staples holding the fence wire to the posts. Insects buzzed around her head and the sun's glare forced her to squint uncomfortably. Beyond the barn, in another field, Galaxy trotted over the crest of a hill toward Ben. The light sluiced over his black coat, the white swirl on his rump flashing like a beacon. The stallion appeared to float over the dry grass, and between him and the boy who waited at the gate was an almost tangible connection of energy. Lara watched, entranced, all annoyance forgotten. At the moment of meeting she expected to see the horse and the boy merge as one and leap from the squalor of the farm into another realm open only to them.

But Ben only opened the gate, the horse ambled through, and Lara brushed impatiently at the flies. When she looked again, Ben and Galaxy had disappeared, but Tom was sitting on the steps of the house with a beer in his hand. She was too far away for him to speak, but she knew he was watching her. Again she felt a prickle of anticipation. She carefully avoided looking at him and yanked another staple from the post.

She wondered how old he was. Old enough so he could get in real trouble fooling around with an under-age girl, that was sure. But he had a crafty, bold look to him — he'd enjoy the risk, she thought with a momentary shiver of revulsion. She set her jaw and strained back against a staple. Too bad. That's what they get for stranding me in this dump with no money, she thought fiercely. Did they think I was just going to sit here and take it?

Suddenly she looked up, alarmed. Tom was climbing the hill and came over to lean against the fence gate. She gave him a look of haughty appraisal, more bold than she felt. He tilted his head. "You gonna need a swim," he called. "You must be gettin' pretty hot."

"There's nothing around here to make me hot," she said flippantly. "I'm used to the sun."

He came inside the gate and propped against the post next to her. "You don't say," he drawled, studying her.

"C'mon, what d'you say? You gonna come for a swim with me?"

"I don't have a bathing suit." She stood her ground blandly while his eyes moved up and down her body.

"Well, who cares? I don't either. Hell, it ain't nothin' but a hole down the creek," he said and shrugged. "What's the matter? Afraid you'll get into trouble at that fancy school of yours?"

"I do what I want," she flashed.

He smirked. "I guess you do." Again she forced down her sudden disgust. He cocked his head. "How old are you?"

"Eighteen," she lied. With contempt, she added, "Old enough?"

"Old enough for me, pretty."

She didn't realize Ben had come up the hill until he was a few feet from them. He gave her an expressionless glance and unhooked a pair of pliers from his belt. "You helpin' out?" he asked, jerking his head at Tom. Lara's face burned and she pulled out a staple so hard she stumbled backward. Tom laughed, shaking his head. "No way, Bennie. I gotta go to town for something. You want me to get anything there for you?" When Ben did not answer, he walked off, remarking over his shoulder, "I'll be back in an hour. Then I'm goin' for a swim."

They worked silently side by side for several minutes. She endured Ben's mute presence, unable to supplant her embarrassment with anger. He worked methodically, pulling each staple with a smooth twist of his arm. Finally he cried, "Why're we always mad at each other?"

"I'm not mad."

"Well, I am."

"I can't help that," she shrugged, and he tore off a whole section of fence wire from the posts so she had to jump out of the way.

After five more minutes Lara dropped her hammer with a deliberate thud. "I brought something to show you," she said. Ben wiped the sweat off his face, looking at her wordlessly. But when she knelt to unzip her pack, he squatted beside her. She drew out a folder. Suddenly self-conscious, she held it closed on her knees. "I've never shown these to anyone, most of them," she said.

He questioned her with his eyes and she nodded. He opened the folder and looked at the first collage intently. Struggling against the sensation that she was plummeting out of control, Lara sat back on her heels and tried to focus on Ben's rough hands as he slowly turned over each collage.

"This is just how I imagined they would be," he said in wonder. "Like I've already seen them or something. I don't know how that could be."

"You knew what they would look like?"

"Not so much what they *looked* like," he said, speaking carefully. "More like . . . what they *felt* like. It's sort of . . . what it feels like to think about you."

"Did you recognize the rocks?" she asked quickly, flustered.

When he nodded and smiled, it was as if they had sealed a private pact. "Sure," he said. "That one was really amazing. I always thought that ledge was kinda scary, but sad, too. Maybe the Indians used those caves for burials or something. Like something could be trapped and crying in those crevices —" He shook his head ruefully. "Strange idea, huh? I guess I'm a little crazy."

"Then we both are."

They stared at each other. Ben gave her the folder and his hand brushed over hers. "I really liked them a lot, Lara," he said softly. "Thanks for letting me see them."

A cloud of dust rose from the drive below and two large horse trailers rumbled into the yard. Ben scrambled to his feet. "I gotta get down there," he said.

She followed more slowly. By the time she arrived, the yard was a confusion of people and horses. Two sets of parents, the trailer drivers, a trainer, Headmaster Crighton, and Bob Davitt, head of Huntingdon's business office, milled around near the barn. Ben stood near the entrance and Galaxy's head poked out of the stall by the door, ears pricked.

Then another man came out of the barn and Lara thought she was seeing Ben's double, an older Ben with a tired, weathered face. Thomas Stahler had the same dark hair as Ben, the same eyes, the same ingenuous smile. He motioned to a girl, indicating she should lead her horse into the barn, and joined Crighton and Davitt as the trainer stooped by a gray gelding to unwrap traveling tape from his legs. The boy holding the horse talked to his parents. Standing unobserved in the shade of an old tractor, Lara could hear everything.

"We understood we'd have some choice of the facilities," the trainer insisted, frowning up at Crighton. "This horse doesn't do well boxed in the middle of a barn. He needs a stall by the door." He glanced around the yard. "I really was given to believe the school had better facilities."

"We're in the midst of expanding," Crighton soothed him. "We want to attract students interested in our developing riding program, and —"

"There's not much to attract a serious young rider here," the trainer said. "Please excuse me for being so blunt. But there's a big difference between a farm and a top-class equestrian facility, as I'm sure you understand. These are not some kid's backyard ponies — they represent a sizable investment for the parents."

Another student led a horse past and Lara could not hear for a minute. When she could, the trainer was asking in disbelief, "You got Bernd von Heiland to come do his dressage clinics here?"

Crighton nodded. "Once a week, yes. And he's seen the place, too," he added swiftly. Something in Crighton's voice made Lara look first at Ben and then at his father. She knew how the farm looked to these wealthy visitors, knew they could see only the sagging sheds bordered with weeds, the fields unmowed and fenced with rusty wire, the riding ring crammed with the junk Ben used for jumps. Then Thomas turned to Ben and said, "Take Galaxy out of his stall, son. We'll put the gray in that one." He smiled at the trainer. "It's a perfectly good stall — my son's been using it for his horse. The gray oughta be comfortable in there."

Lara caught her breath. Ben was staring at his father in disbelief as Thomas gestured toward one of the sheds. "You'll have to keep him in there for now," he said apologetically. "I know — but Galaxy's tougher'n these horses. We'll get that shed fixed up nice, don't you worry."

Ben led Galaxy out into the bright sunlight, his hand on the stallion's withers. Again Lara was struck by the almost palpable bond between them. She was not the only one who noticed. The trainer's eyes were riveted on the stallion. Ben walked past without looking up, but the trainer stepped quickly to Galaxy's head. "This is quite a horse," he said. "Tell me about him."

"He's just a horse," Ben mumbled.

The trainer chuckled. "I don't think so, young man. Don't you know what you've got?" He ran an expert hand along Galaxy's neck. "Quite a lot of muscle," he commented. "He didn't get that by accident. And he's no Appaloosa, despite his color." A glance passed between him and the owner of the gray gelding. "What's his breeding?" asked the owner.

Ben looked at his father in desperation. Thomas grinned. "Oh, he's just an ordinary horse," he said, shaking his head. "Outta my old Nell. Sire was some guy's stallion down the road. . . . He moved away. . . ." His voice became vague and Ben flushed, looking away.

The trainer considered Galaxy and Ben through narrowed eyes. "You must do something with him, for him to have that kind of muscle development," he persisted. "Does he jump?"

"Yes," said Ben unwillingly.

"Would you consider showing me?" He waved his hand at the ring. "I always enjoy watching a good horse, don't I, Mr. Phelps?" The gray's owner gave a thoughtful nod and the trainer continued. "I'm a real sucker for a good horse. Mr. Phelps and I have discovered quite a few in our day. I'd sure like to see what you can do."

Ben walked stiffly toward the ring and the stallion seemed to follow just as unhappily. At the gate he hesitated, looking at his father. "Go ahead, kiddo," Thomas urged.

"Without a saddle?" cried the trainer. "And for God's sake, he has no bridle either!"

Thomas shrugged. "He's been riding him since he was a kid," he explained. "He don't have no saddle." The trainer gave Thomas an incredulous stare and turned his attention again to Ben and Galaxy.

Lara was drawn to the ring with the others. Ben

vaulted onto Galaxy's back. For several minutes the boy and horse stood motionless. It seemed to Lara that each one was waiting for some secret signal from the other. Then, without any visible sign from Ben, Galaxy began a collected canter around the perimeter of the ring. Although some of the jumps had already been dismantled, Lara was familiar with the ones that were left — a brush hurdle, a triple combination, even a water jump constructed from a tarp and some two-by-fours. Ben had created a recognizable Grand Prix stadium out of scraps.

"Ben doesn't seem too happy about doing this," Miss Mik remarked, coming to stand next to Lara.

"That guy can see Galaxy's no ordinary horse," Lara answered shortly.

"What do you mean?"

She shrugged in distaste. "Of course he wants him for himself."

Galaxy lifted over the brush jump nearest them. His muscles bunched and thrust under the gleaming coat and his tail swept out like a banner. With graceful precision the boy and horse continued around the complicated sequence of jumps, lifting without effort over each one. Ben leaned into Galaxy's stride, matching the stallion's fluid movement perfectly. The trainer and owner stood by the fence close together, watching intently.

A tremor of anxiety went through Lara. She recognized the determination in the trainer's eyes; she'd seen

it in her father's eyes when he'd first seen Conquistador, and Timothy had begged to have him. Acquiring
was a game to people like that, she knew.

The trainer whispered earnestly to the owner and
then turned to Thomas. Lara strained to hear his
words. "Where's your son shown?"

"Shown?"

"Yes — where's he ridden?" The trainer was impa-
tient. "Your boy's had some show experience — anyone
can see that."

Thomas looked perplexed. "He just rides around
here when he gets a chance. He's been riding that horse
forever. They practically grew up together."

"He hasn't shown — anywhere?"

"We don't have money for such things," said Thomas
with slow dignity. "He's just a horse — he's my son's
best friend. The kid's kinda lonely out here —"

The owner of the gray gelding watched closely as
Ben dismounted from Galaxy. "He's much too good a
horse to waste," he mused. "He could be developed
into something really special. I swear he's got Hanoverian blood — you say you don't know the sire?"

"He was just some big horse, I told you. We didn't
much care," said Thomas evasively, and the trainer
rolled his eyes. Ben came with a worried expression to
stand beside his father while Galaxy, with a sheen of
sweat over his dark coat, stood alert behind them.

"I'd like to have that horse," said the owner bluntly.
"I can offer you five thousand for him."

Lara slapped the fence rail with both hands. Miss Mik looked at her, startled. "Five thousand!" hissed Lara. "Do you know how much they pay for horses? *Hundreds* of thousands! Conquistador was three *hundred* thousand . . . as a three-year-old! They think they can cheat him!"

Miss Mik put a restraining hand on her arm. "It's not your business, Lara," she said firmly. Lara twisted away and did not answer, trying to catch Ben's eye. But Thomas was already shaking his head.

"Well, thanks," he said. "But I told you — he's my son's best friend. He ain't for sale."

"But —"

"Nope," said Thomas, smiling politely at the men. "I guess I wasn't tellin' the truth when I said the farm's the only thing I'd never sell. Won't sell Ben's horse either." He put his hand on Ben's shoulder. "I'm sure you got plenty of horses already. Galaxy just ain't for sale."

Lara watched the conflicting emotions on Ben's face — gratitude struggling with shame, pride grappling with anxiety and doubt. The trainer and the owner had turned away in disgust. All at once she too was filled with loathing. The farm no longer felt like a haven to her. The smell of horses, of dust, of the relentless, driving urgency of people with money reminded her too sharply of her parents' world, and of Timothy. . . .

Next to her, Miss Mik glanced at her watch. "Dinner's in forty-five minutes," she said. "I'm taking Rick and Jordie back now — you want a ride, or do you want to walk back alone?"

If Miss Mik had given her no choice Lara would have gone with her without argument. Now she hesitated, part of her wanting desperately to stay in the woman's calm presence. But when Miss Mik smiled at her, her emotions grew dangerously unsteady. From the corner of her eye Lara saw Tom come out of the house. He winked at her but she gave him no sign. "I'll walk," she said abruptly and watched as Miss Mik pulled away down the drive. Still she did not leave the fence. Tom flicked a pebble at her.

"Okay, Old-enough?" he called. "You ready for that swim?"

"You'll have to wait until I'm out on the road," she said. "You can pick me up then."

As she went down the drive it occurred to her that she only had to turn to the right, in the direction of the school, and keep walking. Tom couldn't make her get in the truck. She went past the corner of the barn and saw Ben brushing Galaxy through the open door of a shed. She hesitated, her heart pounding, and wished she had a cigarette to calm her. I have to get out of this place, she thought, wrapping her arms around herself. I have to get out. She almost called out to Ben, but the dust had dried her mouth. She remembered the six-pack on the seat of Tom's truck, put her head down, and continued along the drive toward the road.

When she heard the pickup roaring behind her she fought the impulse to run and deliberately forced herself to look back at Tom with a provocative toss of her head. She could handle him. She understood his game. It was worth it, to get what she wanted. And she knew what *he* wanted — but he wouldn't get it for nothing.

At the creek in the woods, she leaned on the tailgate and chugged the first beer she'd had in more than a month. Tom eyed her. "Good?" he asked. She licked the froth from her lips. "Yeah," she replied. He reached in the cab and turned on the radio, blasting the quiet woods with sound.

Tom grinned at her, stripped off his T-shirt, and went gingerly to stick his toes in the creek. "Hoowhee!" he gasped. "This sucker's never warm. Cold enough to freeze my —" She looked bored and he came back to the truck, leaning close to her. He ran one finger down her arm and she shivered but did not move away. "You sure been in the sun a lot," he said. "You got some tan."

"It's not a tan," she retorted. "It's my skin color. I'm Mexican." He slid over until his hips touched her own. "Well, ain't you far from home," he murmured. His finger moved up her neck and over her cheek. "You want another beer, pretty?" She steeled herself against his touch and nodded. He popped another can, watching with a broad grin while she drank it straight down. "You sure got some thirst," he chuckled, flipping open another. She drank the third in the same way, whirling into a reckless limbo where nothing mattered to her.

She didn't care that this man was fingering first her hair, then her T-shirt, or that mosquitoes bit her bare skin when he pulled her shirt out of her jeans, or that he was pressing into her so hard the tailgate cut across her back. "Give me a cigarette," she muttered thickly and he laughed, lit one for her. After she'd inhaled a few times he took it from her lips and said, "Time for a swim, pretty. Race you in."

She tried to walk but realized dimly that the beers had gone into an empty stomach. She peered around, dizzy, suddenly aware of how far Tom had driven down the track into the woods. She had to continue playing this game if she wanted to get out. But her mind felt as fuzzy as her body. "I can't," she whispered. "I feel sick."

Tom glowered at her. "What d'you mean?"

"What I said," she answered through clenched teeth. "I feel sick. Take me back." It took every ounce of her will to speak with a tone of command. She risked moving closer and pressed against him. "There'll be other times," she promised in a husky voice. "I didn't eat lunch — shouldn't have drunk so much." She ran her fingers lightly over his chest. "Take me back, Tom."

He obeyed sullenly. When he turned onto the main road, she saw Ben walking in their direction and hiccuped in relief.

"Where the hell does he think he's going?" snarled Tom.

"It's Ben," she mumbled. "Pick him up."

Tom spun to a stop in front of Ben and said, "Get in

the back." But Ben yanked open the door on Lara's side and climbed in. He didn't look at her. "Where the hell you goin'?" repeated Tom.

"To find you," Ben said.

She was squeezed tightly between them. When Tom shifted gears, he let his hand linger on her leg until he knew Ben had noticed. Then he patted her. "Too much excitement for one day," he grinned. "She ain't feelin' so good." He braked near the house, slammed the door, said to Lara, "Let me know when you're feelin' up to it," and sauntered up the steps.

Neither of them moved for several seconds, although the dust coming in the open window choked her and it was so hot in the cab their skin turned sweaty where they touched. "That was really stupid," said Ben finally. He sounded more frightened than angry.

"I can take care of myself," she said lamely.

"You don't know him," Ben cried. "You don't have any idea, Lara."

"I can handle him," she snapped. "Anyway, just who do you think you are? You don't have any say in my life." Her heart was still racing and she had to swallow down nausea. "What were you coming to find me for? What gives you any right to stick your nose in my business!"

He leaned his forehead against the window, defeated. "I like you. That's what. I like you. I don't want you to get hurt."

She slumped away from him. After a moment he

lifted his head and muttered, "Your teacher came looking for you — Miss Mik. Said your mom called and was going to call back in half an hour."

"What did you tell her?"

"I lied," he said in a low voice. "I said you were taking pictures in the woods."

She giggled. "You're as bad as I am! You hang out with me much more, you'll get really good —"

"Shut *up!*"

She thrust the door open and got out. "What does it matter to you what I do!" she cried. "You're just wasting your time with me, you know. I'm not the kind of person someone like you wants to be with. I'm the kind of person someone like *him* wants to be with." She jerked her head in the direction Tom had gone.

"I am not wasting my time," Ben said, stubborn. When she refused to answer he sighed and pushed open the door. "Get in. I'll drive you back." She glanced involuntarily toward the house and he gave her a half smile. "Don't worry — he can't say anything. This isn't really Tom's truck. Dad just lets him use it 'cause he doesn't have a way to buy one himself."

They drove the half mile to campus in silence. Ben stopped in front of the dorm. "You better get out," he said. "You aren't supposed to ride with anyone but a teacher."

"Who cares," she said tiredly. But he looked so sad as he started to drive off that she called out impulsively, "Ben!" he braked and waited for her. She leaned in the window. "You were so incredible on Galaxy today," she told him softly. "I wanted to tell you. Ben, five thousand dollars is nothing for a horse like him. I *know*. Don't ever sell him. You could really go somewhere with him, Ben — I mean it. You have some kind of magic together. Everyone can see it. You have to believe in it."

He was silent for a long time, pensive, his arms draped over the steering wheel. "Lara," he said at last. "Lara. Please don't get kicked out. Don't. I don't want you to go."

She didn't answer but watched the pickup until it disappeared out the front gates before going reluctantly to her room.

Chapter Eight

By early October the trees had turned orange and yellow. Ben lay on his bed and stared out the curtainless window, letting his English textbook slip into the blankets. He hadn't been able to concentrate on anything, not his studies or his senior project in the auto shop or his farm chores. He sat up listlessly, went to the window and looked for Galaxy. Even quietly grazing, the big stallion seemed cramped in the small field.

Ben sighed and turned away, selected a video, and slipped it into the VCR. But for once, watching the dressage events he'd taped of last year's Olympic Games gave him no joy, and after a few minutes he turned it off. He could hear Tom arguing downstairs with his mother, a thump as something was shoved violently across the floor, a door slam. Footsteps ran up the stairs, and without warning the door was pushed open and Tom thrust his head in.

"Where's that six-pack I had in the fridge?" he growled. "Damn it, Ben, if you been –"

"I don't drink that stuff," said Ben. "Don't you know how to knock?" Tom stumbled across the doorsill. "Damn," he slurred, glaring at Ben. "Better not've been you, Bennie boy. Maybe you're too good to drink, but what about that little bitch you –"

Tom would attack him if he said the wrong thing, so he stared down and was silent. But Tom kicked the door open wider and came in, grabbing the arms of Ben's chair and shoving his face close. "Yeah, what about her, Bennie?" he snarled. "She get you to steal it for her, huh?"

"I haven't seen her for a week," said Ben. He held his breath to keep his voice steady. "I didn't take your beer, Tom. You drank that six-pack last night, remember?" The moment the words were out he realized it was a mistake.

Tom pushed the chair sharply and Ben fell against the desk. He scrambled away as Tom lunged for him, fell again, and caught one glimpse of his mother's terrified face before Tom kicked him. He lay curled tightly while Tom battered him with his boots and his mother screamed out the window for Thomas.

The riding students from Huntingdon were having lessons in the new ring. His fear overwhelmed by shame, Ben gasped, "Don't, Mom! It's okay. Don't . . . they'll hear . . ." He ducked away from Tom and went to his mother, dragging her from the window. She gave him a wild look, as if *he* were attacking her, and he dropped her arm immediately.

Tom sprawled across the bed, laughing. "Man, will you look at him!" he jeered. "It's just a little family argument, ain't it, Mom? Who gives a rat's ass if them kids hear? Pukey rich kids and their stupid horses taking over the whole damn place." He threw Ben's video against the wall so hard the case cracked, and then he heaved himself to his feet. "You ain't nowheres good enough for them, Bennie boy. That ain't your world — don't you know that? You think any of them give a shit about you? You think that girl cares?"

"Tommie —" said his mother, reaching toward her older son. "Tommie, please —"

"Back off, Mom!" he yelled. "This don't have nothin' to do with you."

They all froze when Thomas appeared in the doorway, and then Ben, with frantic haste, slammed the window shut. "What the hell is going on here?" Thomas shouted. Ben was trembling so hard he had to clutch the windowsill. His father's normally gentle hands were closed into fists. Tom dropped his eyes.

"You been drinkin' again?" Thomas demanded. "I told you what I'd do if I ever caught you gettin' nasty drunk on this farm, you little —"

"Thomas," whimpered Betty, but he pushed past her and grabbed his older son. Without thinking, Ben flung himself at his father. "Dad — Dad!" he cried. "Dad — it's okay! Really! Me and Tom was just —"

Everyone stopped, all staring at Thomas. Ben watched the rage on Tom's face dissolve into longing and fear as he looked at his father. "We was only wrestling, Dad," whispered Ben, clinging to his arm. "Honest. Wasn't we, Tom?" Tom made a sick sound in his throat.

Thomas let his hands drop. He gazed for a long moment at Ben and in his eyes was bewildered shame. He turned to his older son. "If I ever catch you drinking here again, I swear I'll kick you the hell out. You hear, Tom? You can live on the streets for all I care."

Before he left, Thomas paused in the doorway and turned to his wife. "Come on down, Bet. I gotta talk to you," he said, and strode out.

Tom suddenly bent double. "Jesus, I'm sick, Bennie," he groaned. "I'm gonna be sick."

His brother was powerfully built. Ben could feel the compact muscles even through their shaking as he helped him down the hall to the toilet. He held Tom's head while he vomited, remembering how much he'd wished he had Tom's muscles when he was younger. He rubbed the heaving shoulders.

"Don't cry, Bennie," muttered Tom thickly. "Cripes. Don't cry. I'm sorry. I'm sorry, Bennie. . . ."

The next day his mother was already home from work when Ben got off the bus, sitting tiredly on the couch in front of the television. "They're cuttin' my overtime," she said, shaking her head. "Told us today. Trying to save money, they said. Cuttin' back on double shifts, too." She managed a brief smile at Ben. "Well, your dad kept tellin' me I should take a break. Don't know how he figured we'd pay the bills, though. Guess I ain't got no choice now."

Later, he made a desultory attempt to stack the dismantled jumps in a corner of the yard but watched the Huntingdon students from the corner of his eye. He was reluctant to ask why Lara hadn't come with the others, but the desire to see her ached in him so he could hardly bear it. He remembered every word of their last conversation.

Five thousand dollars. Lara had said that was nothing for a good horse, but five thousand dollars would mean more to his mother than she could ever imagine. And Galaxy . . . what about Galaxy? For five thousand dollars, Galaxy could have everything: a heated stall, vitamin-rich mash, the best care. And more – Galaxy could have the chance to be a star. A shining, triumphant stallion, winner's ribbons fluttering from polished bridle – Ben could imagine it so clearly he rubbed his arm over his eyes.

Lara had said he had to believe in it. And he did — for Galaxy. But Tom was right. Ben could never fit into that world. He could never give the stallion such a chance. It was ridiculous to imagine otherwise. It *was* money. Wealthy people could let their dreams and desires flourish. In their world, they knew everything was possible. But in Jonesburg it was not so easy for dreams to co-exist with circumstance. Where you came from determined where you could go, Ben thought, tossing another tire onto the heap. And after all, what was so bad about where he was going? Dave Hawley's a good guy, he told himself. I'll be able to get my own place, get a decent car, maybe even have a little left over to give Mom. . . .

From the field beyond the barn, Galaxy trumpeted his high stallion call to the other horses. Ben looked over at him just as a boy led a gray gelding from the ring. "Hey, Alex," Ben called, and the younger boy came over eagerly.

"Guess what, Ben!" he said. "I got Miniver to do a flying change all the way around the ring! Did you see? I really did it!" The gelding blew noisily against the boy's spotless jacket.

"He looks pretty happy about it too," smiled Ben. He liked the younger boy. Alex often stayed late to sweep the barn or to clean droppings from the yard. It wasn't true, what his mother thought, that all Huntingdon students were spoiled. He watched Alex brush Miniver's

101

forelock away from his eyes. "Bernd von Heiland's coming next week," the boy told him, excited. "He's the best — I can't believe the school got him to come here. Hey, Ben, your dad said you'd take the clinics with us."

"Naw," muttered Ben. "Too busy. Listen, you know that girl who used to come down here? With the black hair? Lara? What happened to her? She's never around anymore."

"Oh, her," Alex shrugged. "I don't know. She's still around, I guess. She's kind of crazy. My sister went to school with her last year in Connecticut. She got kicked out the first month."

"Your sister?"

"No." Alex giggled. "Not my *sister*. Lara. She's supposed to be real smart or something, but she's always getting into some kind of trouble. . . ." Suddenly his eyes lit up. "Do you know about her brother? He's so fantastic! He's a Grand Prix–level Young Rider — really great. My dad said he could qualify for the next Olympics. I never met him or anything, but I see him at the big events. He's always winning." He rubbed Miniver's ears. "You wouldn't believe his horse. Anyone could win on a horse like Conquistador!"

"They must know a lot of horse people — Lara's family, I mean," said Ben cautiously.

"Well, sure, I guess," Alex answered. "Greenwood's a well-known stable. Timothy McGrath's uncle was a Grand Prix rider and he's been running it for years. They know everybody."

Ben smiled ruefully. Everybody who fit into that exclusive world of horses and money, he thought. But Lara knew those people — knew people who would pay five thousand dollars for a horse, maybe more. With her help, Galaxy could be part of that world too. His thoughts were interrupted by the sight of Miss Mik coming toward him across the yard.

"Ben," she called. "Ben, Bob Davitt wants a couple of kids to paint those poles they're going to use for the jump course. But I've got to supervise clearing a trail." She smiled. "They always want me to be in two places at once. Anyway, would you mind setting up the kids with the paint? Are you going to be around on Saturday?"

"I guess," he said. Miss Mik paused, frowning slightly. "Ben, I just found out the school hasn't been paying you for the time you put in," she said. "That's ridiculous. I'm going to speak to Davitt about it."

"It's okay," he said, embarrassed. "I don't mind. Really. I'm not doing anything else, anyway."

"I don't believe that," she said, studying him a moment. "I saw you ride your horse. I may not know much about horses, but I can see when someone's put a lot of hard work into something. You don't get that good without working."

He dropped his eyes and did not know what to say. Miss Mik seemed troubled. "Ben —" she began. "Ben, is everything all right? I know it's not my business, but —"

So she had heard the fight. He flushed with humiliation and interrupted abruptly. "Everything's okay. It's just my brother . . . he's out of work, so he gets kinda — you know. It's okay." He forced himself to slow down and continued, "Yeah, Miss Mik. Don't worry about the kids. I'll set them up. Just ask Mr. Davitt to get the paint here by tomorrow."

If she hadn't smiled at him again, he wouldn't have asked. But her eyes were so warm and kind that he blurted, "Will Lara come down to help with the painting?"

"Lara's been working on the brook trail," Miss Mik said. "I sent her up there last week." She hesitated. "You really care about her, don't you?"

"Yeah," he mumbled.

"She's a troubled girl," said Miss Mik thoughtfully. "She needs a good friend like you." She paused again, then added, "She's clearing windfall brush on the trail where it joins the state forest fire road, up behind the gym."

Ben didn't even wait for her to leave before he got on Galaxy. In his relief to be away from the house and his anticipation at seeing Lara, he forgot the reason he'd given himself for wanting to see her in the first place. When he spotted her from a distance she was swinging her shears idly, staring up into the trees. He grinned. "Working hard?" he called as he rode up. She whirled around, but he could not tell if she was glad to see him.

"What are you doing here?" she demanded.

"Hello yourself," he retorted but couldn't lose his

grin. "I wanted to see you. You haven't been around. I didn't know what happened to you."

"Whatever could happen to me?" she mocked, but now she was smiling back. "I'm still here, as you can see. They haven't kicked me out yet. They're gluttons for punishment."

He slid off Galaxy and they stood together awkwardly on the trail. "Are you still taking pictures?" asked Ben lamely.

"I always take pictures," she said.

He squatted and traced an aimless line in the dirt with a twig and she knelt beside him. "I liked them a whole lot – your pictures," he said. "I've been thinking about them. I like the way you arrange everything." He looked at her curiously. "But don't you ever just leave the photo be? I mean, the way you took it? Instead of cutting stuff out of it?"

"No," she said. "I don't like them that way. I hardly ever like the way things are in the photograph. It doesn't seem real. I want to make them into something more real."

"But photos *are* real," he said, confused. "How can you make them more real by changing them?"

"Do you like poems?" she asked unexpectedly.

"I'm not much good in school," he muttered.

"Poems don't have anything to do with school," Lara said, and reached for her pack. "Listen – don't move. I'm going to read you something."

He knew she was trying to explain about her photographs, but he felt nervous and stupid when she took a book out and opened it. The only poetry he'd read was in English class, and English was his worst subject.

But when she began to read in her husky voice, and to sway to the rhythm of the words, he became completely entranced by "The Man with the Blue Guitar." He listened to the sound of her voice lifting and falling with words that seemed to contain a message for him alone. " 'So that's life, then: things as they are?' " On and on the poem went. " 'Where do I begin and end?' " Lara's voice was a powerful wave sweeping him along. " 'Things as they are Are changed upon the blue guitar.' " The words dreamed him into a long-ago night filled with unearthly light and the breath of something mysterious, when under that different sky his self had been newly born within him.

When she shut the book, he could not speak at first. Lara seemed as caught in the poem as he, until Galaxy ambled over and broke the spell. Ben scrambled to his feet. "Lara!" he said. "Lara. Come with me — I want to show *you* something." He held out his hand to her. "I want to show you something . . . like the poem."

Galaxy had never held anyone except Ben on his back, but only a slight shudder went through him when Ben cupped his hand and boosted Lara up. "Slide back a bit," he said and vaulted up front. Immediately, Lara slipped her arms around his waist. He forced himself to pay attention to Galaxy as they walked slowly up the trail. Lara's cheek rested against his shoulder and he felt her breath through his shirt. "Where are we going?" she asked.

"It's a place," he said, "a place I go. Me and Galaxy. It's up the mountain."

After a long silence, she asked, "Did you like the poem?"

"Yes," he answered.

He had to keep asking her questions to make her talk. "Did you ever get hold of your mom, that night?" he asked. "After I dropped you off?"

Maybe because they could not see each other's face, or because she could feel another heart beside her own, Lara began to talk. "Once when I was younger, Veronica told me that she and Dad really wanted a baby but the doctors said she'd never have one. My dad was just starting the company in Mexico City then, so they adopted a baby from there because it was quicker than doing it in America. . . . That was me. But right away, almost, my mom got pregnant after all, and had Timothy." She paused and he felt her thinking. "It's like when she goes shopping. Veronica has this *thing* about shopping. She goes shopping for something she thinks she really wants and buys it. But a few days later she always finds a better version of it — a better brand or something. So she buys *that*. Then the first thing — the dress or whatever it was — just gets shoved to the back of the closet. She never uses it. She always used to drag me along when she went shopping. I hate it."

"Why?"

"Why what?"

"Why do you hate shopping?"

She pulled back impatiently. "It doesn't matter. I'm not talking about shopping. I'm trying to tell you what my mother's like. First she thought she wanted me, but then she got Timothy. So I'm the thing she shoves to the back of the closet."

"I think my mom's the one who gets shoved to the back of the closet in my house," Ben said slowly. "I don't even know what she likes to do. She likes doing crosswords, I guess."

Lara told him about the schools she'd been to. "After Mexico, we lived in Germany for a while — I was still in grade school. And then California. And then we went back to Mexico City for a few years, and now New York. California was the worst."

"I thought California was supposed to be a really neat place."

"It is if you have nice white skin," she said grimly. "Try being Mexican. Dad always had to send us to the *best* schools, you know. Not a whole lot of Mexicans there." He felt her arms tighten and looked at them, at her smooth brown skin that paled to soft cream underneath.

"I don't think my parents ever stopped to think about what it might be like for me," she mused. "I really don't think they knew. Timothy would go to the school too. He was good at sports and popular, and I would be a spic or a wetback or whatever they called Mexicans. I don't think Timothy noticed."

"How could he not notice? He was at school with you."

"Oh, he didn't notice much but himself. . . . He only ever cared about one thing," she said in a low voice. "Horses. He wants . . . he wanted to ride in the Olympics."

Ben turned Galaxy up the trail toward the clearing. Lara didn't say more and he didn't want to ask. A dark abyss seemed to open whenever she spoke of her brother and he felt its chill shadowing her voice.

But the sunlit clearing was warm as Galaxy pushed through the hemlocks and Ben heard the soft intake of Lara's breath. "Oh!" she cried. "It's like another world!"

"It is another world," he grinned. "See? Isn't it like the poem?" He slid from Galaxy's back and she hopped down beside him, looking around. He showed her the mossy bank along the stream where the red-backed salamanders hid, and the rocky cliff from which they could see across the mountains to Jonesburg. "It doesn't look real from here, does it?" said Ben. From the ledge below them late summer swallows dived, and over the grass floated the shadow of a red-tailed hawk.

They wandered into the center of the clearing. Concealed in the grass was the decayed carcass of a doe, hardly more than a skeleton with a few tattered shreds

109

of hide clinging to the white bones. Lara squatted and ran her hand over a smooth, sun-bleached rib.

"I've been watching it for months," said Ben. "Every time I come up here, it's different. It changes all the time."

"It's incredible," she breathed.

"It's sort of beautiful, I think," Ben said. "She must have come here to die – she was wounded somehow. See this broken leg? She's just becoming part of the earth now."

Lara fingered the delicate skull and Ben leaned over her, pointing. "See – first the birds eat it. Crows and turkey vultures. And then the mice gnaw the bones and take the fur. And then the beetles come. Once, in the spring, the whole skeleton was covered in butterflies!" After a moment he said to her shyly, "This isn't all I wanted to show you. This isn't the whole poem yet."

She sat on a rock and he jumped on Galaxy and took him to the center of his marked-out ring. He bowed to Lara as he'd seen the riders do on his videos, and Galaxy and he began to dance. He was aware of her without losing his focus on his work, and it seemed as if her presence was creating this dance. Ben took Galaxy through every routine they had ever worked on, and when he finally bowed again to Lara, the horse was blowing hard. Ben's legs were shaking from exertion when he slid off. But Lara sat motionless, and suddenly he was struck with a terrible uncertainty. He had shown her everything he was.

110

He knelt down because he could not bear to have her look up at him. Without speaking, she leaned toward him. His arms moved on their own to hold her tightly. He laid his cheek on the top of her head, her touch so intense it was like pain. When he couldn't stand it anymore he buried his mouth in her hair, searching for the soft skin of her neck.

After a moment she spoke, and he pulled back a little to hear. "Galaxy is your blue guitar," she breathed. Her breath was warm against his mouth, her lips speaking more sweetly than her words.

But when he drew her down next to him in the grass, she pulled away. He let her go immediately and she sat up. "Don't spoil it," she whispered. He brushed the grass from her hair, bewildered. "It wouldn't be spoiled," he said. "Lara. What's wrong?"

"Nothing's wrong," she insisted. She jumped up and flicked a piece of grass at him, trying to laugh playfully. But the expressions on her face were like a succession of masks she was putting on. He felt a sense of loss so powerful he could only follow her helplessly while she pretended to explore the clearing. She kept at a distance, and he didn't know what to say because he didn't know what had happened. One moment he'd held her contained in his arms, and the next there was only a shell of her walking around. But when he found enough courage to take her hand, she didn't pull away.

"Lara, are you angry?" he asked.

"Why would I be angry?"

"But something's wrong!" he cried. "I just want —"

"I know what you want," she said, suddenly scathing. The vehemence in her voice shocked him. She thought he was . . . like Tom! "No, you don't," Ben said, stunned, dropping her hand. "You don't know at all."

He walked away toward Galaxy, who was grazing at the far side of the clearing. It had been a mistake to bring her here. The clearing would never feel the same.

"Don't be upset," Lara pleaded, following him. "I'm just crazy — don't you know that? Do you know how many psychiatrists my parents have sent me to over the years? You wouldn't believe the files they've got on me by now. They could write a book. I'm not kidding."

"I don't think you're crazy, Lara," he muttered.

"Well, what am I, then?"

"Angry."

"Angry can make you crazy," she said in a low voice. He didn't answer and she put a hand on his arm. "Come on, Ben. I want to watch the sun go down. Please?"

They sat side by side on the ledge. The low sun pinkened the white spire of the church in Jonesburg, and the mountains turned black. "We're going to get awfully cold," Ben worried, and Lara smiled. "We can keep warm, going back," she murmured, leaning against his shoulder.

The problems on the farm seemed so far away up

here. But taking a deep breath, Ben asked, "Lara, would someone really want to buy Galaxy?"

"Sure — you heard that trainer," she said. "But five thousand is a joke. I bet he didn't really believe he was going to get Galaxy for that."

"Oh yes he did," Ben said bitterly. "All he had to do was look around the place. I bet he figured anyone who lived in such a dump would think five thousand dollars was pretty good." He kicked flecks of shale off the ledge. "And it *is* good — do you know what that money would mean to my mom? And Galaxy could —"

"What are you saying?" she demanded, staring at him.

"I have to sell him," he said defiantly but wouldn't meet her eyes. "He *is* being wasted, Lara! That trainer is right. . . . Galaxy could be something really special —" He swallowed. "I'll never be able to give him that chance, Lara."

For a startled moment he thought she was going to hit him. She jumped up and stalked off. He followed warily until she whirled around to face him. "You are such a coward!" she cried. "You really would sell out, wouldn't you! Did you think I would *help*?"

He spread his hands helplessly. "Well, I —"

"That's just horrible!" she raged. "I can't *believe* you would sell him!"

"Lara, I only . . . I just . . . why aren't you listening to me?"

"Because," she said. "Because I thought you wanted

113

to make something different out of your life. I thought you were like me."

"I don't want to sell him!" he cried in anguish. "It's going to half kill me. But he's just going to waste . . . I can't do anything with him. Not like he deserves. Don't you see?"

"And what about you?" she challenged, derisive. "What about *you* going to waste? I guess that's okay. You'll just do that stupid job in Jonesburg all your life. So you can end up like . . . like your mom!"

"I will not!"

"Oh yes you will," she said, smug. "There's millions of people who work for people like my dad, doing stupid jobs they hate. They just let it happen to them. You won't even know it's happening to you."

"What?" he asked, confused.

"Didn't you understand that poem?" Lara answered. "People just go along with things as they are because they're too cowardly to make things different. They don't even *try* to change."

The stallion came trotting out of the dusk. The forest was dark; only the sky held the remaining light. Straight at them the stallion came, then spun at the last instant and galloped away across the clearing. The swirl of stars on his rump flashed. Then back again he came, neck arched and tail flying, rushing at them out of the twilight, rearing, snorting, whirling away once more to race off. The stallion was awesome, a mythic beast blazing with some mysterious command.

114

Now the stallion galloped around them in tight circles, brushing them with the wind of his passing. Never once did he touch them. Ben felt no fear. Lara stood motionless, her lips parted as if to drink in the wild energy. Then, as suddenly as he had begun, the horse slowed to a trot and came to stand docile in front of them.

Ben hardly dared to touch him. The stallion still exuded a force that seemed to spark off his mane and tail. But then Galaxy butted him, blowing softly, and the long mane stirred in the evening breeze. "Galaxy," Ben whispered. "Galaxy." In the half light the stallion's eyes gazed so deeply into his own Ben gasped.

"What?" asked Lara.

"He just . . . I think he said something."

"Of course he did, you idiot," she said. "He was telling you to stay with him. He's your blue guitar, remember?"

Chapter Nine

Beyond the Huntingdon grounds the Buckhorn range was laced by the shadows of wind-driven clouds. If she were in the clearing now, Lara wondered, would she be able to feel the touch of those ever-changing shadows on her skin? She lifted her face to the autumn warmth streaming in through the window.

"Lara, are you listening?" barked the dean. Lara glanced at him before deliberately resuming her gaze out the window. She hoped she'd made it clear that she did not care about the outcome of the discipline committee's deliberations. Miss Mik sat next to her. She had said nothing except at the onset, when she had been asked to relate Lara's failure to report for evening check-in at the dormitory.

"Lara, are you aware that you're at Huntingdon on probation? That any infraction of the rules is going to carry serious consequences for you?" Dean Parker's voice betrayed his irritation at her lack of response, and Lara felt a small satisfaction. These schools didn't like losing students — it didn't look good. They would love to kick *her* out of the school; it was her father's money they didn't want to lose.

"Lara!"

Miss Mik stirred. "Let me talk to her for a minute," she said quietly. For a moment the dean transferred his frown to the woman, then nodded and said, "All right. Five minutes."

Lara leaned against the wall in the hallway and looked bored. Miss Mik had hardly spoken to her since she had arrived more than an hour late for check-in the night before. Miss Mik had taken the dorm monitor's report without comment and told Lara to go to her room. Now she still seemed prepared to say nothing as she stood in the hall with Lara.

After several minutes Lara gave her a mutinous stare and demanded, "What?"

"Lara, I don't want Ben getting into trouble over this. He has more than enough troubles of his own," Miss Mik said.

"What do you mean — Ben?" she protested. "I wasn't with Ben. He doesn't have anything to do with this."

"I'm glad to hear it," Miss Mik replied, her voice betraying nothing. Lara watched her with suspicion and the woman continued. "He's a fine, serious young man struggling to keep his head above water. I wouldn't want him dragged into anything that would cause him distress. So, Lara. What *were* you doing last night then?"

"I was taking photographs," she answered quickly.

"In the dark."

"It got dark. I was just wandering around and . . . I got lost. I didn't know what time it was. And it took me a long time to find my way back." She elaborated as she went along, gauging Miss Mik's response.

"Shall we tell them that then?" asked Miss Mik in a voice as bland as her own. "You were taking photographs in the woods, you lost track of time, and you got lost?"

"I did!"

"Did I say you hadn't?" inquired Miss Mik. Her eyes were so clear — as if she never had to hide anything, thought Lara, and she slumped against the wall sullenly.

"I know you don't trust me," she muttered.

"Do I have a reason not to trust you?"

"No," Lara blurted. She tossed her head. "Yeah — what about my file? You can tell from my records."

"Tell what?"

"Tell that . . . that you can't trust me," she said.

Miss Mik shrugged. "I don't read the records."

"You mean you haven't looked at my files?"

"No," answered Miss Mik.

She felt as if familiar ground had given way to un-mapped territory through which she was being forced to navigate. Her shoulders ached from pressing so hard against the wall. Warily, she asked, "Why?"

"Because I'm only interested in who you are *now*," said Miss Mik. "I'm not interested in what someone else has written about you in the past. People change."

"But my records —"

"Do you *want* me to read your records?" asked Miss Mik quizzically. "Is that who you want me to think you are — the person in that file? The person someone else says you are?"

"I don't care who anyone thinks I am!" Lara spat, but the silence after her words seemed to rattle in the empty hall.

"Then you *could* be a photographer lost in the woods?" Miss Mik's voice was so soft it sounded sad, and suddenly Lara felt as if she *were* stumbling through the woods at night, lost and alone. She wanted so much to tell Miss Mik everything — about the magical clearing and about Galaxy, and most of all about Ben. But all she was able to do was nod defiantly, not trusting herself to speak.

As Lara told the discipline committee how she'd forgotten the time while taking photographs, had wandered off the trail and gotten lost, she saw herself building a tower with each word . . . like the tower she'd constructed of the rock ledge prints. But now it was she, Lara, trapped inside the crevice with her mouth open and mute, and the eyes of the committee members clustered at the opening peering in. She found it difficult to breathe. Miss Mik took her hand gently under the table. Without looking at her, Lara clung to the woman's hand.

"Are you satisfied with Lara's story?" asked the dean.

"I think what Lara is saying is . . . accurate," Miss Mik nodded. "It's certainly easy to forget about time in the woods, and there are many ways of being lost." The dean scrutinized her, and Miss Mik smiled at him. "As a matter of fact, Dean Parker, that gives me an idea," she continued. "I think Lara would benefit from some recognition of her artistic talents. Have you seen her photo-collages?"

Lara jerked up straight in her chair and the dean closed his folder. "Well, no, I haven't — but I'm afraid I've heard from Mr. Pettigrew that —"

"Lara's work is not going to be to everyone's taste," interrupted Miss Mik smoothly. "That's often the case with artists who have something worthwhile to say. I think Lara should put together an exhibit of her work before the Christmas break. I'd be happy to help her. It would give her a goal in something that's important to her."

Lara tried frantically to catch Miss Mik's eye, but the woman was watching the dean for his response. She slumped in the chair, yanked her hand away, and spat under her breath, "I won't do it. I won't."

"Did you want to say something, Lara?" asked Miss Mik pleasantly.

"No," she mumbled.

"I'm not entirely convinced that Lara will still be at Huntingdon by Christmas," mused the dean. "We've already overlooked several infractions, more than we should have, perhaps. The girls in her dorm are tired of her attitude and behavior. As am I." He paused, then added, "I'm not sure what you base your confidence about Lara's work on, Miss Mik. Mr. Pettigrew is less than impressed with Lara's work in Advanced Photography."

Lara opened her mouth to respond, outraged, but Miss Mik spoke first. "Trust me on this one, Dean Parker," she said. "You know I have some idea of what I'm suggesting here. I'll take full responsibility."

"Perhaps that's something Lara needs to take for herself," said the dean stiffly, shuffling his papers and excusing the other committee members with a nod of his head. "Lara, you're on evening restriction for the rest of the marking period. Is that understood?"

Miss Mik walked her back to the dormitory. "I won't have any stupid exhibit!" stormed Lara. "What did you *do* that for!"

But at the dorm Miss Mik indicated that Lara should follow her into her apartment. None of the girls were ever invited beyond the office at the entrance where Miss Mik met with students. Lara hesitated before stepping into a spacious room with a huge, worn Indian rug on the floor. At first she thought she was looking out many high windows but quickly realized the walls were hung with large landscape paintings.

She turned slowly in the center of the room, looking at the paintings in astonishment. Each one was swept with passionate expanses of color, and from the bold patterns of light and shadow she began to discern familiar things — an unruly field, a grove of trees, the massive Buckhorns, a fence line.

"Well?" said Miss Mik. "You're keeping me in suspense, Lara. I don't often show these to anyone." She was standing at the back of the room near an easel with a half-completed canvas propped on it.

"Did you paint all of these?" Lara blurted finally, feeling inarticulate.

"Yes."

Lara sat cross-legged on the floor in the center of the room and let the paintings enclose her so completely she felt the sun's warmth flowing from the siennas and ochers that made up the fields and the shade of the trees. A cloak of forests, mountains, and weather-worn buildings wrapped her in a world as secret and apart as the clearing.

She didn't realize she'd spoken aloud. Miss Mik came to sit next to her and handed her a mug of tea. "The clearing?" she asked.

"The clearing where Ben took me, on Galaxy . . . last night." Her words were almost inaudible. But Miss Mik only sipped her tea. In this room, it did not seem possible to Lara that she could ever lie again. "They are so beautiful," she breathed. Turning to Miss Mik, she asked, "Why don't you let anyone in here to see?"

Miss Mik shrugged with a short laugh, looking unaccountably nervous. "I've never been much good at sharing my work, I'm afraid. I've always been very private. Silly, isn't it?"

"But people must see them when they come to visit you."

Miss Mik looked thoughtful. "I guess I don't have too many visitors."

"But Dean Parker's been here — he's seen them, hasn't he?" Lara said with sudden insight. "That's why you knew he'd listen to you. About me. Because you're an artist."

"Your eye is as keen as your camera lens," smiled Miss Mik. "Yes, he's seen these. He keeps trying to get me to exhibit them in a gallery. But I guess I'm afraid."

"You're afraid?"

Miss Mik looked at her over the rim of her tea mug,

and something in her gaze made Lara uncomfortable. She stared around at the huge paintings. "It isn't anyone's business, what you do with your own work," she muttered, belligerent. "You can keep all these here forever if you want. Dean Parker doesn't have any right —"

"It's certainly safer that way," Miss Mik interrupted, and again Lara felt self-conscious. The woman picked a tiny piece of lint off the rug. "But maybe *safe* isn't necessarily the best place to be," she continued, as if to herself. "You can get lost in your secret world. You can lose your courage. If you keep yourself safe and hidden for too long, something odd happens — nothing seems to have a point anymore."

Lara frowned, staring at the paintings, and thought of Ben performing his beautiful dance with Galaxy in his secret clearing with no one there to see. Had *he* lost his courage? She wrapped her arms around her knees. "Is that why you're making me have an exhibit?" she whispered.

Miss Mik nodded. "I wouldn't want to watch you disappear into your private world and shut the door, Lara," she said. "It might be safe, but there's no one else there. There's no point to it." She paused and then, with a slight smile, asked, "Why do you think Ben took you up to his clearing last night?"

Lara shook her head wordlessly and Miss Mik said, "Because even the safest world isn't complete without other people in it. Because no matter how perfect that

123

world seems, the beauty is too much to bear alone. Letting people in is a risk – but keeping them out is a much greater risk. I know."

Lara thought about the big flat portfolios she kept under the bed, filled with work she'd never shown anyone. Even the few she'd chosen to let Ben see were ones she'd thought he would like. All these years, she'd let her parents think she just took snapshots, and she threw away the unused albums they always gave her. "You mean you've never had an exhibit?" she asked, stealing a look at Miss Mik. "Even though these are so incredible?"

Miss Mik laughed shortly. "No, but I'm working at it." She stood up. "So what about it, Lara? You going to be braver than I am?"

She felt suddenly exposed. "I know what you're trying to do!" she flashed, scrambling to her feet. "You can't trick me into anything! I'll do what I want with my pictures! I can throw them all away if I want."

But what frightened Lara most was that Miss Mik seemed to *know,* to see deeper in her than she would look herself: She wanted that exhibit more than anything, with a desire that burned stronger with every denial. When Miss Mik put an arm around her shoulders, Lara twisted free. "I won't do it!" she cried.

"Lara, you don't really have any other options here," said Miss Mik kindly. "The dean was planning to expel you today. I'll get you an evening pass for the darkroom, and you can still spend some afternoons on

Trails taking pictures . . . but if you stay at this school, you're going to have that exhibit."

It was almost time for lunch. Staring out the window of her room, Lara watched students going toward the dining hall in pairs or small groups. She never went to the dining hall with anyone, or to class, or anywhere. "Severe antisocial tendencies . . . emotionally inconsistent . . ." She'd seen only fragments of notes made by psychiatrists in her file – the file Miss Mik had never read. The notes had given her a perverse sense of security; now she felt strangely adrift. Miss Mik didn't know what the psychiatrists had written, didn't know about the other schools, didn't know about Timothy. . . .

She turned sharply from the window and pulled one of the portfolios out from beneath her bed. Some of the collages were disturbing even to her. There was that series she'd done at the end of the summer . . . She hadn't looked at them since, and now she made herself take them out. But they brought everything back with such a terrifying immediacy she shoved them quickly away and slammed shut the portfolio. She *was* crazy and those pictures proved it. Was *that* what Miss Mik wanted her to share with others?

She wasn't hungry but there was a restless emptiness in her stomach and she wished for the numbing buzz a beer would give, taking the edge off things, or at least for the relaxation of a cigarette. Leaning again on the windowsill, she looked toward the fields beyond the school. It was Saturday; Ben would be at home on the farm. And Tom – he'd probably be there too. She shifted uneasily, propped her chin in her hands. If she wasn't crazy now, she thought, she soon would be.

She had to get away from Huntingdon. If she couldn't get them to kick her out, she'd have to do it a different way. She narrowed her eyes grimly. And Tom . . . Tom could help. She twisted her mouth in disgust. Let him have what he wanted, the stupid idiot – so long as he gave her what she wanted first.

Her eyes rested on the shelf of books and she remembered Miss Mik's suggestion that she'd inherited her taste in reading from her mother. What a joke. How could she have inherited anything from Veronica McGrath? Only Timothy was blessed with that luck. She, on the other hand, had inherited everything from some unknown woman roaming the streets of a Mexico City slum, a wasted prostitute who probably never gave a thought to the baby she'd abandoned years before on the steps of a convent.

Of course she knew how to handle men like Tom, Lara thought. It was in her blood. She knew exactly how to get what she wanted. People like Miss Mik and Ben would never be able to understand.

Chapter Ten

The mood in the house had grown raw and irritated. Ben's mother was home more and spent hours watching television. On Saturday morning, when Ben asked his father for advice about repairing the tractor hitch, Thomas grunted and did not look up from his newspaper. Ben tried again. "Dad, I gotta get that hitch fixed so I can take the tractor over to Drummond's, remember? He said if we wanted that load of hay we —"

"Christ, kid!" Thomas barked. "If the tractor don't work, take the pickup. Ain't you got enough sense to work that out for yourself?"

"Tom's got it," Ben muttered. Thomas slammed the paper down. "Well, where the hell is he?" His father was glowering at him. "What'd he do — take off? He been gone all night?"

Ben sidled miserably toward the door. "It don't matter," he said. "I'll get the hay in Mom's car — it's just that it'll take a few trips."

His mother called from the living room. "Ben! I don't want hay all over my car! I mean it."

He stood helplessly in the yard. Part of the contract with the school involved keeping the barn stocked with hay and grain. But Thomas had not done any haying this year because of his job at the canning factory. Ben sighed, looking up at the overgrown fields. At least the big field was being cared for by the school, now that they were building an equestrian cross-country training

127

course on it. Its neatly cut contours were bordered by the only new fence on the farm, contrasting dramatically with the fields around it.

His mother called to him out the door. "If you're taking the car you better hurry up 'cause I'm going over to Sue's later this afternoon."

Feeling harried, he examined the tractor hitch one more time, and when Thomas joined him, he didn't look up. After several moments, Thomas said, "Didn't mean to take your head off, son. I know we gotta get that hay. Look —" He paused and squatted beside Ben. "Something's been eatin' at you, Bennie. You ain't yourself. What's up?"

"Nothing, Dad."

"That ain't true," insisted Thomas. "I know you better'n you know yourself. Look, I just want to help if —"

"You can't help," mumbled Ben. "I can't even explain it anyway. Honest, Dad. It's just I —" His father was watching him from kind, worried eyes and Ben longed to trust him as he had when he was younger. He took a deep breath. "I have this idea . . . of how I'm supposed to live my life. Of how *anyone*'s supposed to live their life. Except it don't make no sense. There's no way I can live like that without money. But see, Dad, it's not about owning things or anything like that. It's about —"

"It's about having beauty around you — about living in beauty," Thomas finished for him.

"Yes!" said Ben in a low voice. "Yes, that's it. But I can't figure it out more'n that. It's just — I know what *isn't* right for me. I know what *don't* fit into the way I see things. But I can't see what *does* fit. All I have are these stupid dreams."

"Dreams ain't ever stupid, Ben," Thomas said. "Dreams is all we got. An' dreams don't cost nothing . . . they're gifts. It don't have nothin' to do with money."

"But your dreams failed!" cried Ben, anguished. "And it *was* because of money!"

"No it wasn't," Thomas said softly. "It was because of me. *I* failed — not the dreams." He was studying his broad, dirt-stained hands as if they would yield the answers he sought.

"What do you mean?"

"Dreams only work if you have guts, Bennie," he said in a voice that sounded stripped to the bone. "Trouble was, I always got to doubting my dreams. When the goin' got rough, I was afraid. There was you and Tom, real little, and your mom —"

"But why was that wrong — to be afraid? You had to take care of us."

Thomas sighed. "I know. I know. But maybe there's something more important to give your kid than food. . . . I was wrong if I taught you dreams ain't possible without money. 'Cause I know it ain't true. I don't know exactly *how,* but it just ain't." He fiddled with the tractor hitch. "I hate to think I taught you to be afraid," he said, his voice barely audible.

"You didn't teach me that, Dad," Ben cried. "It's not you — it's me. It's just . . . I want —"

129

Involuntarily, he glanced around at the yard and barns, but Thomas caught his look before he could hide it and nodded. "You want something better than this." It was a statement rather than an accusation, but Ben stared down unhappily, unable to reply, and felt that the silence between them could have no possible end. His father put a hand on his shoulder.

"Wanting something better is the only way anyone can change things," said Thomas softly. "I know this place ain't much — besides, it's my dream, not yours. But Ben — don't you ever stop wanting what you dream of —"

The phone rang and Betty yelled for Thomas to answer it. A moment after he went in, the pickup skidded to a halt by the house and Tom jumped out. "Hey, Ben," he grinned. "Lookit I got you." He tossed something at Ben — a book. Ben stared at the title. *Learning from the Masters: Interviews with Olympic Equestrian Trainers*.

"You like it?" Tom asked.

"Wow, it's . . . thanks . . ." Ben stammered, too startled to open it.

Tom waved his hand grandly. "Go on — take a look. Lotta pictures of them fancy horses you like."

He cradled the book carefully and opened it. It was beautiful, and expensive — the price tag was still on it: $38.95. Where had Tom found that kind of money? He swallowed, unable to meet his brother's eyes. Tom slammed the door of the truck and jerked his head toward the house. "Dad in?" Ben hesitated before nodding and Tom narrowed his eyes. "What? He say anything? You tell him anything, Bennie boy?"

Ben shook his head. "He knows you been out all night, though," he added cautiously. "I think he's mad. And I gotta use the truck, Tom. That hay at Drummond's —"

Tom tossed the keys at Ben and strode up the steps to the house. Ben laid the book on the hood of the pickup and leafed through it. Most of the names in the contents were familiar to him from his videos, but one chapter in particular caught his eye: "Horse and Rider — A Meeting of Souls," by Bernd von Heiland. That was the trainer Huntingdon had hired to work with the students in the riding program! He closed the book quickly, afraid to look any further.

He should take it back. Maybe he'd be able to leave it at the bookstore in Jonesburg without anybody noticing. He ran his hand over the glossy cover. Maybe Tom *had* bought it. Because he felt bad about the fight . . . But he knew he was only fooling himself. Tucking the book under his shirt, he went inside and up to his room. For a long time he sat on the bed, afraid to open the book because it would make him an accomplice to Tom's theft but equally afraid to give it up because he was sure the book contained some essential clue that could give form and hope to his dreams.

"Ben!" his mother called. "That teacher's waiting for you outside. You didn't even get the hay, did you? Just when you figuring on doing that?"

"I know, Mom," he said as he ran past her out the door. "I'll get it later. Mr. Drummond won't mind."

Miss Mik was waiting for him in the yard with three other students, but Lara was not with her. He struggled to conceal his disappointment.

"Make sure these guys do the painting someplace where they won't get in the way, will you, Ben? The trainer's coming later and he won't want any distractions," said Miss Mik. She paused, looking at him quizzically, "But do you have time? I thought you were going to take riding lessons with the others when he came. Your dad told me you were."

"Oh, he's always saying stuff like that." Ben shrugged. "It don't ever work out." He pointed toward a pile of long poles. "That's what they want painted," he said. He levered open two buckets of paint, handed out brushes to the students, and went to the barn for sawhorses. When he returned, Miss Mik was gone and the students were playing with the paint and brushes. "Stop messing around!" he growled at them. "You're getting paint all over the place." They looked so sheepish he relented. "Just try to get some paint on the poles," he said more kindly, play-punching one of the boys on the shoulder.

Galaxy called from far off with an eager whinny and Ben went to the fence. The stallion was out of sight high up on the hill among the thickets. Taking a deep breath, he focused on his heartbeat, on the blood pulsing through his muscles, and felt the tension in his body dissolve. At once he heard, from a distance, the low thud of galloping hooves. Galaxy still answered him. Between them they could still create a private world where there was only the powerful, synchronized beating of two hearts. He smiled.

But when he felt a touch on his arm he was not startled and reached out his hand in response. Lara made no sound, stood very close with her hand on his arm, and as long as they touched, the perfect world remained intact. Then, almost against his will, Ben moved. Inexplicably, he needed to break the connection, to look into her eyes, to see himself. Separate.

"You didn't hear me come up, did you?" Lara asked softly.

"I didn't think you were coming —"

She half turned and gazed at Galaxy, who had come to stand by the fence. Ben could not tell if she was pulling away, or waiting, or whether she simply had no expectation of him. He thought a complete stranger would be better known to him than she. He pulled her around, hugging her as a buffer against the painful pressure in his chest, kissing her wherever he could reach. "I thought you weren't ever coming," he whispered. "I thought maybe you didn't want to see me again."

"I got into trouble yesterday," she said, muffled in his shirt. "Because I was late for check-in. They were going to kick me out."

"What do you mean!" he demanded. "It was my fault! I took you to the clearing . . . I didn't even

133

think . . . I forgot you'd have to be back. All I have to do is tell them —"

"Don't you dare!" Lara twisted out of his arms and laughed at him. "Don't be so serious, Ben! It was no big deal. Don't forget I'm an expert. I made something up — they bought the whole story," she said, tossing her head and grinning. "They always do."

"Well, they don't always, or you wouldn't get kicked out," he muttered.

"I get kicked out when I *want* to get kicked out!" she flashed. "I let them catch me. I don't even bother trying to make them believe me."

He stuck his hands in his pockets, watching her in a tumult of troubled delight. She was weaving Galaxy's mane into a row of tight braids, her brown fingers flying through the rippling mass of hair. She seemed to sway to the movement of her hands, as if she was in a trance, and Galaxy stood still as a statue. Then, without changing rhythm, she reached for Ben and wove her hands in his hair. He pressed his mouth against hers and closed his eyes. This was not like the union he felt with Galaxy. With Lara, he gave himself up to something so overpowering it eluded him each time he tried to control it. With Lara, all his movements were a *giving-in* — but in his defeat he felt such an alluring promise. He breathed her in, filling himself with her urgent energy. "Show me something," she whispered, and he kissed each word from her lips.

"What?" he murmured.

"A secret. Anything. Something beautiful." She smiled. "Like you did before." She led him beyond the greenhouse to the hedgerow bordering Galaxy's field. He glanced nervously in the direction of the yard. "I don't want you to get in any more trouble," he said, agonized nevertheless that she would change her mind.

"I'm not painting those stupid poles, for God's sake," she said. "If Miss Mik wants me to have an exhibit, I have to get some photos, don't I? Take me somewhere so I can take pictures."

He allowed her to persuade him, but with one part of his mind he watched himself, astonished. How had it come to be this way? Did nothing matter to him anymore but Lara? Did even Galaxy not matter? "Von Heiland," he muttered with some effort. "That trainer's coming today, Lara. My dad thinks I should meet him." He tried briefly to pull away from her, but her touch was weaving him into such an enchantment he desired only to be held in the spell forever. She traced her fingers over his skin and said, "He won't even get here until two-thirty — I asked Alex. And he's got to work with all the others first." She breathed on his skin and he felt the warm point of her tongue. He gave in without more protest.

Lara followed him without asking where he was taking her, and Ben wondered unwillingly if the only thing that mattered to her was that he could take her away from where she did not want to be. After ten minutes, pausing so they could catch their breath, Ben said, "It isn't very far now. Don't you want to know where we're going?"

"It doesn't matter," she said.

Lara must have followed Tom to the creek in this same way, for the same reason. Ben shoved through a stand of young birches, disregarding the twigs slapping his face. When he looked back, the white saplings seemed like lace over Lara's dark skin and the golden leaves reflected sunspots on her black hair.

He skidded down a bank into a deep, narrow gorge. "Here," he said. A creek undercut low rock cliffs where the air was always cold. Ben jumped the stream and peered up under the ledges. In the dripping wet moss, he saw the first icicles already formed that would stay unmelted through June. "We always called this place Ice Hollow," he told her. "When Tom and me were kids we used to make bets on how long the ice would last into summer. You'd love this place in winter — you wouldn't believe the shapes the ice makes."

But Lara was silent, looking around, already abandoning him as she claimed this little world exclusively for herself. She took out her camera and crept under the cold ledges farther along the gorge until Ben lost sight of her among the shadows. He threw sticks into the stream and tried not to shiver. "This is why the creek hole's always freezing," he called to her, and wished he hadn't. It made him think again of her following Tom, made him wonder if Lara had touched Tom with her warm and magical hands.

Lara did not respond to his calls, so he scrambled up the rocky bank, bruising his knees, and lay on his back in a patch of sun among the birches. She could come find him, if she wanted. He nestled in the leaves with his arms behind his head and closed his eyes. He could think of something else . . . he could think of anything he wanted. He could imagine riding Galaxy into the expectant hush at that moment before they began their dance. And he could conjure up the final moment too, when, after their triumph of perfection, the spectators broke the hush with a roar of applause.

"Don't ever stop wanting what you dream of," his father had said. Ben knew only that he wanted the beauty he and Galaxy created between them. He did not know what this meant beyond itself, or if anything could come of beauty alone. He lay in the warm October leaves and the wanting drove through him with such force he felt he would burst if he did not do something. His eyes flew open and there was Lara, kneeling beside him. Bits of fern and moss stuck in her hair. Ben sat up. "I have to go, Lara," he said. "Let's go. I want to get back. I want to meet the trainer."

She pushed him back in the leaves, laughing, trailing her hair lightly across his face. "The trainer will come next week too," she said, gazing down at him with eyes at once intimate and far away, electrifying him with something he could not define but wanted more than anything. But this wanting frightened him as the other had not. "No," he insisted. "I really want to go back now."

"We'll go back," she murmured. She lay down close to him. "It was so incredible in there," she whispered. "The ice, and those rocks. Like a dark fairy castle. I could see myself reflected in the icicles, Ben — like I was inside them. Can't we stay awhile? I don't want to go back. I hate it there — you know I hate that school so much, Ben. It makes me crazy —"

He groaned and wrapped himself around her and wished he could drown in her until he didn't exist anymore. Maybe he was crazy too, he thought. But it no longer mattered. She wasn't pushing him away this time. He would drown in another minute . . . and then she would get up, brush herself off, walk away, leave him alone in the world of his family and Jonesburg and Hawley's Garage. . . .

"No!" he cried. He struggled to his knees and stared down at Lara. "I thought you understood," he begged. "Maybe that trainer can give me a chance. Me and Galaxy. Lara — don't you think there's a chance?"

She lay passive, her eyes so impenetrable he wanted desperately to take his words back, to forget everything in the touch of her body. Unexpectedly, then, he felt a sharp pang of anger. "Lara," he urged, "don't you think I should take lessons with the trainer? I really *want* to. I don't know if anything will happen. But maybe I could try. I thought you wanted me to try."

She stood up and picked leaves out of her sweater without looking at him. "Okay," she said in a stiff voice. "Let's go."

He wanted so much to give in to her. But the edge of anger would not go away. She hadn't wanted him up in the clearing, she had gone off with Tom, but now . . . it was as if she wanted him now just because there was something taking his attention away from her. He made his way doggedly down through the woods without checking to see if she was following. She was the one who'd told him to believe in his dreams! She had called him a coward for giving up!

Within sight of the barn he stopped and turned to Lara. She was still unresponsive, but she did not avoid his gaze. He touched her cheek softly. "I wanted to stay up there with you," he said. "I did, Lara. But you told me to believe in what I do."

She smiled at him then, a radiant, open smile, like a flower bursting from a desert, filled with nectar so sweet it made him dizzy. She took his hand and kissed the palm, her lips barely brushing his skin. "Don't pay attention to me," she breathed. "I didn't tell you anything you didn't already know."

Chapter Eleven

They parted behind the greenhouse so Lara could go back alone. Ben skirted the yard and went around to the front of the house. An old mattress partially blocked the door and he shoved it aside in irritation, hating the way everything was visible from the road. From his bedroom window he stared down into the yard. At the far side, Miss Mik's students were painting the jump poles. Through the opening of the newly built arena, Ben could make out the shadowy forms of horses and riders. The German trainer was holding his first clinic. Suddenly Ben was overwhelmed with uncertainty. Alone in the woods, it was easy enough to believe; acting on that belief was something very different. He sat restlessly on the bed and leafed through the book Tom had given him, turning each page slowly, drinking in the glossy images. As long as he could remember, he'd gazed at pictures like these – on his videos, in magazines and books from the library. . . . All he'd ever had were pictures, his imagination, and Galaxy.

But now, for the first time, something of flesh and blood intruded past the mystique of those images. A stranger with a foreign name: Bernd von Heiland. Confined to books and videos, that man could be anything Ben wished him to be. But now, a few hundred feet from the house, the real man was conducting a riding class in dressage. Ben went to the window again. He didn't have to meet von Heiland; no one was forcing him. Maybe it would be better that way after all. He could still watch his videos, still ride Galaxy in the clearing. He felt suddenly foolish at the urgency of his conviction earlier.

"Ben! Ben, you up there?" His mother's voice cut across his reverie. Reluctantly he went to the head of the stairs. "Yeah, Mom?" he called.

She stood at the bottom, looking up at him. Smiling. Somehow younger. "Where you been?" she said. "I been lookin' for you. Guess who I run into at the hairdresser's this morning? Pris Hawley! I haven't seen her in ages."

"Yeah?" he said.

She came up the stairs. "Yeah, well — we were talking about you," she said, almost shy, brushing the hair from his forehead. "Pris was sayin' how Dave wanted a partner someday — he's lookin' to train someone in the business, maybe even sell it, if he wants to retire early." He could only stare at her dumbly, but she misinterpreted his expression and gave him a hug. "Oh, Bennie! I'd be so proud if you did that well for yourself! Pris wasn't naming any names, of course — but why do you think she was tellin' me all that? She said Dave talks about you a lot. Thinks you got potential. Can't wait till you get outta school."

"But, Mom —"

"Just think, Bennie — if you work hard and do a good job, maybe you'd have a chance at a partnership with Dave, maybe even have a business of your own someday!"

"But I don't think —"

"I know you'd do a good job — don't think you couldn't," his mother smiled. She gave him a quick hug.

141

"You're a good son, Bennie," she said softly. "I wish we had more to give you. Thank God your dad and Dave are such old friends, 'cause at least I know you'll be okay working for Dave." A shadow lowered in her eyes. "It's Tommie I'm worried about . . ."

He mumbled a reply and escaped outside, where he found Tom sitting on the steps watching the students, Lara among them, painting the jump poles. Tom gave him a grin. "Them kids are worse'n a roomful of fighting cats," he snorted. "Still, it's more fun to watch than TV."

At that moment Lara looked over at Tom with a flirtatious smile, and Ben felt it like a punch in the gut. Tom shook his head and chuckled. "She really is a wildcat, ain't she? You sure you can handle her, Bennie boy?"

"Just shut up," muttered Ben. He deliberately turned his back on the yard and started to walk down the drive, but before he could get away, Rick caught up with him. "Hey, Ben," he complained, wiping a smear of paint off his face with his arm, "Lara's not doing anything. She's supposed to help paint. Tell her to —"

"Look — I don't really care, okay?" snapped Ben.

Rick glared at him huffily. "Well, all she does is mess around with your brother," he whined. "I'm sick of her always getting away with not working."

"Oh, shut *up!*" cried Ben, and he stalked away across the yard. He didn't care what she did. She could go off somewhere with Tom for all he cared. She could go and get herself expelled from Huntingdon, and then she'd be out of his life forever.

Events were beginning to explode around him like firecrackers. The riding clinic had ended; Alex was leading Miniver out of the ring, followed by a girl leading a mare. Then Bob Davitt emerged with Thomas and headed, talking earnestly, toward his car. Thomas looked over at Ben and beckoned. He tried to avoid his father's eyes, but Davitt, the burly business manager, called out, "Hey — where you going in such a hurry? Fire in town or something?"

"Nowhere," muttered Ben. "I'm just going for a ride."

"Well, I got something I want to talk to you about," said Davitt, strolling toward him. Thomas stayed at the car, studying some blueprints spread over the hood. "Take a look at those," Davitt said, gesturing toward the car. "Plans for the cross-country training course and a whole new barn complex."

"I have a lot of stuff to do," Ben said, his face burning. From the corner of his eye he could see Lara coming toward him. "I gotta go —"

Thomas looked up, his weather-lined face animated by enthusiasm. He came over and put his arm across Ben's shoulders. "Hey, not so fast, son." He chuckled. "Give Mr. Davitt a chance . . . go look at them plans. By the time they're done around here, the place'll look like a respectable establishment." He smiled at Davitt, then at Ben. "And — they're going to need a full-time barn manager! So there you are, kiddo — the perfect job! You can tell Dave Hawley thanks but no thanks, if you want. An' you can live at home, spend all the time you want with Galaxy —"

Davitt shook Ben's hand. "So what do you say — will you give it some thought?" he asked.

Lara was wandering around, sometimes pausing near them, sometimes drifting away. Bob Davitt and Thomas both seemed to lean toward him waiting for his response. Ben saw his mother come out of the house to sweep the steps, saw her pause and look across at him as if she, too, was waiting. The sudden blare of the radio in Tom's truck matched the roaring in Ben's head. Miss Mik's car pulled into the yard, and from the dim interior of the riding arena a man emerged and walked toward them. Ben stood helpless, feeling completely paralyzed.

"Ben, come here quick!" cried Lara. "Quick! It's Galaxy!"

He stuttered something so incoherent to Davitt he didn't know what he said and escaped to the fence where Lara was standing. Galaxy grazed peacefully. "Now what's wrong?" Ben groaned.

"Nothing's wrong, you dope." Lara grinned. "I just wanted to get you away from everyone. You looked like you were going to explode!"

He let out his breath sharply. "I was," he said. "How'd you know?"

"I'm an expert on exploding, remember?" she teased, pulling him behind the barn. He could not believe how quickly her moods changed. Again he felt the edge of anger, as he had in the woods. Lara ran her fingers up and down his chest and he caught her hands to stop her.

"Quit it," he said, and she looked at him, her eyes unreadable. He refused to relent. "What's the matter with you, Lara?" he cried. "Do you always have to make trouble? Couldn't you just do what you're s'posed to, just *once?* Now Rick's gonna tell Miss Mik you went off with me, and you wouldn't paint —"

She snuggled close to him. "Don't worry. You worry too much. It's only his word against mine."

It was almost impossible not to give himself over to the touch of her, the smell of her warm skin and the taste of her mouth. A yellow birch leaf was still stuck in her hair. He held himself rigidly stubborn. "Lara, Rick's right —"

She stepped back from him. "You think Rick is right?" she said softly. "You want me to work with someone who calls me names?"

Reluctantly, he muttered, "What names?"

"A spic slut," she answered, enunciating each word clearly.

Just for an instant he averted his gaze, shocked, and when he looked back he saw something passing over her dark eyes like a hunted thing darting for cover. As if she was afraid, by repeating Rick's words aloud, that she would cause Ben to see her in those terms.

"Aw, Lara —" he began.

"Oh, forget it — it's not your problem," she said brusquely. Again she nestled close to him, so his arms went around her automatically. She whispered against his neck, "Don't be mad at me, Ben. I'm sorry I was so bad to you up in the woods. I just wanted you so much."

"I'm not upset," he said softly, believing it, ignoring the persistent edge behind his words. "I want you, too, It's just . . . I get so afraid sometimes, Lara."

"Of what?"

His shoulders sagged. "Oh, I don't know," he said in a low voice. "I guess I'm scared I'll go my whole life *wanting* and trying and failing . . . like Dad. . . ." Miss Mik called Lara sharply from the yard and Ben stopped. "She'll be real mad if you don't answer," he said, dejected.

But Lara took his face in her hands. "You can do whatever you set yourself to do," she said fiercely. "You're going to make something beautiful out of your life."

Ben didn't answer. Nearby, Galaxy wheeled suddenly and began to trot back and forth along the fence. He arched his neck and moved with deliberate precision, as if Ben were riding him. A man had appeared by the fence a short distance away. He didn't look at Ben or Lara but watched only the horse.

"That's von Heiland," said Lara softly. "Go on, Ben. Go ride for him. Show him what you showed me up in the clearing."

He swallowed. "Will you watch?"

She nodded and kissed him swiftly. "Go on. I'll be there."

Suddenly Ben was alone with the stranger, who stood, seemingly oblivious to him, farther down the fence.

In the field, Galaxy whirled around on his powerful haunches. Gracefully, without any apparent effort, the stallion moved into a collected canter, the sun slipping over his rippling muscles. When he finally stopped, he turned his head toward Ben, ears pricked and tail floating like a cascade. The stallion's attention was so focused the man at the fence turned also, and he met Ben's eyes. Giving a short nod, he walked toward Ben with such firm intent he seemed to exude a visible aura. But rather than overwhelming him, the man's presence drew Ben into a shared power. He stepped forward and met the man's outstretched hand with his own. "You are Benjamin Stahler," the man greeted him. "I am Bernd von Heiland. I have met your father. He would like you to ride for me."

Von Heiland spoke with a heavy accent that left no room for small talk. "This is a very good horse," he said, indicating Galaxy. "Your father tells me no one has ever ridden him but you. This is correct also, you have no saddle?"

"Yes . . . I mean, no," stammered Ben. "I never have. We don't —"

"I would teach all young people to ride without a

147

saddle," von Heiland said. "This is the only way to learn true balance. This is how one learns the language of the horse's soul. So. You will ride now."

The discord Ben had felt all day was transformed by the composure of this courteous stranger, and he found to his amazement that he could focus on the stallion without a struggle. Thomas met him in the ring and handed him the old rope bridle. Ben fastened the straps around Galaxy's head and looped the reins over his neck.

Through the entrance, Ben caught a glimpse of Miss Mik with Lara and the students walking toward the arena. Laughter came from the barn where the riding students were grooming their horses. The pickup was still by the house, although Tom was not in sight. From all this Ben now experienced a curious detachment. Without a word, the trainer turned and walked to the center of the ring.

It was the first time Ben had ridden Galaxy inside the arena and he found himself momentarily disoriented. The cavernous structure echoed and in one of the mirrors along the walls Ben caught sight of Lara watching him. But Galaxy went calmly to the center, standing alert a few feet from von Heiland. Ben took a deep breath.

He would think of the clearing. He would find the clearing within himself and ride there for von Heiland. He closed his eyes, seeing the forests on the Buckhorn open into clear sky. He smelled the sun-warm grass and

148

felt the cool air slipping over him. Galaxy waited. Ben found the stallion's steady heartbeat, found the deeper rhythm of the earth rising to meet them.

When Galaxy and he began to move, there was no sound but the muffled thud of the stallion's hooves in the sawdust. Back and forth across the arena they performed their intricate, measured dance. With each graceful transition a joyful sense of power grew in Ben. Never had he and Galaxy moved in such perfect accord. In the silence he heard his own internal answer to the rhythm of the dance: Yes! Yes! Yes!

He took Galaxy at a slow canter past the opening of the arena, responding with a minute shift of balance to every stride as the stallion changed leads from right to left to right. But as he turned from the entrance toward center ring, Ben caught another brief glimpse of Lara. Miss Mik and the students were standing in the open doorway with Thomas, but Lara had slipped away unnoticed and was walking quickly toward the pickup where Tom waited. They disappeared together beyond the greenhouse.

His heart swallowed him down a bottomless hole. He lost the rhythm abruptly and almost bounced off the stallion's back, righting himself with tremendous effort. But the magic was destroyed. The earth jarred up through the stallion's hooves. Ben took him at too fast a trot along the side and scraped his leg against the wall. Galaxy shook his head and faltered, but Ben hopelessly forced him on.

"Enough!" barked von Heiland. Ben stopped immediately and slumped on Galaxy's back. He did not look at von Heiland. The blood throbbed in his head. *Lara.* He was shaking. *Lara.* Galaxy shuddered slightly when the trainer came up and put his hand on his withers. Von Heiland looked up at Ben. For a moment neither spoke, and then, struggling to keep his voice steady, Ben said, "I'm sorry. It was a waste of your time."

They were alone at the far end of the arena. Dimly, Ben was aware that the group at the entrance had gone. Lara. Lara. Even as he sat there, she was with Tom. She was smiling at him and touching him and Tom was —

He slid off Galaxy's back and faced von Heiland. The trainer was looking at him with a serious, inquiring expression. "What do you want?" von Heiland asked quietly.

He knew he had failed irrevocably, failed himself and failed Galaxy. His head was dull and heavy, but he blurted the first thing that came to his mind. "I want to be an Olympic rider." But even as the words came out, unbidden, he averted his face so he wouldn't see the look of disdain in the trainer's eyes.

"That is good," said von Heiland. "I would not work with you if you wanted anything less."

Ben raised his head and blinked. "I don't understand," he said.

Von Heiland smiled briefly. "You have much to learn," he said. "You must never, never lose your focus, or your horse will lose his trust in you. But you have more potential as a rider than anyone I have ever seen."

He thought with turbulent confusion that he had misheard the trainer's words. But von Heiland was running a gentle hand up Galaxy's neck. He inspected the bridle critically. "The bit is too big," he said. "And here, this knot is rubbing his hair — you see?" He picked up Galaxy's right foreleg and examined the shoe. "The wrong shoes can cripple a horse," he commented.

"We can't afford a new bridle," Ben managed to choke out. Von Heiland inclined his head in acknowledgment. "This is not a big problem," he answered. "I believe I have a bridle that will be right for your horse. We will not worry about such things."

"But I have to worry about such things," Ben said in a low voice, and von Heiland raised his eyebrows briefly in question. "It's no use — can't you see we have no money?" he cried, then looked down again, abashed. He kicked at the sawdust. "I just don't have any way of doing this. You'd only be wasting your time with me," he muttered bitterly.

Von Heiland listened thoughtfully, staring at the arena floor and twirling the top of his riding crop in the sawdust. When Ben finished speaking the trainer walked off a few steps, his hands clasped behind his back, still staring at the ground. Finally he turned around. "Tell me about your horse," he said.

Startled, Ben told him the truth. "His mother's Appaloosa — my dad's old mare," he said. "But a kid at

Huntingdon boarded a Hanoverian stallion with us years ago, and he must have bred Nell through the fence."

Von Heiland threw his head back and laughed. "So! This horse is a changeling, yes? Like in a fairy tale? A prince raised among peasants?" He stopped suddenly and regarded Ben with a quizzical expression. "And you — you are a changeling too?"

"What do you mean?"

Von Heiland indicated the farm with a sweep of his arm. "You don't belong in such a place, yes?"

"I belong here," Ben said, stung. "This is my home — what do you mean?"

"But you see a different world for yourself — that is all I am meaning," said the trainer calmly. "You just do not know how to get there. So it is not a waste of my time. You are not the only person to start from this."

He was intrigued despite his defensiveness. The trainer put his hand on Galaxy's haunches. "Your father told me how you watch your videos — but you understand, what you see there is only the end of a long journey. Those videos do not show all the years before. They do not show where those people started from. Understand?"

Ben nodded. Von Heiland tapped the crop against his polished boot. "Yes? Good, then. I know others like you. I have a good friend — a trainer like myself, named Cafferty. He is the son of a poor Irish farmer. I know for a fact my friend did not wear shoes until he was ten — so. What do you think of that? And now he trains all the best Young Riders in America — Olympic-level riders. Patricia Mann, Jerry Holmes, Timothy Mc-Grath —"

"Timothy McGrath?" interrupted Ben. "You mean — the one with a horse named Conquistador?"

Von Heiland nodded sadly. "Yes, that is the one. You have heard of these riders, perhaps? They are all young, like you. It is very sad, that young man — such promise."

"What? What happened to him?" asked Ben.

But Thomas and Miss Mik were coming across the ring and von Heiland turned toward them without answering. The trainer greeted Thomas politely. "I am glad to include your son in the clinics I give at Huntingdon," he said. "However, I wish to work with him apart from the others, as he is more advanced. You have an arrangement with the school, yes? That is good. It is settled, then." He turned to Ben, sternly businesslike. "This is not once a week," he said. "This is every day. You understand? You must work. Do not be concerned about money — there is always a way. I will tell my friend Cafferty about you. Perhaps he will come watch you ride. You see? There are ways."

Ben looked at his father. "Dad, can we do it? You sure you don't mind not getting rent for that big field?"

Thomas smiled. "Listen to Mr. von Heiland, kiddo," he said. "We'll figure out a way. The job at the factory's helpin' a lot, and besides, I got some plans . . ." The fa-

153

miliar gleam in his father's eyes filled Ben with both doubt and confidence, but he smiled. "Thanks, Dad," he said.

The students were waiting for Miss Mik at the car. Lara was there, standing apart, lost in thought. But as the other students got into the car, she sidled up to Ben and smiled. Her eyes seemed especially dark and luminous, with a dreamy heaviness he'd never seen before. "How come you left?" he demanded. "I was riding and you promised to watch."

She leaned against him. It took all his willpower to keep his arms at his sides. "You didn't need me there," she murmured in a placating voice. "You were perfect, Ben. I knew you'd be." She gave him a lingering kiss; he tasted the smoke in her mouth and jerked away. "What are you doing?" he growled. "Everyone can see."

"So what?" she teased him. "Don't be such a dope."

"I am a dope," he cried, trying to push her away. "You're right, Lara. I am a dope to care what happens to you, you know that? Do you think I don't know what you've been doing?"

She was leaning so heavily against him now he had to hold her to keep her balance. "So what?" she challenged. "Didn't you ever smoke a joint before? God, Ben — loosen up!" She tilted her head back and giggled. "I got another one — want to try it? I'll come to the hedgerow by the playing fields tonight, okay? It's late check-in — no one'll notice. Nine o'clock, okay? Come on, Ben! It'll be fun. Stop being mad at me all the time."

He would not look at her. "I'm mad because you went off with Tom. I told you he was —"

She tossed her head. "And I told *you*, Ben — you don't have any say in what I do. Get off my case! I can handle my own life. I'm sick of you being so serious all the time."

Miss Mik blared the horn and they both jumped. For a moment he thought Lara was going to ask him something. There seemed to be a sudden, unidentifiable appeal in her eyes, but she only turned and walked to the car. Without waiting for them to leave, Ben went to Galaxy. He could not stand to see or speak to another person. He jumped on the stallion and Galaxy snorted joyfully, cantered to the fence, lifted over it, and pounded at a full gallop up the hill toward the Buckhorns.

Chapter Twelve

Lara had no energy to work in the darkroom that evening, although she hadn't yet developed the photos taken in Ice Hollow. She sat on her bed, her dinner churning in her stomach, and stared numbly at the film canisters on her desk. In them was that numinous world of ice and rock and moss. She shut her eyes and tried to imagine the place — but it was as remote now as the moon. Its magic had to do with Ben. He was the solid heart at the center, just as he was on the farm. There was a steadiness about Ben, she thought, as if no matter where he was, his heart remained in the beautiful clearing. Every moment he lived seemed to come from that place. Her private world, in contrast, was as disturbing, turbulent, and incomprehensible as the collages she created out of it.

Lara sighed and checked her watch: 8:30. Miss Mik would be in to check on her soon. She went to the window and opened it. Cold October air washed some of the sick feeling from her and she breathed deeply.

Emily flounced into the room and grabbed a sweater, pointedly ignoring Lara. Now that she was going out with Rick, Emily backed all Rick's complaints about Lara with a self-righteous indignation. What stupid geeks, Lara sneered to herself. But when Emily slammed out, nausea rose in her so sharply she bent double a moment to control it. She stumbled against Emily's desk. A pile of papers scattered on the floor and she kicked at them weakly, but felt no satisfaction. Maybe she had the flu. Maybe I really am sick, she thought, and Mom and Dad'll have to take me back home then . . .

She half ran down the hall to the bathroom and knelt in the toilet stall, resting her forehead against the cold seat. She closed her eyes and fought waves of dizziness. This was not the flu, and it wasn't something she'd eaten.

This was because of what Tom had tried to persuade her to do that afternoon . . . it was because of how much she'd wanted that joint and how close she had come to paying the price he'd asked. She squeezed her eyes shut, swallowing down a sick, burning fright. And Ben — most of all, it was because of what she'd done to Ben. Maybe she'd lost him now. She remembered the look on his face when she kissed him. . . .

She clutched the toilet seat and heaved. Nothing came up but a rage so consuming she flung herself back and banged her head over and over on the tile partition. "I know what you want," she sobbed, gasping for breath. "I know what you want. You're just like all the others, you're just like your idiot brother. You can't fool me." Exhausted, she crawled back and hung on the toilet seat, unable to stop crying. She wiped her nose savagely with the back of her hand, her tears smearing on the cold seat, and tried to pull herself to her feet. But she heard some girls come in to the bathroom and scrambled up onto the toilet, holding her breath.

"It's sickening the way Miss Mik always stands up for her," said one of the girls. "I can't believe she buys her lies like that. She lets her get away with murder."

There was a rush of water in the sink and Lara couldn't hear for a few moments. But the girls lingered. " . . . so we can stay up after eleven, Miss Mik said. Did you get that video, the one I told you to get?"

"They didn't have it in the stupid video store in Jonesburg. Can you believe there's only one video store in the whole town? Anyway, listen to this: Rick said Lara never does *anything* – she's always sneaking off with that guy, Ben."

"He's cute –"

"You're kidding!"

"No, he is cute," insisted another girl. "Really. He's always so serious – and he never wears a shirt!" There was a burst of giggling, and the girl continued. "Maybe someone should tell Ben what a total *slut* she is. You wouldn't believe what I heard about Lara from her last school. Anyway, if Ben's so nice, maybe *I'll* tell him. I'm supposed to do Trails next week till my ankle gets better. I was sick of hockey anyway. She's as dark as a . . ."

"Oh sure, you'll tell him," cried a girl in mock derision. "If I know you, you'll *seduce* him! I guess that'd show Lara. I don't know what a guy would see in her anyway. She's as dark as a . . ."

The door banged and Lara heard them racing down the stairs. Suddenly, without warning, she *was* sick, and she slid off the toilet to her knees, retching until she thought her insides would come out. She rinsed her mouth at the sink and crept down the hallway to her room. On her bed she lay curled tightly.

After a long time she got up and went to the pay phone in the hall. She could hear the girls roaring with laughter at the film they were watching. Veronica McGrath answered at the first ring in the New York apartment. "Oh," she said. "Hi, sweetie. I wasn't expecting it to be you. I'm late getting over to the hospital, so I thought —"

Lara leaned her head against the phone and clenched the receiver. "Mom? I'm really . . . cold. Could you send me my heavy sweaters, Mom? It's freezing here and I have to spend half the day outside on this stupid Trails thing."

"I'll get Alberta to pack them first thing tomorrow, sweetie. Is there anything else you need? Toothpaste? Shampoo? You have enough?"

She didn't want to talk about toothpaste and shampoo. Lara took a ragged breath. "Mom, could you . . . could you come visit me? Other kids' parents do — all you have to do is tell the school you're coming."

"Why, Lara? Is there something wrong?" She could almost see Veronica checking her watch.

"I'm just really homesick, Mom." She hated herself immediately, felt the tears burning again and willed them to stop. But she couldn't tell her mother what the girls had said in the bathroom. What was the use? Veronica would think it was all true anyway.

"Honey, you know you always get homesick at school this time of year," said her mother. "Remember? It'll go away. You just have to be patient. Listen, do you have enough film? Are you still taking pictures? Your dorm parent said —"

"You talked to Miss Mik?" Lara cried, incensed. "What did you have to talk to her for?"

"Of course I talked to her," Veronica said in exasperation. "I've called a couple of times but you weren't there. So naturally I spoke with her."

"You have to call at *night,* Mom," Lara said. "I told you that before. It's the only time I'm here. If you call in the day you won't get me."

"You know I can't always get to the phone in the evenings, Lara," said her mother, and there was a sharp silence filled with words neither would speak. Lara slumped in the chair. She knew Veronica called during the day on purpose, so she could fool herself into thinking she really cared. So she could fool herself into thinking Lara would believe she cared.

"Lara? Lara, are you there?" Veronica's voice barely concealed irritation. "Look, honey. I don't have a lot of time right now."

"I'm here, Mom," she answered wearily. "It's okay. I just want the sweaters."

There was another pause, and her mother said with effort, "Look, sweetie. I haven't got my calendar right here, but I could probably come for a day at the beginning of next month. How about a Saturday? Sweetie? I'll just make sure Juan can drive me, if your father doesn't need him. How would that be?"

"I don't care," Lara said in a dull voice. If she played things right she wouldn't be here by November, anyway.

Veronica sighed. "Look, honey – did you want me to come or not? I have plenty to do right here, you know. I'm not sure what we'd find to do anyway — is there much to do on Saturdays at the school?"

Her pride was already dragging on the ground. "I just wanted to see you, Mom. I just was . . ." She swallowed and could not continue.

"Well, that *is* a change, isn't it?" Veronica laughed lightly. "When you're at home, it seems you'll do anything to get away from me." When Lara still did not speak, her mother sighed again. "Okay, honey, look. I said I'll try to come up that Saturday, and I will. We'll figure out something to do — maybe we can go shopping in Jonesburg."

Lara stifled a hysterical giggle. Shopping in Jonesburg — well, if there was anything to buy, her mother would find it.

"Lara? Lara? Are you listening?" Veronica called.

"I'm here, Mom," she muttered. "I was just thinking."

"Well, I hope you're thinking about your schoolwork, Lara. Your midterm history grade left a lot to be desired, didn't it? And what happened in math?"

Veronica knew it was safe to talk about grades. There was a definite right and wrong with grades, and she didn't have to feel responsible if it was wrong. "I hate the teachers here," Lara replied.

"You're much too intelligent for that, honey," snapped her mother. "Now, look — it's after eight and I —"

"I know, Mom. Okay." As the receiver was hung up at the other end, Lara whispered, "Thanks," but she knew Veronica had not heard. Miss Mik was calling her from the end of the hall and she slouched out of the phone alcove. "I was just talking to my mom," she said, defensive.

"You're on evening restriction, but that doesn't mean you can't leave your room," laughed Miss Mik. "Everyone's watching movies in the lounge . . ."

"I don't want to," she muttered quickly. "I'm tired. I want to sleep." The woman studied her with a faintly perplexed expression. Lara climbed into bed without looking at her. She wanted to sleep forever, to be left alone forever.

"Lara." Miss Mik hesitated, coming into the room. "Lara, what's wrong? You can't go on this way. Do you want to talk about anything?"

She didn't have enough energy even to pretend indifference. Thoughts and emotions jumbled around in her like a million Mexican jumping beans, those little beans with a living worm inside sold at the tourist markets in Mexico City. The worms eventually ate away the inside of the bean until there was only a fragile shell left. There was such a pressure at the base of her throat, where everything she wished she could tell Miss Mik was pushing to come out. But how could she tell her about Tom? When it was all her fault anyway? How could she explain what compelled her to be someone she loathed, when she didn't even understand it herself? And how could she explain why it terrified her that Ben cared about her so much?

"I just have cramps," muttered Lara.

After Miss Mik left, the emptiness in the room chilled her more than the cold draft of night air that blew in the open window bringing the smell of wood smoke and wild autumn forests. Something flipped off her desk in the breeze and fluttered to the bed. She picked it up. It was the photograph of Ben. He didn't know how to be anyone other than who he really was, she thought. He hid nothing from her, wouldn't lie to her — because lying meant he would have to pretend he was someone else. And he knew only how to be *Ben*.

With sudden urgency, Lara grabbed her jacket, chose a book from the shelf and a recently developed photo from her folder, put them in her pack along with a flashlight, and slipped out the door.

Escaping from dormitories always filled her with a rush of adrenaline. Tonight she couldn't crawl through the broken window in the laundry room because she would have to go past the lounge. But the tree outside the window in the next room gave access to a low roof near the back entrance, and from there she dropped to the ground behind some bushes under Miss Mik's window. She crouched in the shadows for several minutes and studied the campus with caution. Then she ran to a row of trees along the drive by the playing fields, hid again in the shadows, and stared across the wide expanse of grass.

The hedgerow that formed the boundary between Huntingdon and Stahler's farm looked like a black wall. There was no moon, but the sky was so brilliant with stars it gave the night a quality of ceaseless motion. Unlike the stifling silence in the dorm room, this silence had such vivid texture she could feel it prickling over her skin. She held her breath. Shadows stretched across the silvery grass like paths.

She broke from the trees to run, heart drumming and cold air searing her throat, until she plunged into the black depths of the hedgerow as if throwing herself off the edge of the known world. The stillness here at the base of the Buckhorns was untamed, seemed to be a living thing. Lara tried to penetrate the darkness over the rough fields, searching for the farm buildings below. Gradually, her eyes adjusted so that she could make out tiny patches of light from the house, and although an owl screamed and something squealed in the grasses, she felt suddenly safe.

She was alone, but it did not feel like isolation. Here, with the mountains rising across an infinite curtain of stars, the vast solitude contained her so she no longer felt battered and trapped. And then she saw Ben coming up the hill on Galaxy. She remained hidden, unwilling at first to disturb this newfound self within her. But in a moment she was overcome with the anxiety that he might ride away again before he'd found her, and she pushed through the thickets into the open field. Still enveloped in darkness, the horse and boy stopped. Only the patch of stars on Galaxy's rump was clearly visible. "Is that you?" Ben called out softly, and she moved toward him as he slid from the horse's back.

"I didn't know if you'd come," she whispered.

"I didn't know if you would either," he replied.

She was disconcerted to realize she felt shy. This meeting had a different intimacy to it — as if they had agreed to create a tiny haven in the enormous, inhuman space of night. They stood together unsure, and then Ben pointed up the hill and said, "That's a nice place there, where the deer bed down in the day. There won't be brambles." Lara followed, shrugging off her pack, and sank down next to him in the matted grass.

His eyes were so full of her she could not bear it and turned away. She wanted to curl up in his arms. She knew all she had to do was reach out her hand and he would gather her up and hold her. But she could not risk it. What if she looked into Ben's face and saw what she had seen on Tom's face, saw that familiar hungry claim on her body that left her heart starving? What if Ben had decided that she must want to be treated as Tom treated her? So she could not make a move. Instead, she challenged flippantly, "So — you going to smoke this joint with me?" She dug it from her pocket and lit it. Ben looked helpless but she ignored it, inhaling with a flourish. "Come on, Ben! It'll relax you."

"I don't need to relax," he grumbled. "I hate stuff like that."

"Don't you ever do *anything* fun?" she scorned.

165

"You ever live with a drunk, Lara?" he asked. "You have any idea what that's like?" He stood abruptly. "I'm gonna take off." When he put his hands on Galaxy's withers to jump up, Lara scrambled to her feet, stubbing the joint out on her sneaker.

"Ben . . . don't," she cried softly. She took a deep breath. "I don't know why I did that. It was really stupid." She paused, and when he still did not reply, she went on desperately. "Look. I brought you something. Another poem. I wanted to read it to you, Ben. Really, I wanted to see you."

"Well, you sure don't act like it," he said, voice muffled.

It was easier to talk to him when his back was turned. The stallion seemed such an immense being, warm and solid, and she felt him supporting them both. "I'm afraid you'll turn out to be just like the others," she whispered.

"Well, I'm not like the others," he said, bitter. "I love you. I *love* you, Lara."

She wanted to touch him so much it was a painful ache, but he did not reach for her when he turned slowly around to face her. "Let's go sit in the grass again," he said. "Okay?"

He talked to her quietly for a long time, telling her about von Heiland and his lesson with him. His intensity soothed her. "Galaxy could be as great as any horse I've ever seen on television," he told her. "I don't just mean I believe that, or want it — *I know it*. Galaxy told me. I know that sounds crazy but it's true. I get these

pictures in my head, and it's like he puts them there."
He didn't say anything for a few minutes. Galaxy
grazed peacefully near them. "Lara, I told von Heiland
I wanted to be an Olympic rider."

"I could have told you that." She smiled. He smiled
back. After another pause, he said, "Read me that poem
you brought."

Although they were not touching, they sat so close in
the grass they created a nest of warmth. Their breath
mingled, a momentary mist in the cold air. She took the
book and the flashlight and began, "'I wake to sleep,
and take my waking slow. . . . I learn by going where I
have to go.'" It was a short poem, and when she came
to the last stanza, she read it twice because she loved the
sound of the words, and because all at once she began
to wonder what it meant. After she'd finished, Ben said,
amazed, "I never knew poems were like that – like the
ones you read." He looked down at his hands. "They
make us read poems in English class sometimes. . . .
I'm not very smart, you know, Lara. I don't do real
good in school. . . ."

"If your school is anything like the ones I've been
to, don't worry," she laughed. "They're mostly run by
idiots."

"I don't think Clayton County Vo-Tech is much like
the schools you go to," he said with chagrin.

"Don't be so sure," she said, slamming the book shut.
"I *hate* it when we have to read poetry in school. The
teachers don't know anything about it."

"Yeah, but I bet you don't flunk exams."

"I flunk other things," she grinned. She examined the book thoughtfully. "I wonder what my mom was like when she was in college. She bought this book for a class – all my books were hers in college. I can't believe you could read poems like this and still turn out like her."

"How can poems make a difference?" asked Ben.

Lara ran her fingers over the embossed title: *Theodore Roethke: Collected Poems*. "Poems make you wonder about things," she said slowly. "They make you wonder about the way people are and about the way the world is. It's like in 'The Man with the Blue Guitar' – I mean, if my mom read that, didn't it make her wonder about *things as they are?* Didn't she ever *want* to change things?"

"Maybe she couldn't," said Ben. "Maybe she didn't know how."

Lara was quiet a moment. "I don't think I know how either," she said in a low voice. She put the book down in the grass and added fiercely, "But I want to know! I *have* to!"

He said slowly, "You can learn by going where you have to go. . . ."

"Yes," she smiled. He held her eyes a moment, then picked up the book and leafed through it, shining the flashlight on the pages with a frown of concentration. He hesitated, then said, "Here's one for you . . . for us." He cleared his throat self-consciously and read

In the slow world of dream,
We breathe in unison.
The outside dies within,
And she knows all I am.

His face was such a mixture of embarrassment and pleasure she laughed and kissed him swiftly on the mouth. He put his hands on her shoulders and kissed her back. Suddenly insistent, he pulled her down with him into the grass, his hands tangling impatiently in her clothing as he tugged open her jacket. His urgency thrilled and frightened her. To steady herself, she wrapped her arms around him tightly. His hands moved over her skin with such gentleness she thought she would melt under his touch, and when she looked into his eyes they were so luminous it took her breath away. She could disappear into them and never find her way out. She couldn't think because he was kissing her so deeply. "I love you. I love you," he murmured.

"Ben –"

He buried his mouth in her hair and with an effort she pushed his head back so he would look at her. "Ben," she gasped. "I can't. I can't."

His shoulders sagged. "Why not?" he cried. He lay heavily on her and she squirmed until he rolled off. "Why not, Lara? What's wrong?" He searched her face for an answer but she jerked away and blinked several times.

169

"Why can't we just be friends?" she begged. "Ben?"

"We're not just friends!" he cried stubbornly. "And don't pretend you want to be, because I don't believe you." He swallowed. "Don't you love me, Lara?"

She almost answered "Yes" without thinking, as if it was the most natural thing in the world. "Yes" hovered in her mouth, such a passionate, certain "yes" she had to fight to keep from saying it. But she said only "I don't know" in a flat voice, and watched the hurt appear like a red weal on his face, as if she had slapped him. "I'm not . . . not very good at loving people," she stammered. "I'd only mess you up."

"You're already messing me up," he said, trying to smile. "A little more couldn't hurt." But it was worse to her that he was bravely trying to make light of it. "I can try to be just friends," he said. "I'll try, Lara. I don't want to lose you. I don't know anyone like you in the whole world."

They sat side by side in the grass and Ben made a few awkward attempts at conversation. Lara shivered with cold and barely responded. After a long silence, Ben tried again. "What happened with your brother, Lara? Von Heiland told me something —"

This time she turned to him, startled. "What do you mean? What did he tell you?" Ben seemed so taken aback she allowed herself a tentative relief. He must not know, then. "He had an accident on his horse — he got hurt badly. He's still in the hospital."

"Yes, but why —"

170

"It was just an accident," she said brusquely. "That trainer doesn't know anything about it."

Ben twirled a piece of grass in his fingers. "He told me about his friend Cafferty," he persisted. "He said Cafferty was your brother's trainer." He hesitated, then added, "He told me he was going to ask Cafferty to come watch me ride Galaxy."

"When?" she gasped.

"I don't know — December, maybe. He only said maybe," Ben answered, still bewildered by her response.

When he found out, it would be the end. He wouldn't *want* to know her then. So she had until December. "My brother named his horse Conquistador," she said in a strained voice. "Did I already tell you that?" He nodded, hesitated, then brushed her tears with fingers so light she hardly felt his touch. "Do you know who the conquistadors were, Ben?" She didn't wait for his reply. "They were conquerors, from Spain. In the sixteenth century. They were ruthless. When they took over the New World — like Mexico and South America — they killed millions of Indians. Mayas and Incas and Aztecs. Or else they made them into slaves. They did horrible things."

She took his hand and put it to her face again. He gazed at her. She moved his fingers until he did it on his own, tracing her cheekbone and down her nose, exploring the shape of her face. "I've seen photos of the old Indians," she continued. "They're really different from the Spanish Mexicans. Their faces look like mine . . . same kind of nose, same cheekbones. A lot of the poor people in Mexico are descended from what's left of those Indians. They were pretty much wiped out by the conquistadors. It was really strange, Ben, seeing pictures of people who looked like me."

He was stroking her hair and she leaned against him. "Oh, Ben, I know it doesn't make any sense, but I *hated* that horse! *Conquistador*." She spat the word. "Timothy just thought it was funny when I told him. But it wasn't the horse — of course I know that was stupid. It was just that no one *cared* what he reminded me of . . . that I don't even know . . ."

"That you don't know who you are?" he finished for her, and she nodded. He nodded too and said, picking his words with care, "Like I know who I am. I mean, I know where I come from. I have cousins and aunts and uncles all over the place around here. There's a dozen Stahlers right in Jonesburg. They've been here since forever, I guess."

"It makes me afraid," she whispered. "Not to know. Like I'm not connected to anything in the whole world. Like I'm not even real. I could just disappear. . . . And when I feel like that I get so angry, I just want to hurt something. Anger feels real —"

He gathered her in his arms, rocking slightly. "I'm real, Lara," he said. "Galaxy's real. There's a lot of good things that are real. What I feel about you is real."

"I know —"

172

"Those conquistadors — that was an awfully long time ago, the sixteenth century," he said.

"My mother wasn't a long time ago," she said. "My real mother. She was Mexican Indian. She's alive. Probably. Probably she's starving, or sick . . . and I live with all this money. . . . Ben — maybe I have real brothers or sisters. But I won't ever know. Not ever."

He didn't reply, and after a moment she pulled the photograph out of her pack and smoothed it across her knees. "This is for you," she said. He stared at it under the beam from the flashlight.

"It's me and Galaxy," he breathed in wonder. "How'd you get it to look like that? With all that sky?"

"I was kneeling down when you went over the jump," she said. "I took it from below — you like it?"

"It's beautiful," he grinned. He studied it quizzically. "But you didn't do anything to it — I mean, it's not all cut-outs like your other ones. It's just one picture. I thought you didn't do that."

"I do if it's perfect just the way it is," she smiled.

Chapter Thirteen

She could not bear looking at the picture of Ben she had propped up on the desk. Sometimes she caught him gazing at her as if he could look straight into her deepest thoughts, straight into her heart. Finally she stuck the photograph in a drawer. But very soon she missed seeing it.

Lara sat half turned away from Emily, who was studying at the other desk, and slowly took the photo out again. Ben's eyes disconcerted her, caught by the camera when he thought she was not noticing him. What did he see in her? It was as if he saw something she could not see herself. Staring at the photograph made her feel she was tethered by an invisible rope and she fought it wildly – but she could not put the picture away again, because then she felt lost.

No matter what terrible things she did – and she knew they were terrible – Ben loved her. And Ben loved only good things. Galaxy. The clearing. Beauty. How was it possible that he did not see she was crazy? That it was not in her nature to be good? She was nothing like him – she was not honest, or kind, or responsible. When she got angry, she was capable of hurting whatever was in front of her. Lara put the photo down on the desk and propped her chin on her fists pensively.

Perhaps she could be good. It would mean not cutting classes, not going to the nurse with made-up illnesses; it would mean doing her homework, working on Trails, smiling at Emily, not being surly or late, doing every assignment for Mr. Pettigrew without complaint. She clasped her hands together. Yes, she could do all that. Ben might not be wrong. The resolve flooded her with such a forceful tide of determination she shut her textbook with a loud snap.

"I'm trying to study," said Emily, with exaggerated patience.

Lara opened her mouth to retort, then looked at the picture of Ben and stopped. She would be good. She would. She smiled at Emily. "Sorry," she said.

All week Lara was never late to class or rude. Sometimes she caught the tail ends of thoughts she could not identify, but which troubled her — as if there were some stranger's mind working away hidden within her. She was subdued and vaguely restless. She wondered: Is this what it feels like to be a good person? Is it possible to be crazy *and* good?

In the afternoons, on Trails, Lara raked leaves side by side with Rick, Jordie, and the others. She was aware they did not want her there. She overheard Rick grumble, "Well, I wonder what she's trying to pull over on Miss Mik now."

Later, she asked Miss Mik, "Isn't there anything I can do at the farm? Isn't there anything to paint or something? Can I go down?"

"I guess the arena could use a raking," Miss Mik said, studying her. "Are you feeling all right? You're very quiet lately."

"I'm just thinking," she said, but it wasn't true. She was not thinking. She was lost in an undefinable place, featureless and gray.

"Lara, you aren't to go off anyplace with Ben," Miss Mik warned. "You're to rake that ring. I'll come check it later. Is that understood?"

When Miss Mik left her at the farm, Lara stood staring at the house. If she just gave Ben what all the other boys wanted – would that make him happy? But perhaps it was only possible to make someone happy if you were *good*. She seemed only to hurt people.

The farm was deserted. Lara wandered into the barn, where the horses were stirring in their stalls. Students did not ride on Wednesdays because there were often games at the school everyone was required to attend. She turned slowly around in the barn, sifting the stillness through her. Some chickens were scratching in the dirt near the door, one hen pecking the others with swift jabs. "Stop it," Lara said. "You nasty things." At the sound of her own voice she was overcome with unease, as if she had invaded a place where she did not belong. She took a rake and went across to the indoor ring.

On this cold windy day the tin roof rattled and the beams creaked continuously. Inside, the huge building smelled of horses and sawdust and new wood, and she was reminded sharply of Greenwood. She worked for a while, raking the uneven lumps smooth. When she grew bored, she raked spiraling designs in the sawdust like a Japanese sand garden.

Gradually she became aware that she was uncomfortable in the enormous space. Even her breathing echoed. She dropped the rake but controlled her impulse to run. She could find no reason for her panic. She was aware only of an anxious sensation, as if she were drifting down a sluggish gray river that in the distance, far away, changed into a raging torrent. For a long time she stood holding her breath, powerless to combat the current. Then, like a bright beacon, she heard a high trumpeting whinny. "Galaxy!" she whispered, and ran to the entrance. "Galaxy."

The stallion was trotting down the field toward the fence, and she went to meet him. He pricked his ears and watched with alert eyes as she unlatched the gate. She had never been alone with him and he seemed more massive than when he was with Ben. But she wrapped her arms around his neck without hesitation, pressed against his warm, powerful body, and breathed deeply until her fear subsided, until she no longer perceived them as separate beings, human and horse. She felt his heart beat and the internal rumblings of his belly and the minute twitches of his hide against her cheek. A languorous peace filled her and she leaned against him, and it was a long time before she heard the toot of a car horn.

In the back seat of Miss Mik's car Rick cuddled with Emily, both ignoring Lara as she got in the front. "I can drop you back at the dorm," offered Miss Mik. "Or you can come to town with us. You'll have about an hour while I do a few things if you want."

"Okay," said Lara.

In Jonesburg Emily and Rick went off together and

Miss Mik said, "I have to go in this store, Lara — do you need anything? Your father said if you needed money you could —"

"I don't need anything," said Lara quickly. "I'm okay. Thanks. I'll just look around."

She went listlessly down East Street. On this cold afternoon the old men who usually sat on the bench in front of Dalgetty's Lunch were gone. At the end of East Street she turned down Bartlett Avenue, already nearing the edge of town. She'd never come down this far and found herself on a nondescript street of small businesses in worn cinderblock and shingle buildings.

She'd taken half a roll of film before she noticed Hawley's Garage. The faded sign was hanging in front of a pile of tires. She walked closer. From inside the garage came the static-infested blare of a local radio station, and through the open bay she saw a man in greasy overalls working under a car. Next to the telephone in the entrance was a notice board pinned with flyspecked *Playboy* centerfolds.

She imagined Ben working in this cheerless place, lying for hours on his back on the cement floor. Suddenly she understood the enormity of what Ben was combating. Everywhere in Jonesburg, the atmosphere of depression ate away at people until they looked like those old men outside Dalgetty's or like the slack-eyed girl who was pushing a baby stroller past her on the sidewalk. How did people ever escape a place like this? *Was* it only possible with money? Was it possible that even with the most wonderful dreams imaginable, Ben might still become trapped here?

She did not pay attention to where she was walking and found herself on an unfamiliar street. On the corner was a news shop and next to it a bar with neon beer signs flickering in the window. Before she registered the sight of the pickup truck, Tom came out the door toward her, grinning, and blocked her way. "Well, looky here," he said. "If it ain't my pretty friend."

"What do you want?" she asked.

"You're being pretty unfriendly," he complained. "You wasn't so unfriendly last time we met, were you?" He reached out, cigarette between his fingers, and ran his hand over her hair.

She flashed him a disdainful look and twisted away. "Leave me alone," she said. "You're drunk. I don't want to talk to you." She ducked under his arm and walked away without looking back, but the encounter had disoriented her and she wasn't sure which direction would take her back to East Street. She didn't think he would follow and was completely unprepared when Tom violently grabbed her arm.

"Hey, don't be like that!" he demanded. "You can't be real nice one day and a little bitch the next — don't you know that?" He kept his grasp on her arm, forcing her to walk awkwardly at his pace alongside him. "Hey — maybe you an' me should just take a nice drive in the truck, what d'you say, pretty?"

She refused to reply, looked quickly around. The

street was deserted. Tom grabbed her other arm to push her back against a wall. "I know what your problem is," he snarled. "You got a thing for my baby brother, don't you?" He stared at her until she was forced to meet his eyes. "You think he likes you? He only wants the same thing everyone else wants, Miss Pretty. He ain't no different from anyone, tryin' to take as much as he can get. He's sure got Dad fooled. He'd give Bennie boy the friggin' moon, if he could. Trouble is, he can't. So Bennie's tryin' to get it from you."

She gave him her softest, most suggestive smile and willed herself to relax in his grip. "Hey, Tom," she said, fingering his shirt. "Don't be mad. I was just in a bad mood. I wasn't trying to be unfriendly." She made her voice husky and low, and under her caressing touch he responded as she'd hoped. He was still holding her against the wall but his hands moved up and down her arms now, instead of gripping her tightly. For some reason, now, she did not move away. There was something about his roughness, the possessive push of his hips, his persistent hands . . . All she had to do was look at him in a certain way and he would give her whatever she asked for. For one reckless moment she considered going with him in the truck, letting him take her away, just *away*, anywhere . . .

"I really have to go," she murmured. "I'll be at the farm again soon, you know. You don't have to be so pushy." And at that moment she did not care whether he obeyed her or not. She shivered under his hands and he smiled. If he let her go, she would go; if he pulled her toward the truck, laughing at her with his eyes . . . she would follow.

But he only cocked his head, grinned, and dropped his hands. "Okay, pretty," he said, shrugging. "I ain't up to arguing. But don't you forget. I'll consider that an invitation."

She could feel him watching her as she walked away, and her arms throbbed where his hands had held her. She yanked her sweater straight, bit her lip, and was suddenly overwhelmed with shaking. She felt as grimy as the man under the car at the garage. It was impossible for her to be good. She couldn't do it. She'd almost gone off with Tom. . . . Blindly, without knowing how, she found Miss Mik's car and slumped on the front seat. She wished feverishly that she'd wheedled another joint or a beer from Tom. At least it would have been worth it, to get high. At least for those few numb minutes she wouldn't have to feel anything. Why not? She might as well.

She was already out of the car to go back when Miss Mik appeared and threw some bags in the trunk. "Pretty quiet place, isn't it?" she laughed. "You see Rick and Emily yet? What on earth they found to do in this town is beyond me."

"They're getting it on somewhere," Lara said nastily, but Miss Mik looked at her and she dropped her eyes. She twisted her hands on her lap, flushed, and considered telling Miss Mik about Tom. It would get him in big trouble, she knew; she was underage and he was over twenty-one. He could go to jail. All she had to do was point her finger. She contemplated this fiercely. It would have the double value of shocking Miss Mik.

But Ben would hear about it then too. All at once she collapsed inside, as if the air had been knocked out of her. She leaned forward, pressed her forehead hard against the dashboard, and only grunted when Miss Mik asked if she felt all right. She was not sick. Oh no. She was bad, that was all. She could not be good, even if she wanted to be. And she didn't want to be.

Emily and Rick finally returned, and they headed back to the school. As they drove past Stahler's farm on the way to Huntingdon, Lara stared up at the house. "Why does that place always have to look like a dump!" she hissed savagely, and Miss Mik glanced at her in surprise. "I mean it," said Lara. "It's disgusting." With each word she felt herself purged of something.

Miss Mik turned up the drive to the school and said quietly, "They don't have the money to pay the landfill fees, Lara. And Mr. Stahler told me he can fix that old Chevy and the fridge to sell them. . . ."

"Then why doesn't he!" cried Lara.

"I expect he doesn't have much time. He's got a couple of part-time jobs," said Miss Mik, looking at her with a level stare.

Perversely, she hated that Miss Mik was making excuses for Ben's father, and when the car stopped she slammed the door and stalked off. Her clothing felt dirty and heavy, and she wanted to stand under the full blast of the shower. But Miss Mik caught up with her at the door. "Wait," she said. "I want to show you something."

Lara followed her warily into the apartment. On the easel was a new painting that caught her eye immediately. A rich blue sky swept up from a powerful image of Galaxy at the zenith of his jump, Ben tucked gracefully along his neck. Lara walked closer. "How'd you know about the sky?" she demanded.

Miss Mik shrugged and put her bags down. "Lara, tell me what's going on. I know something's wrong. You're not yourself."

All week she had tried not to break a single rule, had not been rude or lost her temper. All week she'd felt as if some other person had taken up an uneasy residence within her. But obviously Miss Mik had not seen the goodness — saw only that something was "wrong." But it was true — she was not herself. She was disappearing from herself.

Except with Tom. Tom saw her for who she really was. With Tom, she could be someone she recognized. Suddenly Lara could not bear looking at the painting of Ben and Galaxy. She fled the woman's apartment with a mumbled excuse, ran upstairs, and stood under a stinging shower. Over and over her own thought repeated itself in her mind: Except with Tom. With Tom she was her old familiar self. She knew how to play his game with him, knew the intoxication of danger, the excitement of flirting with the edge of control. She might not be *good* with Tom, but she could do something she was good *at*. She shook the water out of her eyes. That was that, then. She'd tried. No one could say she hadn't tried.

And after all, how could Ben or Miss Mik understand? Lara had come from a place where babies had to be abandoned so the mother could sell her body for a few pesos in order not to starve. Could anything good come from a place like that? She rubbed herself dry with a towel so hard her skin felt bruised.

The next day in classes Lara was inattentive and jumpy. Without planning it, she went back to her room and pulled out the portfolio beneath her bed. She thought: I make pictures of where I come from. No matter how much money her parents had or what schools they sent her to, she thought, it wouldn't change the fact that she'd come from that other place. And that would always determine who she was.

She had grown afraid of seeing Ben again. But Miss Mik made her come with the other Trails students to clean up the barn for some visitors who were going to be looking over the school. "Couldn't I just do something around here?" Lara asked, but Miss Mik shook her head impatiently. Lara pulled on her work jeans and sweater with apathy. A faint whiff of Tom's cigarette still clung in the wool and she yanked it off and flung it to the floor. In the mirror she caught a glimpse of herself – but it seemed to be a stranger's face staring back, someone from that *other place* who might at any moment demand: "I know you. I know you. You belong *here*."

For once, Lara was reluctant to leave the group of students and stared at the ground when Ben came out of the barn. "I'm working on the tack room," Ben told Miss Mik. "But there's a lot they could do around the yard, I guess, and the barn –" He paused, looking worried. "My dad said he'd be here, but I don't know where he is. Maybe he forgot those people were coming today."

"It's all right, Ben," Miss Mik reassured him, "Mr. Crighton's coming down soon, and Mr. Davitt, and they'll show the people around."

"Yeah, but . . ."

Miss Mik gave him a little shove toward the barn. "This isn't your responsibility, Ben," she laughed kindly. "Don't worry. Just put these guys to work, and the rest will take care of itself."

Lara trailed after the others and sat on a hay bale while Ben handed brooms to Rick and Jordie, barraging them with such detailed instructions they rolled their eyes in protest. When he turned to her finally, Lara couldn't help muttering, "What do you want me to do – polish the floor with a toothbrush?"

He gave her a sheepish half smile and said, "I just don't want it to look like a dump, is all." His anxiety

185

dispelled some of her own and she managed a weak smile back. They looked at each other self-consciously and Ben blurted, "You could help me in the tack room if you want."

"The tack room's perfectly neat," she said, looking in through the half-open door. "You could eat in there."

"Not off the floor, you couldn't . . ."

Unexpectedly, they both giggled. Ben pushed the door open wider with his foot and reached for her before she could close it behind them. They lost their balance and stifled their laughter as a sawhorse holding a saddle crashed to the floor. Lara ran her hands up under his shirt and lay her head against his chest.

"I missed you," he whispered. "How come you didn't come down all week?"

"I came down Wednesday but you weren't here," she replied. She envied him the certainty of his feelings for her. He kissed the top of her head softly, and when they heard the sound of cars arriving, his arms tightened around her. "I gotta go out there now," he whispered unhappily. "Come out with me, okay?"

"Aren't you supposed to make me sweep the barn or something?"

"Rick can do that. Come on," he urged. "Please, Lara? I don't want to deal with them people by myself. You don't have to do anything."

They untangled themselves, frantically brushing straw from their clothing and hair. Outside, the headmaster of Huntingdon and Bob Davitt were greeting the two sets of parents who had come to investigate the school and riding program for their children. When Ben and Lara came out of the barn, Davitt was having difficulty trying to divert attention from the yard to the new riding arena.

"The horses are stabled in that barn?" asked one of the men, glancing at his wife.

"Well, yes. For now, we —" But Davitt was interrupted smoothly by the headmaster, who took the arm of one of the women and steered the group toward the arena. "We're in the midst of remodeling the barn," Crighton said. "We've completely overhauled the structure and renovated the stall area. I can assure you we've had experts confirm the stability of the building, Mr. Lamont. Now, if you'll just let me show you our ring . . . I think I mentioned, didn't I, that one of the most respected trainers in the East is working with our more advanced riding students? Bernd von Heiland? I'm sure you've —"

"You've got von Heiland here?" inquired the man. "He worked with that mare Crystaline, didn't he, dear — after Henry bought her for his daughter?" His wife nodded, distracted, sidestepping to avoid some boards piled haphazardly near the ring.

"Ben, you have any idea when Thomas plans to get rid of that pile of wood?" called Davitt, turning to Ben for the first time without greeting him. Crighton continued to walk ahead with the parents.

"He hasn't had the time," said Ben softly. "He's

workin' two jobs right now, and he fills in at the feed store on the weekends. I shoulda got to it myself last week —"

"Let's go in the barn now, shall we?" Davitt interrupted, turning away and addressing the parents as they came back with the headmaster. Ben trailed behind the group and then, still unintroduced by either Crighton or Davitt, he held the door open for them and carefully explained the daily routine for the horses. He held himself with such quiet poise that Lara's eyes stung with furious tears.

"You work here, I take it?" asked one of the men when Ben had finished.

"This is my father's farm," said Ben evenly.

The parents avoided each other's eyes uncomfortably, but Crighton said, as if their discomfort was Ben's fault, "Thanks, Ben. I'm sure you've got plenty to do without hanging around with us. When your father returns, send him in, will you?"

Ben inclined his head briefly and Lara stifled a snort of laughter. Ben had mimicked von Heiland's gesture of aloof courtesy to perfection! His silence indicated there was nothing he needed from these people, including their approval, and to make sure they understood, Lara looked at them pointedly with an insolent grin. Crighton gave her a look, the two men belatedly offered to shake Ben's hand, and Lara hardly waited until they were both outside to cry, "What pompous pigs!

188

God, Ben — you were so fantastic! Did you see how they —"

"I don't blame them," he interrupted fiercely. "I wouldn't want my kid riding around here on a million-dollar horse."

"What are you talking about! Don't you dare —"

"No, I mean it!" he insisted. "It's not even safe, Lara! Look — what if some horse bolts into that roll of rusty wire? What about the glass from that busted window over there, and all that loose plastic flapping around? Dad's had time, Lara. He has! He ain't always worked this many jobs."

She stared at him, speechless a moment, then snapped, "Well, if Crighton doesn't like it, he can build his stupid riding program on his own land!" She pulled him behind the barn, ignoring the glares of Rick and Jordie, who were pushing a laden wheelbarrow toward the manure pile. "They don't have any right coming over to your father's farm and passing judgment!" she cried.

"Well, I still don't blame them," Ben said stubbornly.

"Oh, stop it, Ben!" Lara flashed. "They had no right to be rude to you. You're a million times better than any of them, including old fart-face Crighton."

She didn't know who enraged her more, Ben or the visitors, and she stomped back into the barn. She pushed the door open so violently one of the horses shied in his stall and Crighton frowned. "Lara, be a little more careful. Are you supposed to be in here?"

189

"Yes!" she said, grabbing a broom. "I'm sweeping." She swept so savagely the air filled with hay dust and one of the women coughed. Crighton moved the group farther away and continued talking, but Lara could still hear. "We couldn't be in more sympathy with your concerns," he was telling one of the men. "We're experiencing a delay in our plans because of the present owner of the farm, but I can assure you it won't be for long. Frankly, the man is barely hanging on, and I'm confident he'll have to sell by spring."

"We've already drawn up plans," Davitt took over from Crighton, propping one foot up on a bale. Like he already owned the place, thought Lara. Davitt smiled. "We're committed to developing one of the finest private-school equestrian facilities in the country."

"Well," said one woman slowly, looking at her husband. "After all, Janey won't even be ready for Huntingdon until next fall — but you say by spring . . . ?"

"By the summer, I am confident this will be Huntingdon property, and we will begin serious development at that time," nodded Crighton. "Janey will be well accommodated."

Lara threw the broom against the wall. The sucking-up they were all doing would make a cow sick, she thought, loathing the smug expressions on the parents' faces. They'd been so busy trying to impress each other with who they knew and how much money they had — people like that would never stop to consider how it would all sound to Ben, she thought. She was overwhelmed with self-disgust for trying to be *good*, for trying to comply with the rules and behavior people like these parents and Crighton thought mattered. She would rather be bad, if it meant she wouldn't be like them. At least she would be honest. At least she would not suck up to anyone.

But what about Ben? If he had the choice, would Ben leave Galaxy stabled here in a rotting shed, or would he allow himself and Galaxy to become some wealthy man's hobby? But would he even get a choice? If Ben's father lost the farm . . .

She could not imagine Ben and Galaxy separated — as if the boy and the horse drew their life force from each other. She was trapped by her irreconcilable thoughts, knowing how essential it was for Ben to follow his dreams, but knowing, too, exactly what he faced in the world where those dreams could be realized. Where money was involved, someone always won and someone else had to lose. Ben could lose Galaxy, his father could lose the farm, and Ben's dreams could end in Hawley's Garage — it was as simple as that. Making a dream come true took more than just believing in it.

"Lara, Miss Mik's here," Ben called from the door. She brushed past the visitors without looking at them, and Ben caught her outside the door. He smiled into her angry eyes and kissed her swiftly. "Hey, don't you worry none," he whispered. "Them people don't matter to me — I'll be okay. I love you."

Chapter Fourteen

Friday afternoon dragged. The weather had turned cold and gray with the beginning of November, and drafts whistled through the broken caulking around the windows in the English classroom. Ben idly traced the design he'd drawn on his notebook page. It was the ring figures for a dressage test that von Heiland had shown him the week before: 20-meter circle, change of rein across diagonal . . . He frowned, trying to remember the terms. "Your instinct is good," the trainer had told him. "Now you need to learn discipline. Art is instinct wedded to hard work – because instinct is only raw material without discipline. And discipline is empty of life without the creative instinct."

Ben studied the design. "Dressage is about change," von Heiland had told him more than once. "Change is beautiful. Why? Because it is movement. Most people live their lives resisting and fighting change . . . always afraid, yes? You have noticed this? But life *is* change, Benjamin. This is how everything is created . . . *change*. Movement. When you and your horse learn to move from one change to another with grace and courage, that is how it will also become in your life. You will see – it is not so very different, dressage and life."

Whenever he tried to pin down the meaning of von Heiland's words, they confused him. But if he simply remembered them and did not force himself to figure them out, the trainer's words began to connect with what Ben had already observed in his life. It was true, he thought now — most people he knew did seem to struggle against life, resenting the hardships and fighting the unexpected events that brought about change. "It takes tremendous courage to work with change instead of against it," he remembered von Heiland saying. "It is not so easy to live with change so it becomes an act of beauty in your life. That is why you must work, work, work. Work develops courage."

Von Heiland hadn't meant only those precise changes of lead, gait, and direction that were the distinctive mark of the formal choreography of dressage. He'd also meant those inevitable changes in a person's life. Ben propped his chin on his hands. But if he lost Galaxy, or his father lost the farm, how could it be possible to work that change into an "act of beauty" in his life? How would he find the courage?

"Ben!" The voice jerked him to attention. He slumped despondently in his seat while the teacher inspected his notebook. "What on earth is *this*?" she asked, shaking her head and handing it back to him. "Ben, what's going on? You've been slacking off for weeks. This is your senior year — a lot depends on what you do here. I'm getting a little worried about you." She gave him a perplexed smile and he sighed, turning to a clean page in the notebook. The assignment was to write an essay on a human quality, such as joy or pity. He wrote "Love" at the top of the page, then paused, frowning. He erased it and in its place wrote "Courage." He began the essay with von Heiland's words.

All Friday evening, Ben waited for Lara to call, knowing her mother was coming to visit the next day. "You'll hate her," Lara had said. "But I want to meet her, Lara," he'd insisted stubbornly. "Besides, don't you want to show her Galaxy? I thought she loved horses." Lara had given him an inscrutable look. "She only loves *Timothy*," she said. "She'd love a baboon as long as it was Timothy's."

But she did not call. The next morning, he waited impatiently for his mother to give him a ride to Jonesburg on her way to work. "For goodness' sake, stop fussing at me!" Betty cried. "We can go in ten minutes, I told you."

"But, Mom — I have to load up that grain and get back here in time for my lesson," he pleaded. "You know Tom won't wait if I don't meet him when I said I would."

But even though he was on time, Tom was not waiting for him at the feed store with the truck as he'd promised. His mother had already driven off to work and Ben walked, grumbling, the six blocks to the bar. Tom was hunched on a stool at the far end of the smoky room, gazing blankly at a television game show. "You were supposed to meet me," Ben said. "Come on, Tom! I have stuff I gotta do at home."

Tom did not respond. Ben stood uncertain behind him, his eyes stinging from the cigarette smoke, and saw Dave Hawley with Art Fenstemacher, whose hardware store had gone out of business the week before. Dave Hawley grinned. "How you doing, kid? Hope you ain't takin' up bad habits now! I got to have someone workin' for me that's straight — keep the rest of us in line." The other men at the bar chuckled and Dave added kindly, "How's your daddy, Ben? That brother of yourn won't tell us nothin.' Heard the canning factory's layin' off —"

"It is?" asked Ben, startled. Fenstemacher nudged Hawley in the ribs and Hawley coughed. "Well, it prob'ly ain't nothin' to worry about, Ben. Hard times for everybody, I guess — least we're all in the same boat!"

"You ain't in the same boat, Hawley!" growled another man good-naturedly. "Took you a whole god-damn week to fix my Chevy, you said you was so busy."

Ben tried to get Tom's attention again. "Give me the keys then, okay? I'll get the grain myself, and I'll come back and pick you up after. Come on, Tom — I gotta get there before they close at noon."

"For Christ's sake stop buggin' me," snarled Tom, staring at the television without turning. Dave Hawley moved closer to Ben and grunted, "Hey, Tom — give the kid a break."

Tom whirled around. "Shut up and keep your nose outta my business, Hawley," he said.

Hawley put his arm over Ben's shoulder and gently pushed him out the door. "Look, Ben — why'n't you go ahead an' borrow my truck. No, go on – I can get a ride with Art. He ain't got nothin' better to do. You can drop off the truck in the morning. How's that?"

Hawley held the keys out to him and Ben looked at the ground miserably. "Hey, now," Hawley said in rough compassion. "Forget about Tom – he's no good. I know I got no right to say that, but it's true." He hesitated, glancing at the door. "Look, I was meanin' to ask you next week, soon's I straightened a few things out – but I got work for you startin' after Christmas, if you want it. Part-time till you're out of school, or your Daddy'll kill me! When'd you say your birthday was? When you'll be eighteen?"

"December twentieth," answered Ben, struggling to respond politely to Dave Hawley's concern. Unbidden, von Heiland's words came to him again: "It takes tremendous courage to work with change . . ."

"Look, I'm gonna be real honest with you," Hawley continued seriously. "Your dad and me's been friends since high school, and I care for him like a . . . like a brother." He grimaced wryly. "Well, you know what I mean. Anyways, I got the work – an' you need to get yourself outta that house. So look – you know that little room with the kitchenette, behind my garage? You work for me after school startin' Christmas, live in that room so's I don't have to worry no more about break-ins, and I'll pay you minimum to start."

"Thanks, Mr. Hawley," Ben stammered. "I mean, can I think about it? It's a real decent offer, but my mom — well, my dad wants me to . . ." Hawley gave him the keys and thumped his shoulder. "'Course you think about it, Ben," he said. "It ain't easy — family stuff. Just remember you got a place if you need it, okay? Now go get that grain. Go on, get outta here."

He loaded the grain sacks into Hawley's truck, his mind racing. Hawley's by *Christmas* . . . but then Galaxy . . . Tom . . . can't stand being in the house anymore . . . my own place . . . but Galaxy . . . could save some money. . . . How will I tell von Heiland . . . and Lara. . . .

Lara. If he lived in Jonesburg he'd never see Lara. And he'd have to face von Heiland. But what could the trainer offer him, compared with Dave Hawley? Hawley was offering him an immediate, sensible way out. All von Heiland offered was "we'll see" . . . and hope.

He heaved the last sack onto the truck and arranged the charge to Huntingdon. As he drove up to the barn, Galaxy cantered along the fence, his black mane and tail flying in the cold. Ben paused by the truck a moment. His heart always swelled at the sight of the stallion and he could not keep from laughing as he watched Galaxy showing off for him. "Just a few minutes, boy," he called, and slung the sacks off the truck as if they weighed nothing.

In the arena von Heiland was clapping his hands, barking directions to three students. Ben leaned against the wall in the entrance and grinned as the students reined their horses to stand in a half-circle around the trainer. "What did I say about laziness?" von Heiland demanded. "Alex, you are riding a horse, yes? You are not sitting on the sofa watching television? But with you, it is very difficult for me to tell the difference. And Olivia, you are thinking of something, perhaps? The holidays? A boyfriend? Meanwhile, your horse, she goes where she pleases. Now —"

The trainer shot out a volley of commands and then came, shaking his head, toward Ben. He studied him with a critical eye and did not return Ben's greeting. "You look like . . . how do you say it? A bum," said von Heiland brusquely. "Every time I see you, you are dressed in these clothes, like a bum. So. What will we do about this problem?"

"I just got back from unloading grain," retorted Ben, stung. "And don't tell me to go buy new clothes, because you know I can't. Anyway, it's freezing out."

"The cold is of no consequence," snapped von Heiland. "You pay attention only to your work. This is what I have been trying to teach you, yes? So — your horse, he is very beautiful, but you look like a bum. Therefore, nothing happens. Nothing beautiful can be created in this way. To make beauty, everything counts. Nothing is too insignificant. You understand?"

"Yes, but I don't have —"

"It does not matter what you wear, as long as it is clean and neat," said the trainer. "As long as it shows you respect what you and the horse are creating."

Ben went to his room and looked around in a

quandary. Besides jeans and sweatshirts, all he had was the suit he'd worn to his cousin Brenda's wedding — but as soon as he pulled it from the closet he realized how much he'd grown in two years. But Tom had been at the wedding too. . . . He pushed open the door to his brother's room cautiously and found the wedding suit wadded in the corner of the closet. He smoothed it out, polished his boots with the edge of a blanket, combed his hair, and then walked self-consciously across the yard to von Heiland. He felt ridiculous, but the trainer nodded in approval. "Now you are worthy of your horse. Now we work."

It was a difficult lesson and it took all his concentration, so Ben did not notice the black limousine pull up beside the barn. But as he cantered past the entrance, he saw Lara standing there with a man, watching him. The stallion responded to his start of surprise with a momentary break in stride, and Ben forced himself to focus. He could feel von Heiland's eyes boring into him. But he could not force from his mind the impression of Lara's eyes as he'd cantered by. Something was wrong.

He kept his head straight and held himself in rigid control. Von Heiland called, "You are not a block of wood, Benjamin. Relax. Go with the horse," and he strolled across the ring toward the man and Lara.

The acoustics in the arena were unpredictable, and as Ben trotted along one side of the ring he could hear very clearly the man asking von Heiland, " . . . Never shown? But how did he get to this level? What does he intend to do with the horse?"

"He's a complete natural," he heard von Heiland reply. "He's trained himself and the horse – most extraordinary, is it not? I have asked Cafferty to come see him."

"Cafferty? Is he coming?"

"He said he would come," nodded von Heiland, and looked sharply in Ben's direction. "Don't let him push his head out like that, Benjamin! Look how it throws his shoulders off." He turned again to the man. "I think Cafferty will agree with me. But this boy, he has no money, you understand. He comes from this –"

Ben caught the gesture of von Heiland's arm from the corner of his eye and flushed. He was painfully aware of how he must look dressed in the rumpled suit, riding without a saddle. But as if to belie his thoughts, Galaxy snorted, arched his neck, and collected himself into a beautiful canter, the light a soft sheen over his supple muscles. Once again, as Ben passed the entrance he overheard a few words of the conversation. ". . . Exactly what I'm looking for, for my son," the man was telling von Heiland. "A horse like that – gentle, but loads of potential. You agree? Now that my son has decided to become a trainer himself –"

When von Heiland called him to halt a few minutes later, Ben slid off, breathing hard, to stand by Lara. "This is my father," she said without greeting him. "Dad, this is Ben." She spoke without expression, with neither interest nor animosity, and seemed to look through them both when William McGrath extended his hand to Ben. "Lara couldn't wait to get me down here," McGrath said with a laugh. "Said the farm was the only decent thing about the school." But even as he spoke, his eyes kept shifting from Ben to Galaxy. "That's a fine animal you have there, son," he said. "Lara's told you about her brother, Timothy, of course. . . ."

Lara stared at Ben with eyes he could not fathom, eyes that seemed like flat water disturbed by shadows moving beneath the surface. "Yes," Ben replied. "She's told me everything." He kept his eyes on Lara's face and added carefully, "I'm very sorry. Would you like to see the barn when I put Galaxy away?" He felt as though he had plunged into Lara's eyes and was swimming blind.

"Barns all look pretty much the same after a while," smiled McGrath. "I'll just chat a bit with Herr von Heiland – Lara, you go on with Ben, if you want. I'll be right here – there's no hurry."

When they were out of sight beyond the barn, Ben turned to her intently. "Lara –" She was unresponsive in his arms. "Lara, what happened? How come your mom's not here?"

"She couldn't come," shrugged Lara. "It's no big deal."

Despite how she always spoke of Veronica McGrath, Ben was sure Lara had been looking forward to her mother's visit more than she would admit, because of how many times she had mentioned it in the last weeks. "Why?" he asked. "Is she sick or something?"

"No," said Lara. "She isn't sick. "She just didn't want to come, I guess. I don't know. Dad just showed up this morning and said she was busy or something."

"You mean she didn't call you herself?" he asked, incredulous. Beneath her nonchalance he saw her hurt, and he felt it as if it were his own. He pulled her tightly against him. "That's really rotten," he murmured. "That was a shitty thing for your mom to do." He tried to kiss her but she pushed him away.

"She's very busy," Lara said. "Don't do that, Ben. I don't feel like it."

McGrath was deep in conversation with von Heiland when they walked back to the arena. "I was telling Herr von Heiland how much I admire your stallion, Ben," said McGrath. "I've been hearing about Huntingdon's plans for an equestrian center. What do you think of them?"

There was something too calculated in McGrath's question, something beyond casual interest that suggested he was thinking of more than the conversation he'd been having with the trainer, and Ben suppressed a flicker of foreboding. "Well, the school wants my dad to sell the farm," he answered bluntly. "They're putting a lot of pressure on him. But they're letting me have these lessons here. So it's hard for me to say what I think."

There was a pleased look in von Heiland's eyes at the reply, but McGrath regarded Ben with sharp assessment. "Yes." He nodded. "I would imagine it puts you in a difficult position. I'm only interested for my son, of course, who may decide to return to school in the fall —"

"Ben's father won't sell the farm," Lara suddenly interrupted. "This is his home. He loves it. The school has no right to pressure him."

McGrath laughed. "Well, business is business, Lara," he said. "That's the way the world runs, I'm afraid. If Ben's father really doesn't want to —"

"They know things are hard for him right now," Lara said hotly. "That's why they're putting the pressure on. It's like kicking someone when he's down."

"Now, Lara —" began McGrath, but Ben broke in. "My father can handle it. The school will have to be satisfied with leasing our land and the barn. Their money won't make no difference to my dad."

When von Heiland went to check on his other students in the barn, the three of them stood together awkwardly in the yard. Finally, McGrath asked, "Where's your horse, Ben? I wouldn't mind taking another look at him. I don't know when I've seen such a fine animal, not since —"

Lara caught his eye and again Ben felt the foreboding, as if her unreadable look was a warning. Reluctantly he led McGrath to the field beyond the barn where Galaxy grazed along the fence. To his amazement, Lara suddenly hung on to her father's arm like a young child and began to chatter, so McGrath was forced to pay more attention to her than to Galaxy. "So when I come home for Thanksgiving, let's do that, okay, Daddy?" she wheedled.

McGrath looked uncomfortable. "I thought your mother had talked to you about Thanksgiving," he said.

"I haven't talked to Mom. What do you mean?"

He hesitated a moment, troubled. "Well, honey — it's hardly worth the trip, is it, for a long weekend? And the Beechams are just up in Wilkes-Barre — they're really looking forward to seeing you."

"I don't *want* to go to the Beechams!" she cried. "I want to go home."

"They're your godparents, sweetie," McGrath frowned. "And you know we'll be spending most of the time at the . . . well, you know how difficult it'll be for your mother if you're home and Timothy's . . ."

"Okay, Dad," Lara stopped him. "Fine. It's fine."

"Now, look," suggested McGrath, "how about if I ask your Uncle Ralph to bring you down here the day after Thanksgiving — you could spend some time with Ben. Wouldn't you like that? Would that be all right with your family, Ben?"

"Well, I —"

"Give it up, Dad," Lara snapped contemptuously. "I don't give a shit where I go. I said it was okay, didn't I?" She looked straight at McGrath. "So I don't suppose I'll be coming home for Christmas either."

"Well, of course it's up to you, honey," said her father. "It really depends on what's happening with everything else. Your mother was thinking you might like to have a real holiday — in Florida, with your Uncle Henry and Aunt Pat? You know — the beach, the sun . . . They'd love to have you stay, sweetie. Since they moved down there they don't get much chance to be with family."

"Well, they won't exactly get *family* with me, will they?" she sneered.

Ben felt as if he were being forced to watch a horror movie, unable to close his eyes when the monster opened its maw to tear everything to shreds. Lara was putting up a valiant fight to keep the monster at bay, but he could not help her. It was a monster he could not see and did not understand. "Lara can stay with us for Christmas," he offered, knowing even as he spoke how terribly impossible that would be. He thought of Lara watching his parents bicker as they sat around the kitchen table, the television blaring and Tom sprawled drunk on the sofa. "Lara, will you stay with us for Christmas?"

And then, because this was a horror movie, Tom drove up at that moment, coming within inches of sideswiping the limo when he skidded to a halt. Standing with McGrath and Lara, Ben could only resign himself to the situation. "It takes tremendous courage to work with change" came von Heiland's words again, like a voice-over in the film.

Tom walked toward them. "Hey, Bennie," he said, poking the suit jacket with a grin. "You sure are a fancy dude today." He cocked his head at Lara. "This here your daddy? You must be real proud of this pretty girl of yours."

McGrath took Lara's arm and headed to the limo. "Ben, thank you for the invitation, but I think Lara would prefer to spend her holidays with her relatives in Florida." He held the door open, and when Lara got in he closed it firmly and walked around to the other side. Ben knocked on the window and Lara rolled it partially down. "What?" she said.

"Lara, don't . . . don't shut me out," he cried in a whisper. "Please. I need to talk to you. Will you come down tomorrow? Or meet me somewhere?"

"I don't know."

He held on to the window with both hands, no longer caring if anyone saw. "Lara, you *have* to," he pleaded. "I mean it. Please talk to me. If you don't talk to someone you'll go crazy. Come on. Tomorrow —"

"I'm already crazy, Ben." She smiled softly. "I told you that before." The window rose with a hum and he had to snatch his fingers away. He could see nothing through the dark-tinted glass.

The limo backed up slowly, turned, then stopped. Once more a window was rolled down and Lara's father looked out. "Ben," he said. "I'd like to give you this. I'm very interested in your stallion. Lara tells me you won't sell, but in case you change your mind – I'll give you a fair price, I can assure you. You can reach me at this number." McGrath pressed a business card into Ben's hand, and without further discussion he settled back in the seat and spoke to the driver. The window hummed up, the limo pulled away, and the card seemed to burn Ben's hand to the bone.

Tom was laughing at him. "You wouldn't go and sell out, would you, Bennie boy? Thought you was too good for that."

Ben lunged at his brother, flailing with his fists. But even drunk, Tom was stronger and he threw Ben hard against the truck. "What d'you think you're doing, you little piss-head!" he growled. "This about that sweet little girl of yours, huh? Grow up, Bennie! Let me tell you what your precious Lara likes to do."

Ben tried to jam his hands over his ears but Tom held him by the arms and thrust his face close. Every word Tom spoke was like a fist in Ben's gut. Even after his brother was pulled away by von Heiland, Ben could not catch his breath.

"Get up, Benjamin," commanded von Heiland. "Get your horse. You will ride."

He squinted at the trainer in disbelief, but von Heiland took him by the shoulders and pushed him toward the fence. "Benjamin. Get the horse."

He walked shakily to open the gate and Galaxy followed him to the arena, his muzzle nudging his shoulder. The stallion's touch made him tremble. Von

Heiland paid no attention, cupping his hands to boost Ben up and barking, "Get up now. On your horse."

He made him canter Galaxy around the ring, calling instructions so fast Ben was dizzy. He bounced on the stallion's back, slipped, hauled himself up, slipped again, and began to laugh. He laughed so hard he fell forward against Galaxy's neck and the horse stopped. Von Heiland strode up and, without warning, hit him a stinging blow on the thigh with the butt of his riding crop. Ben hiccuped at the pain and gasped, "Why'd you do that?"

"You are hysterical," said von Heiland. "Now stop. I want you to focus. You understand what I am saying? *I want you to focus.*"

The trainer seemed to be infusing him with his own will through his steady gaze. More gentle now, von Heiland said, "Focus, Benjamin. This is important. If you can find your focus even when you are in pain, you will find your own power. That is true beauty."

Ben closed his eyes. Each time he struggled to concentrate, the pain caused by Tom's words tore through him. But von Heiland would not leave him alone. "Focus, Benjamin. Find your focus."

Once more he forced himself to breathe deeply, tried to match the steady breathing of the horse. This time he did not lose it. This time he found the energy rising as it did in the clearing, rising up through the sawdust floor and coursing through flesh and bone until it joined

Galaxy's heart with his own. They were no longer separate. As one undivided being, they began to move.

Von Heiland stepped back. He gave no further commands. With every stride of the stallion, Ben rode deeper into his own heart until he found the center of that forceful rhythm. And he did not lose it, even after he and Galaxy came to stand in front of von Heiland. For a long moment, neither of them moved. Then, when he slid from the stallion's back, the trainer put his hands briefly on Ben's shoulders. "I am very proud to work with you," he said, and without another word he turned and walked from the ring.

Chapter Fifteen

When the bus dropped Ben off after school on Monday, he trudged up the drive and loitered around the house until, driven by a restless misery, he went out to wander in the yard. Gray clouds draped over the farm and the air smelled heavy with snow. When his mother came back from work she found the kitchen door wide open.

He couldn't tell her he was listening for the phone. She grumbled at him when he came in, so he retreated to his room. After supper he forced himself to open his homework, but the pages blurred as he read. Finally, at nine o'clock, he jumped up and went downstairs to the phone.

A bored-sounding girl answered after several rings. "I don't know where she is," she said impatiently when he asked if she would call Lara to the phone.

"Do you know when she'll be back?" he asked.

"No."

He paused and swallowed. "Well, could I leave a message for her?"

"I don't have a pencil."

He pressed his forehead against the wall. "Could you . . . could you just tell her I called?" he begged.

"Look," said the girl. "I don't really see Lara. Besides, I wouldn't talk to her anyway. *I'm* not going to get my head snapped off. Why don't you write her a letter or something."

He considered this now, slumped at the desk with his head propped in his hands. His handwriting was messy and he wasn't a good speller, but he pushed the neglected homework to one side and wrote "Dear Lara" at the top of a page. But how could he ask her about what Tom had told him? At eleven o'clock, Ben crawled into bed and lay staring into the darkness. He knew he was angry, but it felt only like pain.

On Thursday, a light snow fell, the first of the year. But even the sight of Galaxy cavorting like a colt stirred no joy in him. Then, at three o'clock, Miss Mik arrived with her Trails students, and the last person out of the car was Lara.

Rick was already complaining. "You always let Lara off working, Miss Mik!" he cried. "It isn't fair."

"Rick, I gave you a free day last week, and you left early for the weekend too, so I don't even want to hear about it," snapped the woman. "Lara, if you want to take photos, get busy. I want to see you working."

Lara said "Hi" as she walked past, without a flicker of expression. She was already taking her camera from the case, studying the yard around her and heading for the old tractor dusted with snow. When Ben followed, she said quickly, "Don't mess up the snow." She squatted, then looked up again. "You're standing in my light."

"Lara —"

She angled the camera close at the tractor's rusting grillwork, frowning in concentration. Ben leaned against the large back tire and watched for several minutes. Then, as offhand as possible, he asked, "So how'd the rest of your weekend go?"

She rocked back on her heels. "I don't want to talk about it, Ben." After a moment's silence, she added, "I'm really busy. I want to get these shots before the light changes." It was apparent she was making an effort to be polite.

Ben turned and walked away. At the gate, he fumbled with Galaxy's bridle, dropping it twice in his haste.

He hauled himself onto the stallion and went down the road until he came to the track leading along the creek up into the state forest. When he was completely hidden by the dark hemlocks, he began to cry. For a long time Galaxy made his way without any direction.

On Saturday he moved automatically through his lesson with von Heiland, until the trainer called him to stop and studied him with arms folded. "Today you are a robot, yes?" he demanded. "Today I am watching some kind of cartoon on television? What was that you just did, tell me please?"

"I don't know," mumbled Ben.

Von Heiland stepped closer. "This is what you were to practice all week, Benjamin," he said. "Did you practice?"

"No."

"Why not, please?"

He did not even have the energy to think of an excuse. His thoughts seemed to unravel the moment he became aware of them, and his mouth was so dry he could not speak anyway. Von Heiland tapped his boot with his crop. "Get down," he ordered, and when Ben slid off Galaxy, the trainer continued, "This work is crucial, Benjamin. There is something you want from all this, am I correct?"

Although he no longer cared, Ben nodded. The trainer's words were hitting him like hard, stinging pellets. "I see. There is something you want. And this is why I agreed to work with you in the first place." He switched the crop back and forth in the sawdust, as if deciding something. "You know I have asked my friend Cafferty to come here, Benjamin. He is a busy man, you understand, but I am thinking it would be worth it, for him to see you. Yes? But while I may choose to waste my time, I cannot waste his. So. If you want to be in love, it is perhaps better for you to forget *this*." He gestured at Galaxy.

"What do you know about it!" cried Ben, goaded into response.

Von Heiland smiled. "You think I do not know about such things? You imagine I am not a human being?"

To his horror, Ben's eyes began to blur with tears. Mercifully, the trainer cupped his hands and boosted him back on Galaxy without another word. Then he stood, half turned away, thoughtful. Finally, without turning back, he said, "Cafferty can make all the difference, you understand. I know who you *are*, Benjamin. You must show Cafferty who you can *become*."

The lesson with von Heiland seemed to shake something loose in Ben, relaxing the grip of misery enough for him to think more clearly. What was happening to him? He couldn't sleep, he couldn't study, he had no appetite. He could not stand to go on like this.

In math class he looked up once to catch a girl smiling at him. He smiled back with reckless confidence.

Dawn. Dawn Gillespie. She'd always been nice to him. He toyed with his pencil, algebra sums forgotten.

What a total idiot he was. Lara didn't want him. She didn't want him. Did he need it announced on the radio or something? She'd told him who she was enough times, after all – it wasn't as if Tom had revealed anything new. He had to forget about her. He'd ask Dawn out, or something. Anything. He thought about Saturday's lesson with von Heiland and bit his lip. "Cafferty can make all the difference. . . ."

Dawn Gillespie whispered something from across the aisle and he leaned closer to hear. She wanted to borrow a pen. Her hair smelled fresh, as if she'd just come in from outside, and she gave him a frank, friendly smile from her blue eyes. . . . Nothing like Lara's smile. Nothing elusive, nothing unpredictable, nothing to doubt.

He frowned at his textbook in determination. He had to pay more attention to his schoolwork. And when he got home he would ride Galaxy in the ring. No matter what, he would practice every day with Galaxy, just as von Heiland ordered. He rubbed his face with his hands. He was *telling* himself to ride Galaxy, for God's sake! What was happening to him?

So he did work. He rode Galaxy, and on Tuesday he passed an English exam, and that afternoon he rode Galaxy again until it grew too dark to see. And on Thursday afternoon, the phone rang.

He'd just gone out the door. Galaxy was waiting eagerly by the fence. Ben let the phone ring several times, perversely unwilling to answer. But he told himself it could be his mother's car had broken down, or his father needed something. He answered.

"It's me," said Lara.

"Oh."

She paused. "Miss Mik said I should call you." Her voice was as expressionless as before, but now he felt a vague apprehension. "Why?" he muttered.

There was another pause. "I guess . . . she thinks you should come over," said Lara.

"To the school?"

"Yes."

He took a breath. "To see you?"

There was no answer. He strained to hear through the silence. After a moment, he said anxiously, "Lara?"

"Just come, Ben," she said, and hung up.

To his astonishment he was reluctant. He'd been looking forward to the afternoon with Galaxy, had even thought about riding up to the clearing one more time while the trails were still passable. He stood undecided, looking out the kitchen door, but in the stillness he kept hearing the persistent little echo left from Lara's expressionless voice. Another flicker of apprehension shot through him, stronger this time, and he bolted from the house and ran the half mile to Huntingdon. He was out of breath by the time he reached the dorm and knocked on the door of Miss Mik's apartment.

Miss Mik opened the outer door. "Why'd Lara call?"

Ben asked, still gasping slightly from the run. Beyond Miss Mik's office, the door into the apartment was open and he caught sight of Lara sitting on the floor.

"I thought it might be a good idea if you came over," said Miss Mik quietly. "Go on in, Ben. I have to go talk to the dean for a few minutes, but you can stay here with Lara."

Lara did not look up when he went in. Spread around her on the floor were fifteen or twenty of her photo-collages. He knelt down beside her. Then, to his horror, he saw that the black-and-white collages were scrawled over with messy, glossy-red words: *Slut. Bitch. Suck-up.* Over the prints was smeared a gooey substance and he smelled a heavy perfume – shampoo. He looked at Lara. "What happened?" he choked.

"Oh, just a little token of my peers' respect," replied Lara airily, waving her hand at the collages. "I made the mistake of leaving them overnight in the art room so I could cut mats today for my exhibit." She turned to him suddenly. "I didn't think you'd come."

Still in shock, he gasped, "Why?"

"Because I've been so mean to you."

He didn't know how to reply, and picked up a bottle near him on the floor. "It's nail polish remover," she explained. "They must have used a fortune in red nail polish. Miss Mik's trying to figure out how to clean them up. I think they're ruined. The shampoo comes off, but –" She shrugged.

216

She appeared so unconcerned he was uneasy. He did not know what to do. He was afraid to touch her, but impulsively, without looking at him, Lara put her arms around him. He shifted so he could hold her tightly, lay his head against hers, felt the pulse in her temple. After a long time she whispered again, "I really didn't think you'd come."

"I didn't know if you wanted me to," he said. "You just said Miss Mik wanted me to come."

"She made me call you."

"Didn't you want me to come, Lara?"

She was reserved. "I didn't think it was right to ask you," she said. "I wish . . . I wish you didn't care about me so much, Ben. I'm only going to hurt you."

"You don't mean to hurt me."

She laughed a little. "But it comes to the same thing."

He didn't care anymore. The warmth of her body was like a balm over the misery of the last two weeks, so sweet it was intoxicating. He gave up struggling against what was happening to him. He closed his eyes because hers contained too much for him to hold and searched for her mouth blindly. "I would come anywhere if you needed me, no matter what," he whispered against her lips.

After a while she pulled away and said, "Miss Mik might come back. And I have to clean these up."

He experimented by scrubbing at one of the collages with a rag and got most of the shampoo off. "Who *did* this!" he cried. "Lara? Why would anyone —" He stopped.

"Why would anyone do this?" she repeated in self-disdain. "Why do you think? It's not the first time something like this has happened, you know. I'm used to it. I've been called a lot worse." She gestured at the words scrawled on the collages and tossed her head. "Besides, I asked for it, didn't I? I hate everyone."

"Why do you say things like that about yourself?" he asked, anguished.

She leveled a scornful look at him. "Now you sound like one of those stupid shrinks," she said. "How do I know why I say things like that? If I knew, I wouldn't be crazy, would I?"

"Stop saying that!"

She grinned, passing the open bottle of polish remover under her nose and inhaling deeply. He snatched it from her hand. Then her expression sobered. "It's not really that I hate *people*," she said pensively. "I just hate being told what to do by people I don't respect." She looked at him with sudden intensity. "You know I just want to be left alone. But in a place like this, if you're different that way, it scares people. They'll hate you for that. So I hate them back."

"You didn't hate me, even at first."

"You're different, too. I could tell right away," she said slowly. "You're always . . . *you*. And you aren't scared that I'm different." She smiled and touched his face; then, restless, she picked up a collage and studied

218

it. "The polish remover will ruin the prints," she said, dropping it. "It takes the surface right off. So that's it, I guess. They're ruined."

Ben picked with his fingernail at the hard blobs and a bit of red chipped off, leaving the glossy surface of the print undamaged. With his pocketknife, he pried tentatively at another blob and it broke off under the blade. Lara leaned nearer to watch. "It'll take a while," he said, carefully chipping at the edges of the dried blobs. "But you could get it off." He held the collage at arm's length in front of him, frowning. "I know what you should do!" he said, incensed. "Lara! You should exhibit them just the way they are! Just leave the words on – hang these up with your other ones!"

Her eyes widened. "That's an incredible idea!" she cried. "God! It's fantastic! And the labels I put under these could say: 'By Lara McGrath and Anonymous Students'! That would really make them squirm! It would be perfect – all those parents coming for the holidays . . . that'll show them what kind of school their precious kid goes to. The dean'll have a *fit*."

He was already regretting his suggestion, but when he gazed around him at her violated work, anger matching her own filled him. Her collages were so beautiful – complex and disturbing, the way Lara was beautiful. Ben gave her the pocketknife. "Keep it," he said. "You can scrape some off if you want, but leave other bits. That way, you can sort of make them yours again."

She poked at the collage nearest her. "Now do you see why I have to get out of this place?" she asked, almost dreamily, nestling closer to him. She sighed. "I'm really, really glad you came," she murmured. "You're the best friend I have." She paused, laughed a little. "You're my *only* friend."

Chapter Sixteen

Ben did not see Lara again before she left for Thanksgiving. On Thanksgiving Day it snowed, blanketing the hills with wet, heavy drifts. He let Galaxy out into the field and started toward the barn to tend the other horses. Behind him the stallion snorted and galloped in a circle, and Ben watched happily. Galaxy loved snow and would roll in it several times before he had a chance to ride him. It was a good thing von Heiland wasn't coming this Saturday, he thought, imagining what he'd say about a slush-caked horse.

His mother had to work the day after Thanksgiving, and Thomas had gone into town to buy a roll of chicken wire for the hutches he was building to raise Angora rabbits in. Tom slept until early afternoon. When Ben finished the chores he went eagerly to Galaxy, but the stallion limped toward him. "Oh, *great!*" Ben muttered, examining the icy hoof. "Did you have to go and throw your shoe again, boy? You just got new ones!"

He went to the house to call John Wilcox, the farrier who looked after the school horses. He had to step over Tom's legs sprawled out from the chair. There was a six-pack on the kitchen table and Ben said, "You better not let Dad see that. You know what he said."

"Yeah, I know what he said," Tom answered. Ben dialed Wilcox's number from the phone in the passageway. Tom pushed roughly past, then hovered next to him while Ben spoke to the farrier, and Ben's heart beat faster. No one else was around. He felt a rush of relief when Wilcox answered. "Look, I can fit you in early next week, but today's out," said the farrier slowly. "And, Ben — I've got to get paid for the last time, okay? Your dad said he'd send a check, but I never got it. You think it got lost in the mail or something?"

"Naw," said Ben, struggling to keep his voice even. "He prob'ly didn't send it. I'll tell him."

He hung up, stomach tense, and tried to move away from Tom into the kitchen. Tom leaned close. "So — you plannin' on telling Dad about the beer?" he asked.

"I ain't telling," Ben said. Tom gave him a long look, then sauntered into the living room. "Better not," he said over his shoulder. Ben went to his room, locked the door, and tried to study for the rest of the afternoon.

That night Betty put the cold leftover turkey on the table. "You can make sandwiches. I'm too tired to fix anything." She shoved a bag of soft bread toward her

221

husband. "Don't know why they bother to sell this stuff day-old," she said, shaking her head. "It lasts three weeks anyway. Lucky they do, though – it's half the price."

"It don't go bad 'cause it don't have a single good thing in it," snorted Thomas. "Just air and sawdust."

"Well, if you think we can afford better, you go right ahead and get it, Thomas Stahler!" Betty snapped, and Ben said quickly, his mouth full, "Dad, Galaxy threw a shoe today. So I called John Wilcox, okay?"

"Well, sure – can't ride him without a shoe, can you?"

Ben looked down at his plate. "But you gotta pay him for the last time, Dad. Else he won't come out."

Betty pushed herself back from the table. "That guy was just here!" she cried accusingly. "What do you mean, he lost a shoe? Can't you just go find it and put it back on?"

"He musta knocked it off under the snow," Ben muttered. "It could be anywhere, Mom – that field's at least two acres."

"Well, you ain't doin' much else with your time . . . go look for it!" She grabbed the plate of turkey and put it in the refrigerator.

"Aw, Mom . . . why're you always mad at me? I can't help it he lost a shoe."

She sighed. "I know you can't help it, Bennie," she said, then continued with more force. "But that horse costs a lot of money! Do you have any idea how much he costs? Food, vet bills, shoes, whatnot –"

"Betty, leave the boy be!" Thomas growled.

"No!" she cried. "I mean it, Ben! All that horse does is cost money. He don't even have a chance of earnin' any. Don't you ever *look* at the bills? You don't, do you?"

He stared at her, stricken. It was true. But he'd not even known about bills at the age of twelve when his father had given him the colt. He'd never thought about the cost. Galaxy had always been his, part of himself. He glanced at his father guiltily. Some of his mother's wages went to pay for the stallion.

Tom wiped the back of his mouth with his hand and complained, "I don't know why you don't make him pay for that horse himself, if he wants it so bad. I had to pay for that motorcycle I wanted –"

"That was different!" cried Ben.

"Yeah? How? I had to work after school for it. Anyways, you can start payin' for things now Hawley's got work for you after Christmas," retorted Tom, sly.

Ben's face burned and his mother looked at him sharply. "What do you mean, after Christmas?" she said. "Ben? Hawley say you can start working then? How come you didn't tell us? I wouldn't have made such a fuss about losin' that overtime at work –"

"I haven't decided about it yet."

"You haven't *decided!*" Betty sat down with a thump.

"You're offered work and you have to *decide?* Do you know how many people are outta work in this town?"

Thomas put both hands on the edge of the table and stood up, towering over his wife and Tom. "I don't want to hear another word," he said in a low voice. "This kid's gonna be workin' soon enough. I want him finishing school first." He swung around to Tom. "Which *you* didn't bother to do, an' see where it's got you." He glared at Betty. "The boy's trying to do something decent with his life, Bet. He's learned more from caring and working with that horse than he could ever learn at any job, an' I ain't gonna let anything get in his way. You understand?"

"You're gonna turn him into a loser just like you, Thomas Stahler, just see if you don't. The boy's chasin' dreams, just like you always done," Betty muttered, bitter.

Tom leaned toward Ben as he left the kitchen. "Too bad you can't get your way with your pretty little Lara the way you always get it with Dad, huh, Bennie boy?" he hissed. But Thomas grabbed his older son's shoulder and shoved him toward the door. "Get out," he said quietly. "I've had enough. I don't want to see your face around here."

For a moment neither man moved, as if waiting for a sign to explode. Ben reached for his father's arm. "Dad – Dad," he pleaded. "Please –" Tom twisted out of his father's grasp and slammed out the door. In a minute they heard the truck start up and speed away down the drive.

224

Ben was already asleep when the phone call came. He heard it ringing and when he saw the time on his clock — past midnight — he got out of bed and ran downstairs. All he could think of was Lara and how she'd looked when he last saw her, surrounded by her ruined work, and how she was only an hour north of Jonesburg with people she didn't want to be with. . . .

But it was not Lara. Both Thomas and his mother were already in the kitchen, his mother clutching the receiver. "What, Mom?" Ben cried. "How come you look like that? What's wrong?"

Thomas sat heavily at the table. "Tom's in jail." He looked first at Betty, then at Ben. "Well, it shouldn't surprise you. He's been headin' that way for a long time." He sighed and studied his hands. "He was drunk. He rammed a coupla parked cars leavin' the bar and just about run some guy down on the sidewalk. They took his license away. They're only holdin' him downtown overnight — won't kill him."

Ben didn't have to see the look on his mother's face to know it was his fault. The whole argument, all because of Galaxy . . . and Tom and his dad never getting along . . . and Ben only making it worse because Thomas always stuck up for him . . . and Tom hating them both because of it . . .

"Mom," he said desperately. "It might not be so bad. No, listen! They might make him go to one of those places . . . you know, those rehab places, where if you got a drinking problem you have to talk to the doctors and —"

"Oh, Bennie," she cried softly. "You're always dreaming the best of things, ain't you? But it hardly ever works out that way in the real world." Her voice broke and she was crying, and his stomach contracted with pain.

"It works sometimes," he said stubbornly. "It does. The judge made Harvey Fisk's dad go —"

"Oh, don't, Bennie," she whispered.

He stared at her. She didn't sit down but kept standing with the phone still in her hand. A persistent beeping came through the receiver and Ben took it gently from her and hung it on the hook. "Mom, I was gonna tell you about Hawley's job," he said. "I was. It was a surprise. I was going to tell you . . . for a Christmas present." He swallowed, afraid to look at his father. "I'm gonna take it, Mom. You don't need to worry about that overtime. Okay, Mom?"

All week he planned how he would tell von Heiland. He didn't even notice that Lara still had not called several days after Thanksgiving break was over. When she did, on Thursday, he hardly knew what to say. "I can't come down until Saturday," she told him. "I have to put up my exhibit." He hung up numb with resignation. But when Saturday arrived, he still had no idea how to tell the trainer he was going to quit.

In spite of Ben's preoccupation, Galaxy was in top form. He seemed to take commands directly from von

Heiland without waiting for Ben's signals. At one point the trainer threw back his head and laughed. "This horse, he does not need you!" he called. "You are just along for the ride." He gestured for Ben to come to the center of the arena.

If von Heiland berated him again, he didn't think he could stand it. He slid off Galaxy. Now was the time — he had to tell him now. He opened his mouth to speak, but the trainer interrupted him.

"Last night I spoke to Cafferty," he said bluntly. "He has a busy schedule, you understand, so it was not possible for him to give me more warning. But his pupil for tomorrow is sick, so — tomorrow he will come." The trainer made no attempt to hide his concern. "So, Benjamin. What will I tell him? Will it be a waste of Cafferty's time?"

If Galaxy had not suddenly reared up on his hind legs and wheeled away, Ben would have told von Heiland the truth. I have to quit, he would have said. I have to start working at the garage in a month. I promised my mother. Tell Cafferty there's no point.

But Galaxy had begun to race at full gallop around the perimeter of the arena, with each turn spiraling closer and closer to the center. Von Heiland watched in astonishment. Around and around the stallion flew, weaving a powerful web of energy that held Ben transfixed. He was mesmerized, caught in the rhythm of pounding hooves until it seemed to be his own heartbeat throbbing in his head. And then Galaxy spun sharply around, slowed to a trot, and came to press his muzzle against Ben's chest.

And in that moment, Ben knew he could keep no promise that did not include this horse, this creature who gave his own life meaning. He laid his face against the broad forehead of the stallion. On that long-ago night when the horse was born, some ethereal elements had drifted down from the flashing sky and mixed with the air they both breathed, so the stallion and he were irrevocably bound together. Once again, Ben surrendered to a force greater than his will. "It won't be a waste of his time," Ben answered quietly. "Tell Mr. Cafferty to come."

He didn't trust himself to face anyone after his lesson, so he climbed the ladder into the dark barn loft and curled in the hay. He was half asleep when Lara's head appeared in the opening. She threw a snowball at him. "Cut it out," he grunted. She stumbled through the hay and fell to her knees beside him, laughing. "What're you in such a bad mood for? I thought you'd be glad to see me."

"I am glad to see you."

"Well, why don't you show it then?" she teased, tickling his face with a hay stalk. He lay still, startled to realize he'd lied. He wasn't at all sure he wanted to see Lara. "What's the matter?" she demanded. "You look like someone died."

"Well, Tom's in jail," he answered. "I suppose you'll miss him."

228

"Why'd you say that?" she retorted.

"I didn't mean anything," he muttered. "It's just . . . it's just that everything's a mess. I promised my mom something, and now I've told von Heiland something else, and I can't even make up my own mind." He told her about Dave Hawley's offer and about his mother, but when he told her Cafferty was coming so unexpectedly the next day, her face appeared to lose all color and her eyes got huge. "What is it?" Ben asked, worried. "You don't like Cafferty, do you? Every time I mention him —"

"I don't care about Cafferty!"

"Then what?"

"Nothing!" Then, relenting, she said, "He sometimes sponsors young riders . . . that's why von Heiland wants him to meet you. He wouldn't have asked him here if he didn't think there was a chance. Cafferty only works with the best."

He refused to be sidetracked. "I still don't know why he bothers you so much." But she paid no attention to his words. She bent close over him and when she kissed him, he could no longer resist her. He closed his eyes because the joy was so sharp it hurt. Her lips ran lightly over his eyelids, she breathed into his ear, found his mouth again.

The hay was a sweet darkness, holding them together in rustling warmth. She lay so close to him he could not tell where she began and he left off. Lara filled him with such sweetness, the bitter taste of doubt

229

dissolved, and he pulled her to him urgently, whispering her name, pushing his hands under her clothing. Then without warning she jerked back and scrambled away from him.

The shock of hurt was so intense, he could not catch his breath. She was slapping the hay from her clothing, breathing hard, and after a moment she demanded furiously, "Is this the only reason you want to know me? You always do this! It always ends up like this! Why do you always have to do this?"

He got up on his knees to face her. "You do it with Tom," he said. He did not recognize his own voice. The words seemed to come from a stranger.

He did not pull away under her attack. It was almost a relief to him, to have her pound her fists against him. "That's a *lie!*" she screamed. "You . . . you . . . that's a lie!"

"No it isn't," he said. "Tom told me everything."

"What did that filthy pig tell you!"

He told her, just as Tom had told him, and she fell back in the hay. She made no noise, but he knew she was crying. He could not bear hating her, but he did. Ever since the fight with Tom, he'd struggled against his doubt, against losing his love for her. Now, knowing it was gone, he felt like his heart had been torn from his body.

"It's a lie," she repeated in a dull voice. "He was lying. I never did anything like that. Ever. With anybody. I just made it up. I made it all up."

230

"I'm sick of your games," he said. He rubbed his arm over his mouth and examined the blood on his sleeve. "You broke my tooth."

She was rocking back and forth looking utterly alone, lost in a universe far away from him, but he no longer cared that he couldn't reach her. She leaned toward him and inspected his mouth. "It's not broken," she said. "There's only a little cut." She paused. "I've done a lot worse. Cafferty will tell you tomorrow."

They sat silently for a long time, oblivious to the cold and dark. Finally Ben challenged sullenly, "So why don't you tell me? If it's such a big deal."

She shrugged. "Cafferty's a blabbermouth – he'll tell you. You can ask him if he doesn't."

"I don't care."

She smiled faintly, and the low twilight found its way to her eyes. "I want you to ask," she said softly. "Then you'll know who I really am."

Despite himself, he recognized the courage in her words. He understood, with sudden insight, why she could not tell him herself. Saying the words aloud would make whatever it was real – not just for him, but for her. "It's about Timothy, isn't it?" he whispered.

Lara's form was indistinct in the evening darkness, but her voice was so clear it seemed to have its own shape. "I almost killed Timothy," she said. "That's why my parents don't want me at home." She climbed over the bales to the ladder. "It makes me crazy that you love me so much," she told him. "I can't stand it, Ben. I can't let you. You think I'm someone I'm not. You don't know who I am."

He could not answer or move. Before she disappeared down the ladder, she added again, "Tom did lie to you, Ben." In that instant, as he saw her recognize the disbelief in his eyes, he panicked. He was wrong! He struggled to speak. He *did* love her. He did. Tom had lied – of course. Tom always lied. Now he believed her with a terrible certainty, but even as he got to his feet, Lara was gone. He sank down again in the hay and stayed there until the cold stole all feeling from him. He heard his father's car pull into the yard, a door slam, and silence. All at once he wanted his father's comfort more than anything in the world.

But when he went into the house, Thomas did not look up from the kitchen table. His mother was staring out the window over the sink. "What?" whispered Ben. "Is it Tom?"

Thomas roused himself and shook his head. "Naw, don't worry, kiddo. It ain't nothin' like that. They just laid off a coupla us part-timers down at the factory, is all. Happens all the time. I knew they might when I took the job. . . . It's just, I thought they'd maybe give us some warning . . ."

He went slowly up to his room. From the book Tom had given him he took out the business card and went to the extension phone in his parents' bedroom. It seemed to ring for a very long time before anyone answered.

"McGrath Compton Corporation," said a woman. He asked for William McGrath. "It's a little late," said the woman. "Let me check if he's still in. Whom may I say is calling, please?"

He was there. "Mr. McGrath," said Ben. "You said I should call you if I ever wanted to sell my horse —"

It didn't take very long and it wasn't complicated. McGrath named a price and Ben agreed. It was twice as much as Thomas could earn at the canning factory in a year. "Don't you want to think over my offer?" asked McGrath, after a pause.

"No," said Ben. McGrath said he would like to bring Timothy to the farm soon to see the horse — he would make the final decision after conferring with Cafferty. "Okay," said Ben, and hung up. He looked up Dave Hawley's number and dialed again. When he had finished speaking he went back to his room, and without turning on the light got into bed with his clothes on and fell asleep.

Chapter Seventeen

Lara walked for several hours along the unlit road. Whenever she tried to pin down her thoughts they scuttled away, so she kept walking until she was numb from cold and she had forgotten what had driven her out into the night. She did not stop walking or look around when a car slowed, stopped, and backed up toward her. But when the passenger door was pushed open, Lara got in without looking to see who was driving. It did not matter to her what happened, or even that Miss Mik turned the car sharply around and headed back the way she had come. "I'm not covering for you this time," said Miss Mik grimly. "Do you have any idea how long you've been gone? I was about to call the police!"

Lara watched the headlights sweeping the darkness ahead of them, as if to keep it at bay. Miss Mik set her jaw. "Your parents called earlier — before I knew you were gone," she said. "I told them you were still at the farm. They're coming to Huntingdon tomorrow with your brother to see your exhibit, and your dad said something about Ben's horse — do you know anything about this?"

The headlights seemed such a puny defense against the night. There was a long silence, broken only by the sound of the car. "You call your parents back when you get in, and then go to your room," Miss Mik said finally. "We'll deal with this in the morning. I'm afraid I'm on the dean's side this time."

Lara watched the passing road and thought: I walked there. My feet touched there, and there, and there. The white line streamed at her out of the darkness and the words formed into a mesmeric chant

234

within her. She felt herself dissolving into nothing and welcomed it.

It was after eleven when they got to the dorm. The girls doing late homework in the lounge glanced up when Lara came in but said nothing. Only Emily, already in bed reading, spoke to her. As Lara unlaced her wet sneakers, she said in a smug voice, "Dean Parker's going to kick you out for sure this time." Lara opened her closet without responding and Emily closed her book with a loud snap. "Serves you right, anyway, for putting up those stupid pictures. You think that was funny?"

"Someone apparently did," said Lara without turning around.

"You don't know who did it," said Emily. "You can't prove anything."

"I don't need to," Lara replied, emerging from the closet. She looked pointedly at Emily's fingernails, painted vermilion.

"Half the girls at Huntingdon wear red nail polish, and you know it," Emily muttered, shoving her hands out of sight beneath her blankets. Lara put her sneakers on the radiator to dry. Emily watched her for a moment, then added, "I bet you were making out with that kid, Ben. You'll have to tell the discipline committee about it, you know."

Lara came swiftly to lean over Emily, saying calmly, "If you say one more word, Emily, I will wait until you're asleep and I'll hack off all your hair with a knife. You won't even know it till you wake up. And you know I will." Emily's mouth stayed open in midsentence, but when Lara smiled, she scrambled off the bed and fled into the hall.

Now all the thoughts that had evaded her before came crashing into her with devastating force. Tomorrow, Cafferty was coming. Tomorrow, Ben would learn everything that had happened last summer. She wrapped her arms around her stomach, remembering the look in Ben's eyes as he'd told her what his brother had said. How Tom must hate Ben! Like she hated Timothy. . . .

"No. I don't. I don't," she whimpered, curling into a tight knot. "I don't hate you. I don't. I never wanted to hurt you. I was only trying to . . . I was trying to keep you . . ." She was so tense she could not cry, but the pressure against her throat made her cough until she retched. Why were they all coming tomorrow? Why was Timothy coming too? She strained the pillow to her mouth.

She hadn't thought he could travel yet. For six months she hadn't been told anything. She only knew where he was, and that her parents were with him. From their continued silence she knew he was alive. That was all. She never asked. Now everything was jammed up inside her head and she couldn't sort it out to think. Tomorrow she would have to face Ben after Cafferty told him the whole story. Tomorrow she would have to face Timothy, too, for the first time since the accident. And the dean wouldn't care that her parents were visiting – he'd hold the discipline committee anyway. Her parents could watch this time while she got expelled. They wouldn't want her at home any more than they had before, but where would they send her this time?

There was nowhere left for her to go. All her disjointed thoughts led around to that. Unless . . . unless she could figure out how to get to Mexico City, find her real mother, live with her in a cardboard shanty. No one would ever be able to find her in those slums. She would look like everyone else. She just had to get to a place where she could hitchhike, like the interstate truck plaza outside Scranton. Yes, it was possible. There was no ocean to cross between Pennsylvania and Mexico. Just roads. She could hitch there.

She fell asleep. When she woke and sat up stiffly, the dorm was quiet. Emily's bed was empty. The digital clock read 2:30. She was still wearing the clothes from the evening before, and a bit of hay scratched inside her sweater. Her first thought was of Ben. He would help her. He could drive her to Scranton in the truck – he'd do it, if she asked. But as her mind cleared she remembered that he hated her. He was the reason she had to leave.

She shivered, wrapping her arms around herself and rocking on the bed. Her parents must not have called again or Miss Mik would have come to get her. She would have patted her gently awake, brought her down to the apartment to take the call, maybe made tea, and Lara could have told her everything.

But again she remembered: Miss Mik had said, "I won't cover for you this time." She stared at the clock, watching it flick from one number to the next. Maybe it wasn't too late to tell Miss Mik everything. To ask her for help. She was the dorm parent – she had to listen. Lara pulled on her still-wet sneakers, took her jacket, and went down the stairs to Miss Mik's apartment. In the silence her knock seemed to reverberate through the whole building and she held her breath before knocking again. The door clicked open under her touch.

Then Lara saw the note tacked to the door frame. "I'm at Hopkins Dorm if you need me – Call ext. 458. Miss Mik." She hesitated, but the apartment lay open and she went in. "Miss Mik?" she called softly. "Miss Mik?"

A rising moon's light streamed in the windows over the paintings. The canvas of Galaxy and Ben was still propped on the easel and she walked toward it. In the moonlight the brilliant colors were washed to cool paleness, and the painting seemed like a window through which Lara could see Ben and the stallion, unreachable, poised forever at the zenith of the perfect leap under an infinite sky.

She ran her fingers over the canvas, caressing the figure of Ben. But it was only canvas. He was gone from

238

her forever and she would never be able to touch him again. She jerked her hand away in unexpected fury. She didn't need Ben. She didn't need anyone. She never had. She'd always wanted to be alone.

She yanked on her jacket, her fingers grazing something in one of the pockets. Ben's knife. She flicked it open. There was still a fleck of red nail polish on the blade. She slashed at the painting on the easel until it hung in shreds from the frame. Then she closed the knife, turned, and noticed Miss Mik's wallet on a table. Inside was ninety dollars, which she folded with deliberate care and put in her pocket with the knife. Then she went out into the frigid December night.

The moon cast shadows in front of her across the road. Over the bare branches an unearthly light spilled, turning every twig into silver filigree. When she reached the farm she kept to the shadow of the barn as she surveyed the yard.

She knew the Stahlers never locked their cars or took the keys. Carefully, she opened the door of the pickup and found the keys hanging in the ignition. Light still shone through a first-floor window of the house, but the upstairs windows were dark. She stared up at them, imagining Ben asleep in his bed, wondering if the house was unlocked too . . . but then she turned away sharply and pushed the clutter of empty beer cans and fast-food bags off the truck seat. Wrapped in a smelly coat she found a bottle. Whiskey, almost full. The first two swallows were like hot knives slicing down her throat into her empty stomach, but she stopped shivering immediately.

"Well, hey, pretty girl," exclaimed a low voice just behind her. She gasped and jumped back, but Tom grabbed her. "Ain't this a surprise," he grinned, his eyes glittering. "I come out here for a little nightcap, but I sure got more'n I bargained for. What's up, pretty? You miss me while I was doin' time?" He held on to her arm tightly. When she jerked away he pinned her against the truck.

Lara glanced involuntarily again at the upper-floor windows, and Tom snorted. "Don't bother. Bennie wouldn't hear a friggin' bomb go off. He sleeps like a baby."

"I don't care," she shrugged, trying to force a teasing note into her voice. "What're you doing out here anyway?"

He propped himself unsteadily against the truck, holding her as much to keep himself from falling as to prevent her from leaving. "The old man has a fit if I keep any booze in the house, so I keep it out here where it's nice an' chilled." He sniffed her and grinned. "I see you've helped yourself to a nightcap too, Miss Pretty. Now how come you didn't just tell me you wanted to party, huh? But this ain't a good place — too cold."

He half dragged her to the shed behind the barn, kicking the door open and shoving her ahead into the pitch darkness. She slammed hard against a wall and for a moment the wind was knocked out of her. Then,

240

in a flash of clarity, she realized she was still clutching the whiskey bottle. Tom stumbled toward her, trapping her against the wall.

Suddenly there was a heavy thud, and in a violent flurry of movement a huge form rushed past them from the darkness. Tom was knocked to his knees and Lara was thrown free of his grip. "Shit, I forgot Bennie's damn horse was in here!" Tom giggled, scrabbling around on his knees. "Stupid thing almost killed me. . . . Hey, pretty, where are you? C'mon down here."

He lurched at her, grabbed her leg, tried to pull her down. Lara swung the whiskey bottle with all her strength at his head. Tom collapsed into the hay without a sound. Frantically she raised the bottle again and bashed it down, but she was shaking so hard the bottle glanced off his shoulder and flew out of her hand. She stood gasping for breath.

The moon hung over the ridge of the Buckhorns and lit the yard outside the open shed door. Motionless in the silvery light stood Galaxy, watching her. The horse did not move, but the moonlight seemed to dance all around him. Gradually her heart stopped pounding and she could think again.

Up in his room, Ben was as far away as the moon. In the darkness behind her lay Tom. She had killed him. No one could help her now. There was nothing else to do but to leave. She put the truck in neutral and let it roll down the drive. When it stopped she turned the key and held her breath. The gas gauge read below empty. But the engine caught. Cautiously, checking the house in the rearview mirror, she turned out onto the road.

Halfway to Jonesburg she realized it was early Sunday morning and no gas stations would be open. Almost crying in panic, she swung the truck around. She had to get away. She had to. She would try for Scranton, forty miles north. Lightheaded from the whiskey, she could not control the images swarming through her mind – the slashed canvas, the crumpled body of Tom – and she clutched the steering wheel.

The moon followed her. Below the ridge of the Buckhorns the forest was an impenetrable darkness, but the snow-covered fields sloping up from the farm glowed with light. Then a black form burst from the shadows and raced up the white hillside as if to join with the moon. *Galaxy.* Lara braked so suddenly the truck skidded on the icy road. She watched until the stallion disappeared again into the shadows. Opposite where she had stopped she saw a track leading into the woods and recognized it as the way to the creek hole. Ben had told her the track continued up to meet the power-line cutting . . . and off the cutting, she remembered, was the smaller trail leading to Ben's clearing.

She imagined the clearing, silent under the eternal moonlight. It seemed to Lara suddenly that Galaxy had showed her the way to go. She shifted the truck into low gear and turned onto the snowy forest track.

Ben jumped awake just before dawn at the blare of the telephone. Foggy with sleep, he stumbled down the stairs and yanked the receiver off the hook. Thomas came into the kitchen and flicked on the light as Ben tried to make sense of Miss Mik's frantic questions. "Ben, is that you? Ben, is Lara with you?"

"Lara?" he asked groggily.

"Lara's missing, Ben. . . . I think she's been gone most of the night." Miss Mik rushed through the explanation. "She's taken some money, and destroyed . . . some property, and . . . I think she was very upset about something last evening. Ben . . . Ben?"

"She isn't here." His mouth felt thick and he could hardly form his words clearly. "We had a fight," he mumbled, glancing at his father.

"She was asleep in her room when I went to check her in," Miss Mik said. "I was out talking to another dorm parent after lights-out, but I never thought . . . I just went to bed when I got back, so I didn't notice anything until I got up to put the heat on ten minutes ago —"

He had a sick feeling when he hung up the phone. His mother came down and wrapped a robe around him, but he could not stop shivering. "What's wrong, Ben?" Betty asked, looking questioningly at Thomas.

Ben couldn't answer. From the window he could see Tom's truck was gone. He turned to Thomas and saw

243

apprehension on his father's tired face. "Dad!" Ben whispered. "Dad! What should I do? Lara's missing! Tom could . . . Tom could hurt her, couldn't he, Dad? Would Tom do something to her?"

Betty clutched her husband's arm, but Thomas only slumped down in a chair. For a moment they all stared at each other, and then Ben flung himself at his father. "Dad! Get up! We have to do something!" he cried, shaking him.

"You better call that teacher back, Ben," sighed his father. He got up heavily to go to the door. Betty sat crying at the table. Thomas peered into the predawn darkness, then asked softly, "Ben, what's Galaxy doing loose?"

They found Tom in Galaxy's stall, huddled in the hay in a drunken stupor, clutching an empty whiskey bottle and bleeding from a gash on the head. As the first gray light showed over the mountains, bringing with it sluggish flakes of snow, the yard filled with state troopers, Jonesburg police, and Huntingdon School officials. The kitchen grew steamy from the people crammed inside, and Ben was wedged uncomfortably between the table and the door, answering the same questions over and over. What happened last evening? We had a fight. What kind of fight? Just a fight — you know. Did she say anything about leaving? She always talked about getting kicked out. . . . What was her relationship to your brother? I don't know. You don't know? I don't know.

244

One of the state troopers looked down at Tom on the living room couch and said with barely concealed disgust, "See if you can't sober him up. He wasn't hit too hard — he musta drunk that whole bottle. Hey, didn't you just book this guy on a DWI, Joe?" he asked a Jonesburg policeman. He turned to Betty. "Look, just pour coffee down him or something. We're gonna have to bring him in for questioning, but we may as well see what he can tell us about the girl now." His mother could not seem to move, so Ben put the kettle on to boil.

"There was hardly any gas in that truck," Thomas was telling a trooper. "She couldn't get too far —"

"How much gas?" barked the trooper. "How far could she get? How was the truck on mileage?"

Thomas glanced at Ben helplessly. "I siphoned out all I could," he said. "So's Tom wouldn't be tempted to drive without his license." He sighed. "I don't know . . . I really don't know."

"Could she have got as far as Scranton?"

"I don't see how —"

The troopers went out to their cars while the headmaster, Miss Mik, and the Huntingdon dean, Larry Parker, spoke together in low tones. Ben wandered around the yard, hardly aware of what he was doing. If Tom had done anything to her . . . if anything happened to her . . . he would die.

The radio in the state trooper's car crackled and one of the men answered it as the others leaned against the car talking. The snow was falling in thick flurries and already the Buckhorns had lost their definition against the white sky. Where was Lara? Ben considered every possibility. Why hadn't they found the truck by now? But she was too smart for that, he thought. She'd ditch the truck where they wouldn't find it, hitch a ride . . . but where? Where on earth did she have to go?

Galaxy lifted his head and trumpeted a high, wild call. Ben looked up. Again the stallion screamed, and again, until the troopers looked over at Ben in puzzlement. "What's got into him, son?" one of them called, chuckling. "Too bad he can't talk, huh?"

Galaxy trotted back and forth in agitation along the fence. Ben walked slowly toward him, thoughtful; the stallion threw his head up and down, the snow swirling from his mane like a storm. Ben opened the gate and the stallion leapt out, skittering around him in a tight circle. "Where is she?" he whispered. "Where is Lara, Galaxy?"

The horse faced him, motionless, so taut he quivered, and the snowflakes trembled off his black coat. *"Where is she?"* Ben whispered again, urgent. "Show me where she is." He closed his eyes and lay his hand on the stallion's neck. *Show me. Show me.* He willed his breathing to slow and deepen, drew the cold air down through his lungs, into his heart, down his arm, and through his fingers into the body of the horse. Together they breathed, together their vision synchronized into the pure sight of dreams. . . .

246

And Ben saw an open place vaulted over by an infinite sky, a clearing of silence surrounded by forest. In silence the snow drifted down. In silence the hemlocks held the open place in dark embrace. In silence a girl stood alone, her face turned to the snow-heavy sky. Slowly, almost imperceptibly, she sank to the earth.

"I know where she is!" Ben cried, racing across the yard with the stallion trotting behind. "I know where she is!" he cried, bursting into the kitchen. They listened to him with dubious expressions.

"What makes you think she'd go up there, son?" a trooper asked when Ben finished speaking. "There's an awful lot of woods up there on the Buckhorn — we could waste days searching, if she isn't there. Seems hardly the place a girl would go . . ."

"But I *know* she's there!" he insisted. "I *know*."

"Geez, son — you told us before you didn't have any idea." The trooper frowned, exasperated. "If you know, how come you didn't tell us before?"

"I only just thought of it," he stammered, looking at Thomas for support. How could he explain about Galaxy? He pulled at the trooper's sleeve. "Let me go up there then — I go all the time. I know the place. Let me go look for her!"

"Better wait till we get a search team together, son."

"But that could take hours!" he protested. "Besides, they couldn't find this place. No one knows where it is but me. I can go on Galaxy right *now*."

Miss Mik looked at Ben and said something he couldn't hear to the troopers. They conferred quietly. "When'd you say the parents should arrive?" they asked Dean Parker.

"We notified them immediately," replied the dean. "They should be here within an hour and a half if the snow doesn't get worse."

The troopers again spoke together, pausing when Miss Mik said something and listening to her seriously. Finally a trooper turned to Ben. "Okay, young man," he said. "You go ahead and give it a try. Take this radio — here, just press this button when you want to speak — and you call us every fifteen minutes, you got that? If you find anything, give us a shout. And take some flares. . . . Get him some, will you, Brad? We'll get the helicopter to stand by from the hospital in Scranton, but we might have to send a team in on foot if the snow's too bad —"

The trail was slippery and overhung with hemlocks sagging under the weight of the snow. But Galaxy trotted with confidence, jumped the creek, and headed up the steep incline beyond. In half an hour they reached the power-line cutting. There, plowed into a thicket of young pines, was the truck. Ben fumbled with cold fingers to get the radio off his belt and pressed the button. After he spoke, he reclipped the radio and continued up the mountain through the deepening snow.

• • •

Her entire lifetime seemed compressed into the hours Lara huddled in the truck waiting for dawn. Only the white expanse of the power-line cutting was dimly visible; all around her was darkness. Finally she realized she could find her way by following the power-line poles. Her thoughts moved even more sluggishly than her legs, but she got out of the truck and began to walk. She stopped frequently to peer into the forest, terrified she would miss the break in the trees that marked the trail to Ben's clearing. She struggled on, slipping often, her heart pounding. By the time she paused again to gasp for breath, the sky above the mountain had begun to pale.

It was a dawn without sun, without warmth, without definition. By the time she found the smaller trail, the snow was falling so thickly she could not see more than a few feet in front of her. She no longer noticed anything, not the snow or the cold or her own body. Nothing else existed but the urgency to reach the clearing. She no longer knew why. She could only plod dully on, stumbling over hidden roots and into drifts, but somehow keeping to the trail.

When she pushed through the hemlocks and looked at last across the clearing, a flat dismal grayness met her eyes. The mystical image of the shimmering snow bathed in moonlight was vanquished by the featureless

249

expanse she now saw. She stood stunned, the snow matting heavily in her hair. Slowly she scuffed through weeds fast disappearing under drifts, following the paths Ben and Galaxy had made. Her wet jeans were stiffening and her sneakered feet were so numb she had difficulty keeping her balance on the uneven ground. She knew she had to keep moving, but exhaustion was suffocating her. Why had she come here? What was this place? She struggled to gather her thoughts. On the road with the moon hanging like an unreachable beacon over the mountains, the stallion had been her wild, magical guide and the clearing had been a promise — the only place on earth she felt she could go.

Because Ben had given it to her. She trembled, wrapping her arms around herself, and stumbled on. Today they would find a dead man, and a slashed painting, and money missing and a truck stolen. . . . Today Ben would know she was not only crazy, but dangerous. It would not even matter now that Ben would also meet Cafferty and find out what had happened last summer. She continued to drag herself around and around the clearing, her legs moving automatically.

Something tripped her and she fell hard on her knees. Half concealed beneath the snow was the skeleton of the deer. Snow had softened the lines of the skull and rib bones. As Lara touched a smooth, arched rib, her brown fingers against the whiteness seemed strangely beautiful to her, as if they were not her own. The deer seemed so peaceful, her remains nestled so deeply into the earth she was now a contour of the land itself. Moment by moment, season by season, the earth was receiving her back. The deer lay folded between ground and sky like a child held sleeping by its parents.

In a motion more natural than walking, Lara sank down beside the skeleton, lying close with her arm over its rib cage. The snow drifted over her until she felt drowsily warm. In this place, she was safe. Like the deer, she fit perfectly into the earth.

But as she settled deeper into the snow, something poked uncomfortably into her hip and she dug in the pocket of her jacket. Ben's knife. For a long time she held it, then opened the blade and lay it flat across her wrist. She gazed at it. In the swirling snow, earth and forest and sky had lost all division from each other. She alone was separate. She drew the blade across her wrist, feeling nothing, and lifted her arm slightly so the red blood dripped over the deer's white bones and into the white snow. It was beautiful. She smiled and closed her eyes.

For what felt like hours Ben cradled Lara in his arms, his coat wrapped around her, his own legs and arms long numbed. Every few minutes he bent close to feel for her breath against his face. Sometimes he was not sure he could feel it, and then he massaged her arms and legs frantically. Straining all his senses, he scanned the sky for the helicopter. Twenty minutes, they'd assured him — keep her warm, keep pressure on her wrist, and they'd be there in twenty minutes. He clutched the flares, ready to light them at the first distant *thump-thump* of the chopper.

Galaxy stood close by, mist rising from his warm body, and Ben wished there was a way he could wrap the stallion's heat around Lara. Galaxy turned his head. Gracefully, his dark eyes watching Ben, he sank to his haunches in the snow and folded his forelegs beneath him. For a moment Ben was too stunned to move. Then, tugging at the unconscious girl, he sandwiched her between himself and the horse. Sharp pains shot down his half-asleep legs and his arms burned with the strain, but he held Lara tightly against the warm body. The snow drifted down and covered them all.

When the helicopter landed with a roar of wind and flashing lights, it felt to Ben as if a universe had been shattered. He was strangely unwilling to surrender Lara to the paramedics. They held him back gently, wrapping him in a silver blanket, and he tried to sort through the barrage of questions. "I'm okay," he kept repeating. "Yes, I can make it back. I won't go without Galaxy. No, I'm not cold. No, I don't need anyone to come with me."

And then, suddenly, he and Galaxy were all alone in the silent clearing. The horse tossed his head impatiently, shuddering snow from his coat, pawing the ground. Ben found that his legs were too cramped and stiff for him to get on Galaxy. He finally had to walk, slipping and stumbling, down the steep trail. Galaxy followed closely, and each time Ben faltered, the stallion nudged him roughly. The radio the troopers had given him hung forgotten, and he hardly registered where he was when he got to the intersection of the two trails.

Twenty feet beyond the abandoned truck, a man was walking toward them. Ben could not even lift his head to greet von Heiland. The trainer made Ben drink steaming hot chocolate from a thermos, and then hauled his dead weight onto Galaxy's back. "This is better?" von Heiland asked, keeping his arm around Ben so he wouldn't fall off. "You can hold on?"

"Yes," said Ben as the warmth of the chocolate and the stallion's body began to revive him. "How come . . . you're here?"

"I came this morning like we planned, remember?" replied von Heiland, smiling. "I was all night in this awful motel in Jonesburg . . . never again! I wake up and think: Cafferty will be coming later, so I will go make sure Benjamin is ready. . . ." The trainer strode steadily along the track at Galaxy's head, his calm voice warming Ben even more than the chocolate. "So of course, what do I find when I get to the farm but all this mess, and then Cafferty comes, and we all sit around in your parents' house and wait to hear what is happening. And then Cafferty tells me an unhappy story."

Von Heiland paused, opened the thermos, and handed another cup of chocolate to Ben. When he had finished, the trainer shoved the thermos into the pocket of his big coat and began to walk again. "I think before you return, you must hear this story. It will help when you are thinking of your friend. Now, I know you have decided to sell Galaxy —" He held up his hand when Ben started to speak. "Yes, yes, I know all the reasons — your father has told me about losing his job. I understand. But still, I will tell you this story. My friend Cafferty, you understand, has been working with McGrath's horses and with the boy Timothy for many years. He knows the family well. Last summer the boy — he had a terrible accident, so he will never ride again. He had Olympic potential. It is no small thing, to say he will never ride again." He paused to shake snow from his hat.

"Cafferty tells me this boy and his sister were at their parents' estate in Connecticut last summer, but one night the parents were not there — why, I do not know. So this is a good time for a party, yes? There are young people in and out, having a good time, but the girl does not know all of them. Some are . . . how do you say it? Crashing the party? And of course, they are all drinking and being stupid. Everyone is drinking, even Timothy, and after a while the girl tries to make everybody go away. . . . Except she cannot. No one is listening to her. One boy is bragging about his father's racehorses, telling everyone they are the fastest horses in the world . . . you know how it is with boys, such ridiculous nonsense. So Timothy says *his* horse is faster. His horse can beat any racehorse."

Ben was completely alert now, his eyes riveted to the back of von Heiland's head as the trainer led Galaxy down the track. Von Heiland was going to tell him what Lara was so afraid he would find out – and suddenly, *he* was afraid too. He thought of her small, still body on the stretcher as the paramedics lifted her into the chopper. In his exhaustion, Ben could not fight off the tears, but von Heiland gave no indication of noticing.

"This is what is so stupid about drinking, yes?" continued the trainer, shaking his head. "People say stupid things and get into fights about such nonsense. So – Timothy tells the other boy that Conquistador can beat any racehorse alive, and the boy of course dares him to prove it. So Timothy gets his horse from the barn, and everyone else piles into a car – it is night, you understand – and Timothy says he will race the car to prove how fast his horse can run.

"Now, your friend – Lara. She is trying all this time to make everybody go away, but she is also very drunk, so they just laugh at her. Then she tries to make her brother get off the horse, and of course he will not. So they have a big argument and are yelling at each other. Then Lara stomps off and gets in the car with the others, except she makes them let her drive. The brother is galloping the horse faster and faster, and the car is going very fast. . . . Very stupid, you agree? Horses cannot run on hard roads –"

Suddenly von Heiland interrupted himself and said,

"You love this girl, so this is difficult for you. Do you want me to go on?"

"Yes," whispered Ben.

Von Heiland said nothing for a moment, standing on the trail, then shrugged. "Well, this is all Cafferty can tell me, you understand — only what Timothy remembers. Just that he is galloping, galloping, and all the young people are hanging out the car windows yelling at him and thumping the sides to make the horse go faster. . . . Six, maybe seven kids. And who knows what happens next? Maybe the horse shies or slips on the road, or maybe the car swerves up on the bank — it is impossible to know. The car hits the horse, the boy falls off under the car, the car flips over — so. The horse must be put down, the boy is in the hospital for many months, everything broken. No one else is hurt — this is a miracle. This is what Cafferty told me."

The track was so narrow the snow-laden trees closed around them like a tunnel, the silence denser than the shadows. Von Heiland stopped and looked at Ben. "She is very troubled, your friend. She is angry in her heart with the world — with her brother?"

Ben nodded, unable to speak.

"So — she imagines this was not an accident," mused von Heiland. "Yes. I see now. There was the argument, and she thinks maybe she hurt her brother on purpose."

"But she drove the car!" cried Ben, doubt tearing at him. He leaned in anguish against Galaxy's neck.

"Why didn't she go call for help or something? Instead of driving the car when she was drunk?"

"Is this so difficult to understand?" asked von Heiland, coming to stand close to Ben. "She is afraid for her brother. But she is so drunk she cannot think straight. So she says to herself: *I* will drive the car. Then I can make sure nothing bad happens to my brother. But all those kids in the car, yelling and jumping around — perhaps they knock her arm as she is driving, perhaps she is just too drunk . . . who knows? The car goes too fast, it swerves, and poof! She loses control."

Ben closed his eyes. Timothy was like him — the favored one. And Lara . . . Lara was like Tom, forever on the outside. He clenched his fists against the stallion's neck. How could Lara ever know, *for sure,* that she had not hurt her brother on purpose?

He didn't care that von Heiland could see him crying. "I can't . . . I can't . . ." he gasped. Von Heiland reached up and put his hand on Ben's arm. "You can't what?" he asked.

"I can't *help* her! I can't *do* anything!"

"No," agreed von Heiland gently. "You cannot do anything about another's pain, this is true. It belongs to them and not to you. But you can love."

"But that's just pain, too!"

"Yes," von Heiland nodded. They had reached the road.

Chapter Eighteen

It snowed every weekend that winter. By late February, new snow was falling onto twenty inches of packed snow that had lain unmelted since the weekend in early December that Ben marked as the end of his old life. He could almost anticipate each weekend's arrival by the lowering of the sky outside the classroom windows on Friday afternoons, just as time began to crawl toward the end of the day. The truck was reliable in the snow, so it wasn't worry that stole Ben's attention away from his schoolwork as each Friday advanced. It was rather that, by the end of the week, he began to shift from the world of the farm and Jonesburg to a world he would drive five hours northeast to find. By three o'clock on Friday afternoons since the beginning of the year, the reality of Clayton County Vo-Tech disappeared, replaced by the sprawling barns and neat white fences of Haybrook Farm Equestrian Center outside the small Connecticut village of East Haybrook.

Rob Cafferty greeted Ben's arrival late each Friday evening with a huge meal and lively stories of the week's events. Ben's tiredness always dissolved as soon as he walked in the door and heard Cafferty's booming voice. "For the love of God, Benji, is it you again? D'you mean to tell me it's Friday already?" And after the food and the loud, good-natured bantering it had taken Ben weeks to get used to, the trainer would shoo away his four children and say, "So — is there anything else you're wanting to do before you go to bed?" Ben, shyly at first but, as the weeks progressed, with a laugh matching Cafferty's, would reply, "I'll just have a look around the barn, Mr. C., if it's okay with you."

Ben was not the only one to wait for the end of the week. On this late February evening, as he crunched across the frozen ground to the barn, he listened as he always did, smiling in anticipation. . . . And as always, he heard it: an eager whinny, hooves thumping against a wooden box stall, another high squeal. "Galaxy!" he called, breaking into a run. "Galaxy!"

Cafferty joined him in the warm, spacious stall a few minutes later, slapping the stallion on the rump with affection. "He's still fighting that saddle, the great worthless creature. But he's no match for our Tim – that boy'll make as good a trainer as he would've been a rider." He gave Ben a wink. "Now tomorrow, I'm sure you'll be happy to know, that meddling spy von Heiland's coming."

"Herr von Heiland?" cried Ben in delight. "I haven't seen him for a month!" He nuzzled Galaxy and grinned. "How come you call him a spy, Mr. C.?"

"Weren't you knowing that man's a spy and a thief, Benji? He's forever spying on my riders so he can steal the best of them for himself."

"But you stole me from him," Ben laughed.

"I'm sure it's only temporary. You'll get tired of being my barn manager after a while," grunted Cafferty in mock despair. "And then he'll scheme out a way to steal

259

you back. . . . Now, there's another thing, Benji —" The trainer paused and gave Ben a rare sober look. "I had a call from McGrath — he's coming here Sunday morning. Said he hoped he'd find you here."

Lying awake in Cafferty's spare bedroom that night, Ben told himself it would be no different from the other two meetings he'd had with McGrath, when they drew up the agreement terms concerning Galaxy. But now that the terms were set, why did McGrath want to see him? He rolled on his stomach and pushed his face into the pillow. He'd determined long ago that he wouldn't think about her. He wouldn't wait, he wouldn't hope — nothing.

But despite his resolve, Lara stole every reflective moment from him. Ben managed his week at school, but on the long drives each weekend thoughts of her crept out in an ambush he welcomed even as he fought against them. He could stay focused on his lessons with Galaxy and on his work during the busy weekends at Cafferty's farm, but at night she was waiting for him. The only news of her came sporadically from Timothy, but Ben hardly saw Lara's brother, because under the terms of their agreement Timothy rested on the weekends, leaving Galaxy for Ben while he was at Haybrook Farm.

Now he tossed restlessly in the bed, fighting down all the old questions. Why had she not answered any of his letters? Why wasn't he allowed to call her? What was happening to her?

Miss Mik told him what she knew. "The Wilson-Pratt Center for Children and Families," she said, giving him the address just before Christmas. "It's a private facility — sort of a highly specialized residential school, but with a psychiatric staff as well. They'll want to get her stabilized emotionally before she has contact with anyone outside her family, Ben — but don't worry. She'll get help there. Places like that have lots of experience handling young people like her."

The only person he could talk to was von Heiland, when he came on his infrequent visits to Haybrook. "I miss her," Ben told him one bitterly cold Saturday in January. He put his mittened hand on his chest. "It hurts right here. I mean, it really *hurts*."

Von Heiland smiled sadly. "I know this hurt," he nodded, tapping his own chest. "Yes. There it is — old pain, but it is there."

"Why won't she answer any of my letters? I know I don't write too good, but —"

"I do not think it is your writing," von Heiland smiled again. "This girl — she is very far away right now. You understand? She is still lost in a dark forest, in a blizzard, all alone. You must be patient. Sometimes it takes a long time to find your way home."

When Ben woke the snow had stopped and the dawn sun brought an unexpected tinge of warmth. As he walked across to the barn, he was sure he could smell a faint hint of spring. At home on the farm, the great horned owls up on the Buckhorn had begun their early evening hooting, one of the first heralds of winter's end. At Haybrook, the horses felt it too, and when he let them out into the paddocks, they bucked and squealed playfully.

He worked hard at his lesson with von Heiland on Saturday afternoon, knowing the trainer rarely would have the opportunity to be in Connecticut on weekends. But when von Heiland took him out to dinner in East Haybrook, Ben couldn't keep his mind on the conversation. At last the trainer gave him an exasperated look and asked, "You are not really here, Benjamin. Where are you?"

"With Lara," he blurted, and flushed, adding in a mutter, "I'm sorry."

Von Heiland pushed his plate back. "Ah, yes. Tomorrow McGrath is coming to see you. And you think maybe it is about Lara? But perhaps he is coming to offer you the position of barn manager at Greenwood, hmmm? He heard from Cafferty how good you are, he offers you more money, and poof! You are gone."

"I wouldn't leave Mr. C.!" cried Ben hotly before he caught the teasing twinkle in von Heiland's eye.

Although he did not allow himself to hope, he was not surprised the next day when, after a perfunctory handshake, William McGrath said, "You must be wondering why I wanted to see you, Ben — because of course you must know I'm very pleased with the way our arrangement is working out." He paused and cleared his throat, and then continued bluntly, "Lara wants to see you, Ben. She can have visitors other than family now. I'm going up today and I'd like you to come."

So he found himself on Sunday afternoon in the limousine with William McGrath, being driven through the Connecticut countryside. After an hour they turned through a stone gateway and up a drive past a discreet sign that read "The Wilson-Pratt Center." He was startled at how ordinary the place seemed — sloping snow-covered lawns and bright, modern buildings of yellow brick, a large playground, and, beyond, playing fields very similar to Huntingdon's. He'd expected bars on the windows and drab institutional buildings. Only last week he'd watched the movie *One Flew Over the Cuckoo's Nest* on television, adding another secret anxiety to the ones he already had: Lara might be getting shock treatment or drugs that turned her into a zombie. . . .

"Here we are," McGrath announced somewhat uncomfortably as the limo drew up to the steps of the main building. Four boys were shooting baskets on a shoveled court nearby and two girls came out, talking, with books under their arms. They stared frankly at Ben as he followed McGrath up the steps.

"Lara's in the library," said a small man with round glasses, checking them in. "I'll take you down there — why don't you just leave your coats here."

He saw her immediately when they reached the sun-lit library. She was pointing at something in a book to a younger girl who stood close by her side. When the girl looked up, blinking her eyes rapidly as McGrath approached, the man with glasses smiled. "Lara's got some visitors now, Marybeth," he reassured her. Ben hung back in the doorway, suddenly uncertain.

She looked exactly as she always had, with her familiar black jeans and T-shirt, her Walkman earphones draped around her neck. When McGrath spoke to the man with glasses, Lara tossed her head and looked so bored in her usual disdainful manner Ben couldn't help grinning. Then McGrath leaned toward her and said something, and her eyes flew suddenly to Ben and everything else disappeared.

She came toward him slowly. "Hi, Ben," she said. "Dad said he'd try and get you to come today."

"Hi," he managed to croak, staring at her in an agony of joy.

"Well, there's no sense hanging around this dump," said Lara brightly. "Dad'll be hours, now old Spec's got hold of him. It doesn't matter. Dad doesn't really know what to do with me when he visits anyway. He only comes because Mom won't."

"Your mom doesn't come?"

"Why're you so surprised?" she said, raising her eyebrows. "I told you about my mom and me. She's not going to change *now,* you know, just because I landed here."

She grabbed Ben's hand and pulled him out the door, whispering, "My coat's in my room — meet me at the front of the building," and ran off.

Ben waited by the entrance and when Lara appeared

she announced, "Well, Marybeth thinks you're cute." He flushed and looked away. "And I think she has good taste," Lara added softly. Then she shoved open the door and ran down the steps.

They walked along a shoveled path past snow-covered gardens and a boarded-up fountain, but by the time they reached a tall hedge bordering the fields, neither of them could think of what to say. They stood awkwardly looking across at the woods.

"Why did you stop writing to me?" Lara cried at last.

"But you didn't answer any of my letters!" he said. "I thought you didn't want me to write."

"I didn't know how to answer," she said in a low voice. "I didn't know what to say to you."

They started walking again, sometimes silent, sometimes racing through their words. "I can stay here until I graduate if I want," Lara told him. "I could leave earlier, but then I'd have to find another school, and besides, I don't really mind it here."

"You *like* it?"

"Isn't that bizarre?" She grinned. "I kind of like it. Don't get me wrong — the rules are full of shit just like anywhere else, but I don't know. . . . The kids here are — different." She paused. "They're so . . ."

"What?" he prompted.

"They're so messed up," she said. "*Really* messed up, some of them. You wouldn't believe the stories I've heard. Like Marybeth. Her father used to . . ." She glanced back at the main building. "She really has

265

a lot to deal with in her life. She has a lot to be angry about."

"You have something to be angry about," he said.

Lara didn't answer for a while, but when they reached the end of the garden walk, she stopped. "Dad's okay, you know — he's really trying. I know he cares in his own way. And Veronica —" She shrugged. "She's not going to change, I guess."

Ben watched her face as she talked, saying nothing, feeling her voice flow through him, loving her. After a while she grimaced at him. "This is supposed to be a *conversation*, Ben. You know — I talk, then *you* talk? You're as bad as when I first met you!" He blushed and she took his hands. "I loved your letters, Ben," she whispered. "I read them over and over. I kept them all. You sure can't spell, can you?"

They trudged through the snow in silence until they reached the woods. Just inside the trees was a ten-foot-high chain-link fence. Lara followed Ben's eyes. "Yeah," she said. "That's to keep us loonies from escaping."

"You're not a looney!" he cried, shocked. For a moment they stared at each other, and then Lara threw herself against him fiercely. He held her, afraid to move, afraid even to look at her. They clung to each other for a long time, their breath mingling in the cold air. Finally, she pushed him back and took his hand. She pushed up her sleeve and exposed a pink scar across her wrist. Unwillingly, he let her put his hand on it.

"Maybe I'm not," she said. He closed his hand around her wrist and pulled her close again.

"Has this place helped, then?" he asked softly.

"Not the idiot shrinks, if that's what you mean," she replied, tossing her head. "They're just like all the others." She smiled self-consciously. "Well, maybe one or two here aren't so bad. . . . Anyway, it isn't them. It's the other kids — like Marybeth. I don't know how they help. But they do."

"Because you help them."

She said nothing, but after a moment she put her arms around his neck. "I missed you, Ben," she murmured. "I missed you so much."

He kissed her face damp with tears, tasting the salt like a warm sweetness in her mouth, and felt his own eyes burning. He opened his coat and she nestled in closer against him. Without warning, and without pulling away, she asked, "Do you still think I was lying, about Tom?"

The memory of that night could still pierce him, and he gasped, "Lara. Lara. I believe you."

"You have to tell me the truth, Ben," she insisted. "I mean it. I keep thinking about it."

"I am telling the truth. I believe you. I believed you that night, only you'd already . . ." He could not finish and crushed her to him, terrified he would see again the look in her eyes that had haunted him for months. What he felt for her had nothing to do with believing.

"I haven't . . . I never really did anything with Tom. Not like he told you," she said passionately. "No, Ben, let me talk! You have to listen to me. Those other boys at all those schools — I made that up. Everything."

"About your real mother, too?"

"No —" She paused a moment. "I really was left at a convent. And prostitutes really did leave babies there."

"Why'd you make all that other stuff up, then? About the boys . . . and you let me think that Tom . . ."

She disentangled herself and went to stand by a tree with her back toward him, looking past the fence into the deeper woods. "I don't know if I can explain it — I think it was partly because I *could* make people believe those things about me," she said. "Then all I had to do was act the way they expected — you know? I could do the act really well, and all the time inside I could be a totally different person, so it was sort of like hiding out. Besides, it made me feel —"

"What?"

She tilted her head back and looked straight up through the trees. "Oh, I don't know . . . like I was my mother. My real mother. So she was . . . more real. It was the only way I could feel like she was part of me. Oh, I told you I couldn't explain." She dropped her head and didn't say anything more for a moment. Then, in a small voice, she asked, "What happened to Tom?"

Ben swallowed. "He's doing okay for now, I guess. He's got a job in Wilkes-Barre."

They turned at the same time and walked along the edge of the woods. Ben tried several times to say something and finally blurted out, "Can I come here again? To see you?"

"You'll see me most of the summer," she teased him, evasive. "Dad told me Cafferty's training you to be his barn manager after you're out of school, and I'll be around at Greenwood . . . anyway, at least until July. Dad's taking me to Mexico City when he goes, so I can take pictures. He said now I'd finally let him see what I did with my camera —"

"Lara!" he interrupted.

"What?"

He pulled her around so she had to face him. "I just want to see you. It's months till we graduate."

She wouldn't answer him until they had walked back across the field to the fountain in the middle of the garden. She kicked at the snow with the toe of her boot. "I still have a long way to go, Ben," she said at last. "It still happens to me – the rage. Mostly I'm fine. But something can happen, just any stupid thing, and I'll lose it again. I'm never sure —" She looked quickly at him and smiled. "I'm not so afraid of it as I used to be. I mean, I know I can make choices even when I'm feeling it . . . so it's not like before. But Ben – I need to do this by myself. When I'm with you I feel so —"

"I thought you felt like when you were alone," he said, trying to speak lightly.

"I do," she said. "That's what I mean. It's like we're part of each other. . . . But we're *not,* Ben."

"But why —"

The sun caught in her dark eyes and he saw himself reflected in their depths. "Oh, Ben. I love you so much," she cried. "But I get so lost in you — it's like I want to *be* you! Don't you understand? I can't stand up to that yet. I hardly know how to be *me.*"

But he understood only her first words. She loved him. *She loved him.* "Okay," he said simply. They went into the building and he thought they would go back to the library, but Lara hesitated, looking unaccountably shy. "What?" he asked.

"Well, I want to show you something," she said. Ben followed her, curious, into a small lounge off the main hall. There he stopped in amazement. On every wall hung framed photographs. He walked through the lounge slowly. Something about the composition, the light and camera angles, struck him, and he knew immediately that this was Lara's work.

But these were not the collages he remembered. On the nearest wall was a series of portraits — not composed from torn fragments into a disturbing collection of images, but single photographs of people. The camera had focused on their eyes, the depth of expression in their faces, the momentary moods; he felt he could hear them think. On another wall were photos of wide-open spaces, the sky constituting three-quarters of each composition. In each one there was a small human figure, distant and tiny in the huge expanse. But the figures acted as vital points of energy and he was drawn to them, enthralled.

She was standing just inside the door. "They're mine," she said anxiously.

"I know," he smiled.

"It's my portfolio exhibit," she explained. "For college. Miss Mik thinks I should apply to Rhode Island School of Design."

"Miss Mik?"

"She writes to me," said Lara. "She thinks I need to find a school with people like me. She doesn't think I'm crazy. She thinks I'm an artist."

"Well, I could have told you that," he muttered.

She laughed. "You're jealous of Miss Mik!"

He looked away sheepishly, and she came to him and took his hand. "You didn't see these yet," she said, leading him to the wall at the far end of the lounge.

It was the farm. A pile of discarded tires; the tractor's rusting undercarriage; a broken pane of glass in the greenhouse that reflected the clouds; a lichen-covered fence post; a spider web in the old Chevy; rolls of wire fencing dusted with snow so it looked like lace ... photograph after photograph, everything achingly familiar. He gazed at them. "But it's so *beautiful*," he breathed. He couldn't stop looking at them. The junk and clutter had been transformed into graceful lines and powerful angles, into patterns of light and shadow and texture.

"'Things as they are Are changed upon the blue guitar,'" she said and, stepping close to him, she placed her hand over his heart. "The blue guitar is *here*," she whispered. He laid his hand over her heart and closed his eyes.

Then Ben said, "I brought your Christmas present. I know it's late, but I wanted to give it to you myself." He pulled a videocassette from his coat pocket. "You want to watch it now?"

"There's a TV in the library," she said, "But Dad's probably there. Is that okay?" He nodded and when they got to the library, Marybeth slipped from a corner where she had been reading and came to Lara, glancing warily at Ben. "Could Marybeth watch, too?" asked Lara, and he nodded again.

William McGrath was sitting with his back to the door reading the newspaper and didn't notice when they came in. But the man with glasses frowned, excused himself from speaking to another student, and approached Lara. "Lara, you know you are meant to sign out and let someone know where you're going when you're with a visitor unsupervised," he snapped. "You've been gone forty minutes. You know better than that."

Ben saw the rage then, like the remains of an old illness. Lara tensed, opened her mouth to flare a retort. But at the same moment, Marybeth flinched and seemed to cower behind her. Lara glanced at her, so quick a look Ben almost did not notice.

"I'm sorry," Lara said evenly. "I did know. I wasn't thinking."

The man with glasses hesitated, then nodded kindly. "Your father's been waiting," he said. "Just let me know when they're ready to go, so I can sign them out and say goodbye, all right?"

Marybeth relaxed and followed Lara to settle next to her on the couch in front of the television. Ben squeezed in on the other side. "I hope it's not X-rated," said McGrath dryly, leaning over the back of the couch to watch.

"Well if it is, you can just close your eyes, Dad," scoffed Lara, but she was smiling when she spoke, and Ben saw McGrath's hand rest as if by accident on her shoulder.

"It's not that great," he said, embarrassed, fiddling with the remote control to the VCR. "Herr von Heiland showed me how to work the camera, but I'm not too good with it."

"Oh, shut up and play it," said Lara.

The music came on too loudly but she put her hand over his. "Leave it," she whispered. "It's beautiful."

Beethoven, von Heiland had stated firmly after he'd seen the video. It was the only music big enough to fit the subject. Ben had studied the video twenty times to make sure it was absolutely perfect, but today Lara was watching with him, sitting so close he could feel her body stir as she breathed, could smell the cold air still lingering in her hair, could still taste faintly the salt from her tears. Her hand tightened around his. "Oh!" she cried, enraptured. "He's *perfect*. He's so perfect."

Galaxy was galloping into a winter wind over a field of early morning snow, solitary and magnificent, his mane and tail streaming behind him like a dark vapor trail. At the end of the paddock he wheeled, a great spray of snow flying up from his hooves. He flung his head down and snorted, snow mixing with the cloud of his breath, and galloped straight at the camera. Mary-beth jumped when the camera jerked and the picture was momentarily blotted out. "He was showing off," grinned Ben. "He wasn't really going to run me down. That's his way of playing a joke."

The scene changed and now Ben rode Galaxy as he trotted by the camera, neck arched and tail held so high it floated over his star-white haunches. Ben was dressed impeccably in pale gray jodphurs, polished boots, and a black coat. Galaxy had a saddle on. The music soared from the film and for the first time, Ben noticed that Galaxy seemed instinctively aware of it. Then some trick of sun on the lens caused the snow to flare into brilliant lights, so the stallion appeared to be galloping through a shower of glittering stars. Lara watched, spellbound, and when the video ended she sat back and did not speak.

"I wanted you to see me and Galaxy in our new home," said Ben shyly.

"He looks so happy there," Marybeth said unexpectedly. "He is, isn't he?"

"He's real happy," said Ben.

Suddenly Lara turned to him. "I'm so glad you didn't sell him!" she cried passionately. "He couldn't belong to anyone. You're the only person who can keep him without owning him."

"I couldn't own him," said Ben. "He's part of me."

He realized Lara's father was still standing behind them, and he looked up uncomfortably. But William McGrath only laughed. "There's not much I haven't been able to buy," he admitted. "But leasing Galaxy from you so Timothy could train him until you both are ready to compete was the best thing I could have ever done for my son." He paused and smiled at Lara. "And my daughter made me see that I didn't *need* to own him."

Ben met Lara's eyes in wonder, but she shrugged with her usual nonchalance. "I only told him that he wouldn't be able to buy Galaxy's heart," she said. "That had to stay with you. It was a package deal."

"When'd you tell him that?" he marveled.

"When I was in the hospital," she said.

After McGrath said goodbye and went to wait outside, Lara reached for Ben and hugged him. "How did you know where to find me?" she whispered. "How did you know where I was — that day?"

"Galaxy told me," he answered, and kissed her.

She smiled. "I thought so." She waved from the steps until they had driven out of sight.

Epilogue

Was it a dream? Was it?

The boy sat on a horse under a sky so wide and blue it seemed nothing could ever be hidden in the universe. Everything existed in this single moment. He closed his eyes and remained absolutely still, until his heart was joined by the other heart and he could open his eyes and let the dance take them both.

They could have been in the clearing with the grass-soft earth, the ember of a fox burning through the hemlock shadows, and the swallows darting under the cry of a red-tailed hawk. The stallion and he spun the dance from air and from their own bone and muscle until the measured rhythm formed its own life and became more than the two of them together. Gracefully they wove back and forth across the arena, and when the movement came to its perfect end they stopped in the center of the ring and became once more a boy and a horse.

But although the crowd cheered and applauded and although the judges marked on their pads, the boy still sat on the horse under a sky higher than any sky he had ever known and did not move. He did not hear the crowds or the announcement on the speakers. He listened only for a single heart beating. He searched until he found the girl and saw the light filling her dark eyes. She raised her hand and he bowed to her, and for that moment all three were held together under the sky.